The Last to Pie

Also available by Misha Popp

Pies Before Buys Mysteries
A Good Day to Pie
Magic Lies and Deadly Pies

The Last

to

Pie

A PIES BEFORE GUYS
MYSTERY

Misha Popp

CROOKED LANE

NEW YORK

Published in the United States by Crooked Lane Books, an imprint of The Quick Brown Fox & Company LLC.

Crooked Lane Books and its logo are trademarks of The Quick Brown Fox & Company LLC.

Library of Congress Catalog-in-Publication data available upon request.

ISBN (hardcover): 978-1-63910-645-5
ISBN (ebook): 978-1-63910-646-2

Cover design by Stephanie Singleton

Printed in the United States.

www.crookedlanebooks.com

Crooked Lane Books
34 West 27th St., 10th Floor
New York, NY 10001

First Edition: May 2024

10 9 8 7 6 5 4 3 2 1

To everyone on team murder pie—
thanks for continuing to hang with my
murder girl!

Chapter One

There are times I wish I made murder pies for people of my own choosing.

Like today.

If I were the kind of pie-sassin who didn't care about keeping to boundaries, the first on my list would be whatever overpaid office-dweller decided the ideal time to do roadwork was smack in the middle of the day.

You know, that time when cars have to actually go places.

Like, for example, across the bridge I'm currently stuck in the middle of.

With a cop behind me.

I sigh, and Zoe, my brown-and-white pit bull, yawns in return. She stretches out across the ancient pickup's bench seat and drops her blocky head on my thigh.

"I know." I ruffle her floppy ears and try not to look at the state police SUV in my rearview.

Or at the stack of pies on the floor.

It's not easy. The white boxes are tied with pink-and-white twine, and six of them are completely harmless. Apple, cherry, and blueberry—as classic as it gets.

The seventh is different. Tucked in a freezer bag for safekeeping, the chocolate chip cookie crumb crust holds a creamy filling packed with mounds of cookie dough. The top is awash with rainbow birthday sprinkles and edged with alternating swirls of whipped cream and whole cookies.

It's festive, sweet, and absolutely deadly.

Because it's not just any cookie dough cream pie. It may look like a simple cookie dough cream pie, but each and every element is laced with enough magic to permanently put down the worst humanity has to offer.

So, yeah, nothing like being on your way to deliver a murder weapon to make you feel comfortable sharing a traffic jam with a cop.

"I'm being ridiculous," I tell Zoe. After all, I could feed the cop a slice and he would be fine. This particular blend of murder magic is finely tuned to act only on its intended recipient.

But still.

Nerve-racking.

Ahead of me, brake lights blink off as cars begin to creep forward, and I exhale in relief.

Finally.

I make it off the bridge, and GPS announces my next turn. I signal well in advance, hoping the cop will go around me. The last thing I need is a babysitter the whole way there.

No such luck.

I bite back a groan as he makes the turn with me, then curse as he chirps the siren and lights up my rearview with the red-and-blue harbingers of nothing good.

I pull into a gas station parking lot off the main drag, and he tucks in close to my bumper. Zoe sits up, alert and excited like we might be getting out to play.

I grab the registration and give her a stern look. "Be good."

Her tail thumps once in response, and she gives a little yip when the officer appears at my window.

"Shh." I roll my window down and hand out my papers without comment. Zoe stands on the bench seat, eager at the prospect of meeting a new friend.

The cop is an older white guy, closer to retirement than not, with the signature buzzed haircut they must get a discount on. "You know why I pulled you over, miss?"

I put a hand on Zoe's chest, and she sits. "I definitely wasn't speeding," I say, giving my sunniest smile. The problem is I actually don't know. I have zero idea, and while that makes me nervous, I'm not going to show it. I'm aware of the myriad ways this could go wrong, and I am more than willing to play the ditzy blonde girl to get out of it.

He laughs. "No, I'd say not." He knocks the edge of the truck bed with his knuckles. "You know you have a brake light out? This side. You have someone who can fix that for you? Father? Boyfriend?"

He has the decency to not say this in a leering, creepy way, just in a plain old misogynistic way. I manage not to roll my eyes, but barely.

"I'll get it sorted as soon as I'm home," I promise.

He scans my license and seems to note that I'm not local. "Daisy Ellery. Out for beach day?"

I nod.

"Good weather for it." He considers the license again. "If I run this, am I going to find anything? Outstanding fines? Warrants?" He winks when he says this, like it couldn't possibly be that.

I force a laugh. "Not even a speeding ticket."

"Well, I'm required to check anyway, but it'll only take a second."

"No problem." And it's not. My record is spotless, but it's not because I'm an inherently responsible driver, it's because I know better than to draw unnecessary police attention to myself. The habit started as soon as I left home, when being caught would've led to too many questions I couldn't answer.

The cop returns a few moments later and passes the license and registration through the window. "All set. Just make sure you get that light fixed."

"Will do. Thanks."

I feel stupid thanking him, but I am thankful. I'm thankful to be driving off not only without a ticket but without harassment, and I am fully aware of how lucky that is. Had I been Black or if Zoe had been anything less than perfectly friendly, all of this could've gone very wrong.

I pull back onto the street, annoyed that I'm even further behind on my delivery.

GPS promises me a ten-minute trip, and I know I'm in the right place after five. The street I turn onto is already lined with high-end cars even though the party isn't supposed to start for another half hour. It's far enough into the offseason that they have the run of the place, but even if it weren't, something tells me these people wouldn't care. Folks with this kind of money rarely do.

I had wanted to be in and out well before this many people showed up, but between the traffic and the cop, it looks like I'll be making an entrance.

"Good thing I'm dressed for it," I tell Zoe. The nice thing about dressing like a fifties housewife is that it's quirky enough to seem deliberate, whether I'm showing up at a frat party or a swanky soiree.

Today's choice is a full-skirted pink floral affair topped off with a yellow cardigan. It's a dress that doesn't transition well into the colder months, and this will probably be its last outing for the year.

I pull right up the driveway, as I was instructed. My truck, a full decade older than I am, feels like a relic from a different world as it lumbers past sleek Teslas and the kind of crossovers rich people get when they don't want to admit they need minivans.

I park and take it in for a minute, this different world. The house isn't a new build, so it has the weathered character of a proper beach cottage, but it's sprawling, with a wide wraparound porch overlooking the lawn on one side and the sea on the other. A pack of kids race around the beach, attempting to get their kites in the air. Zoe whines, clearly wanting to join them.

"Not yet," I tell her, typing out a quick text to the client announcing my arrival.

As I wait, I slide the cookie dough cream pie from the freezer bag, making sure the box of birthday candles is securely taped to the box, and begin arranging the rest of the pies in two stacks on the hood of the truck. "Be good," I tell Zoe, closing her in. She hangs her head out the window, breathing in the salty air.

The woman who comes out to greet me is not what I expect. She's dressed casually in linen, her graying brunette bob sleek despite the ocean breeze. She's elegant in the offhand way Frenchwomen are, but with an undercurrent of steel beneath that cool facade.

She does not look like a woman who needs me to save her.

"Lovely that you could make it," she says, holding out a manicured hand. Her fingers are slim, but her grip is iron. "I'm Evelyn. I hope the snarl on the bridge wasn't too dreadful?"

"We survived," I say, sliding a stack of pie boxes off the hood of the truck. "Sorry I'm a bit late. Where would you like these?"

She waves off the apology, and I appreciate that, despite our obvious difference in class, she's not one of those women to treat others like the help, even when they are. "May I see it first?"

There's no trace of fear or hesitation on her face, simply curiosity. I set the boxes back on the hood and lift the flap of the one in question.

"Charming," she declares. "And it's safe otherwise?"

"Completely." I've explained the details of this already, after she signed the contract, but it's a normal question. It's easy to think of the magic as poison, an indiscriminate danger, but it's not. While most of my pies, the ones I make for the farmers' market or Frank's Roadside Diner, are laced with general magic, murder pies are the epitome of bespoke baking. The magic is tailored to one person and one person alone, but still, hearing that and truly believing it are two different things.

Before I even realize what she's doing, Evelyn snakes one of those slender fingers into the box and scoops the smallest bit off one of the whipped-cream peaks, right where a candle will go. Eyes locked on mine, she brings her finger to her lips and licks the cream off, grinning in a manner that can only be described as wolfish.

If I were a different kind of pie maker, I might be scared.

But I'm not that kind of pie maker.

I know if she wanted to, Evelyn Greco could arrange for any number of brothers or cousins to see to the death of her father-in-law. They're the kind of family where it would only take a phone call. But it would get loud and messy and it would no longer be under her control.

And after what she's been through, Evelyn has earned control.

"Delicious," she says, taking the box from me. "Let's get these put out, shall we?"

Chapter Two

The diner's parking lot is nearly empty when I finally get back, which is typical for a Sunday night.

I pull around back where Penny, my vintage pink-and-white RV, is parked. Even though I spend most nights at Noel's these days, I keep Penny here. The arrangement I have with Frank, the owner, is too good to let slip, and besides, Penny is more than just my home. She's my legacy.

And she's freedom, which is something I will never take for granted.

I let Zoe inside, and she promptly puts herself to bed, spent from the afternoon beach zoomies.

The RV's interior bears little resemblance to the mobile salon my mother used it for, when the small space was dominated by a curved hair-washing sink and brightly lit mirrors. Now it's crowded with cabinets full of baking equipment, and the sulfur stink of perm solution has long been chased away by the scent of sweet fruit in buttery crusts.

The magic remains, though, as does the original black-and-white flooring.

The RV has been handed down through the women of my family in much the same way as the magic. Its interior has been reconfigured to reflect each iteration of the magic, having started life as a sewing studio where my grandmother consulted with the women for whom she'd stitch magic into dresses. It was a space of her own in a time when women were rarely granted such things, and the magic she worked into her seams was equally uncommon. Several of those dresses still hang in the RV's tiny closet, their skirts full of confidence, luck, and strength. Little things to make life better.

It's strands of the same magic that my mother styled into the hair of her clients and that I work into each of my pies.

The exact flavors may have varied throughout the years, but its core, the Ellery family magic, is all about making the world a little bit brighter for the people in it.

And yes, sometimes that means murder pies.

But not tonight.

Tonight I owe Frank another round of diner pies, my payment for parking Penny behind his restaurant and tapping into his water and electricity, and the only magic those need is a dose of happy nostalgia.

I let myself in through the staff door at the back and find Juan shimmying in front of the flat-top, singing along to the radio into a pair of tongs. I let the door close with a thud, and he turns, clicking the tongs twice at me.

"Solo!" he demands, not the least bit embarrassed.

I wave him off. My singing, even in jest, is not fit for public consumption. "Slow night?"

"It's always dead on Sundays," he croons. "And I think I've lost my mind."

"It does look that way," I agree, ducking into the walk-in to get the pie dough I prepped the day before.

When I come out, Juan slides a steaming bowl of gravy-smothered fries at me.

"You're the best."

"And you're an adult," he says. "Who isn't going to talk to me about dinosaurs."

I laugh. "Says who?"

"Says me. Please." He groans. "It's Sunday. Do you know what doesn't happen on Sunday? School. Do you know who hasn't accepted that fact?"

"Isn't the whole point of homeschooling that learning can happen anywhere, anytime?" I say, parroting back the words he said when he announced he and his husband Eric would be homeschooling their daughter.

"The point of homeschooling is to have school at *home*," he says. "Where she can't be shot. I have not, however, quite ruled out feeding her to a dinosaur."

I drop a block of chocolate on a cutting board and grab a chef's knife. "This single-parent thing not all it's cracked up to be?"

"I don't know how people do it. Seriously. It's been three days and I'm exhausted."

As if on cue, Ana bursts into the kitchen, dragging one of the servers by the hand. "Papi," she says, "Did you know Amanda doesn't even have a favorite dinosaur? She doesn't even know *any*. Not even brachiosaurus."

Amanda, for her part, looks appropriately chagrined by this egregious lack of knowledge.

"Did you finish eating?" Juan asks.

Ana nods. "And I helped fill up ketchups. Can Amanda borrow my dinosaur book?"

"Then you won't be able to study it," Juan says, and instantly seems to realize that might not be the worst thing ever.

Ana considers that, and I take the opportunity to jump in. "Hey, pie pal, let's whip up a surprise for your dad, yeah?"

"His plane lands at midnight," she says skeptically. "You can't have pie at midnight."

"Says who?" I kick the milk crate into place beside me and gesture for her to join me.

She hops up, brow still furrowed. "I don't get to eat pie at midnight."

Juan clicks his tongs at her. "Because you're sleeping at midnight."

An impish grin splits her face. "Says who?"

*　*　*

She's still at my side, painstakingly arranging sprinkles into the shape of a T. rex atop a coconut cream pie, when a familiar pattern of knocks sounds at the back door.

It's unlocked, but this man is nothing if not polite.

"Go see who it is," I say, nudging Ana with my hip.

She scatters a handful of green sprinkles across the bottom of the pie for grass and jumps down to get the door. She opens it with a flourish and looks as pleased as I am to see Noel on the other side.

"Zoe said you all were making pies," he says with a wink.

"She was too tired to help," Ana says seriously. "She got to go to the beach today."

"Lucky dog," Noel says, grinning. He comes over and drops a kiss on top of my head. "Hey you."

I let myself snuggle back into his tall lanky frame for a second before fetching a box for Ana's pie. "Hey yourself."

"I'm staying up till midnight to have pie with Dad," Ana announces.

"No, you're not," Juan says as he double-checks that all the knobs are off. Out front, the dining room is dark and the servers are gone. As much as I love the bustle of busy shifts, this is my favorite kind of diner time, when it's peaceful and homey.

10

I write *Welcome Home* on the top of the box in looping cursive and hand it to Ana. "Straight in the fridge when you get home, right?"

She nods solemnly and sits on the milk crate to wait for Juan to finish closing.

I turn into Noel, wrapping my arms around his narrow waist. "This is a nice surprise."

"I knew you were busy, so I didn't want to make you drive across town. Doesn't mean I didn't want to see you, though."

"Missing me so soon?" I tease.

"Always."

I don't bother hiding my smile. I spent a lot of years on the road after my parents died, and it's nice to have this. All of it. Noel, the diner, people to care about.

A home.

"You're the best," I say, stretching up on tiptoes to kiss him.

"Not you guys too," Ana moans. "Why are grown-ups so gross?"

"Being in love is not gross," Juan says in a way that makes me think it's not the first time.

"Mouth kissing is totally gross," she insists. "It's like getting spit in your mouth that's not yours."

"It is kind of like that," Noel agrees, and I laugh.

Juan just shakes his head. "In addition to the dinosaur phase, we're also in a cootie phase. All right, monster, let's go."

She hands him the pie box and turns to Noel. "I want to climb the mountain."

"Ana, leave him be," Juan says.

"It's cool," Noel says, reaching his hands out. "Mountain time!"

She grabs his hands, and he swings her up and around, letting her scale his back until she perches atop his shoulders.

"Master of the mountain!" she declares, fists raised.

Holding her legs, he trots her out the back door to Juan's car before reversing the process.

After a chorus of good-nights, they drive off, and I'm glad my trek home is only across the parking lot.

Zoe greets us at the door, and Noel, saint that he is, offers to take her out while I shower. When I'm done, I find them both stretched out on the bed.

"Kettle's hot, if you want tea," Noel says.

"Did I say the best earlier? I meant perfect." I root around in my tea stash and drop a pair of orange spice bags into mugs. "Thank you for humoring Ana too, by the way. She adores you."

He sits up, propping himself against the cabinets that act as my headboard. "It's mutual," he says. "She's a riot."

"And a handful," I say, passing him both mugs to hold while I clamber in beside him.

"Yeah, but in a fun way."

I laugh. "Tell Juan that."

He peers at me over the top of the mug.

"What? You know I love her," I say, and I do, with my whole heart. "But there's something to be said for being able to send her home."

He cocks his head in the way Zoe sometimes does. "But someday?"

I nearly choke on my tea. "Hot," I lie, desperate to cover how flustered I suddenly am. When he doesn't say anything, I force a laugh. "What happened to the farm and some dogs?"

He shrugs, the movement bringing him closer to me. "Totally still in the cards," he says. "But I mean, the magic, right? It's passed from mother to daughter? So someday, right?"

I'm saved from having to answer that, a question he can't possibly believe is actually innocent or anything remotely resembling easy, by the chirp of my phone.

It's the tone reserved for the Pies Before Guys account, and by now, Noel recognizes it too. He's quiet while I read, all scary future life decisions temporarily forgotten.

"That's weird," I say, more to myself than Noel.

At first I think the message is spam, although the account is so well protected that rarely happens.

The murder pie side of my business is strictly word-of- mouth, and there's an established protocol for soliciting orders. A referral is critical, although thanks to my friend Melly's meddling, this line has blurred a bit. But even so, Melly's clients are always linked to her.

This one doesn't seem linked to anyone.

The username is simply *JodieL*, and that's the first thing out of place. No zip code. Part of the referral process is instructing new clients in how to identify themselves, which is always first name and zip code. No exceptions.

My stomach knots at the memory of the only time I had an order that didn't follow that rule, a person hiding behind the username *RememberRemember*.

It wasn't a good time.

But I remind myself that it was also a one-off. It doesn't mean it's remotely connected to this new request.

No.

As I read, I realize that would've been easier.

Chapter Three

"What is it?" Noel asks.

"Odd request."

JodieL, no zip code or referral, has attached three photos, which isn't the odd part. It's the contents. I know Noel doesn't want to see them, so I keep the phone angled away as I scroll through again.

All three are close-up shots of mottled bruising, well lit, with two so zoomed in it's hard to make out exactly where on the body they are. In the last, the barest hint of earlobe is included above the black band of broken blood vessels along the sharp curve of jawbone.

No identifying features. Nothing beyond white skin to show that these are even on the same body.

I could almost get past that if the other factors were in place. Maybe, when I was first starting, I could've even looked past all of it and followed up immediately, but no. That's not true and I know it. Because the biggest red flag, combined with the lack of identifying information, is the fact that the target's occupation is listed as police.

Noel nudges me with his shoulder. "What, did you get an order to kill the president?"

"Not quite." I meet his warm brown eyes, wondering, just for a moment, if a lie would be easier, safer, before remembering that he signed up for this knowing full well what I am and what I do. "A cop."

He pulls back, brows knit in concern. "Is that a good idea?"

I pin him with a look. "Cops are something like forty percent more likely to commit domestic violence than your average person, so yes, in normal circumstances I would think it's a very good idea."

He raises his hands in surrender. "Sorry, you're right. I just meant that it's probably safer for you to avoid cops? It's one thing to help them in a murder investigation, but pieing one? I just don't want you to get hurt."

"I think it's safe to say I won't be playing detective again anytime soon." There's still a part of that experience that feels surreal. It was wild enough getting to compete on *Bake My Day*, America's attempt at co-opting *The Great British Baking Show* for their very own, but that wasn't the half of it. During filming, one of the judges—a man I was supposed to be delivering a murder pie to—was killed before I had the chance to do it myself, and I found myself in the unlikely position of helping the police rather than hiding from them.

It did nothing to help with show nerves.

I read back through the scant details of the request: *I need help. I'm afraid my boyfriend is going to kill me, and I obviously can't go to the police. They'll take his side. They have before. I don't know who else to ask. I have to get out.*

That's it. No specifics.

A trap?

Leaving the message open, I hand the phone to Noel. "Does this sound legit?"

He reads, then blows out a long breath. When they meet mine, his eyes are clouded with concern. "I'm just a farmer." He runs a hand through an already messy mop of dark hair. "This is above my pay grade."

I give him a playful nudge. "Right. Just a farmer. You're just a farmer running one of the hottest craft cideries in the country."

Normally the reminder of Hollow Hill Orchard's massive success would be enough to garner a grin, but not tonight. He hands the phone back like it might detonate. "I don't know if it's legit or not. It sounds like it to me, but I'm not an expert."

I'm about to lay out the details of my hesitation, the theory I really don't want to admit to, but he continues before I have the chance.

"Either way, I think you should leave this one." His expression is earnest, full of the sweet concern that's second nature for him but something else too. Fear. "If it's not legit, fine, then you're ignoring some weird scammer, no harm, no foul. But if it's real, I don't think it's worth the risk. You can't walk into a policeman's house with a murder weapon. You can't."

"It would only be a pie," I remind him. "Same as the others."

He shakes his head. "No. I understand what you do. Maybe not all the details and maybe not in ways I want to think too hard about, but I get it. I do. You have the power to help people who can't help themselves. But you can't do that from jail. You can't do that if you're dead."

Zoe, sensing the change in atmosphere, uncurls from the foot of the bed and wiggles up the middle. She drops her blocky head between us and stares up with soulful eyes. I ruffle her ears, and she sighs.

"Can't see her from jail either," Noel says softly.

"That's low."

"It's true."

And it is. It's the reason I ran so many years ago, after I first discovered that the magic I'd inherited from my mother could be used for more than comfort and light. I hadn't meant to make a murder pie that first time, but I did, so I hid the body and hit the road, traversing the East Coast with Zoe, knowing that getting caught meant getting separated from her.

And pit bulls, even cream puff ones like Zoe, don't fare well in shelters.

"It's not worth the risk," Noel says. "We—*you* have a good thing here. Maybe let this one go. For your own sake."

I set the phone aside, knowing he's right.

I should probably let this one go.

I just don't think I can.

Chapter Four

F all means back to school, which means all the cutie pies I can make, because no one buys more of the portable pastries than Turnbridge University students.

The campus is at its best this time of year, when the leaves are changing colors and everyone is still excited about their new courses. Early-semester pies are fun to make, filled with energy and curiosity and bursting with local ingredients. Come December, when finals strike, the lines outside Penny will get even longer and the magic more potent, blends of focus and stamina helping students get through their big assignments.

Of course, no one knows the pies are performance enhancing. They just know they're delicious and easily available, and that alone is enough to turn a profit with college students. The boost is a free gift with purchase, a benevolent iteration of the magic I so often use for darker purposes. It's closer to what my foremothers worked, quiet magic made to lift the spirits and offer confidence, comfort, and joy. Working with the gentler magics always makes me feel a little more connected to them.

It can be hard to think about the other Ellery women without wondering how they'd see my murder magic, but I don't dwell on that as I work through my line of customers. Zoe is hanging out below the serving window, happily soaking up attention as people pay. If I'm honest, there are some days where she's as much of a draw as the pies.

At the end of the line, I finally spot a head of sapphire curls and am glad the midday rush is winding down. She's not here for pie.

She lets a few stragglers cut in front of her, grinning widely at me when she catches me watching. I shake my head and can't help smiling back as I get the remaining customers pied and on their way.

"So Pie Girl," Melly says when she reaches the RV, "fancy blowing this pie stand?"

"Two seconds," I say, already sticking the BE BACK SOON sign to the window. I grab Zoe's leash and slip my phone into the pocket of my pumpkin-colored dress before locking Penny's door.

Melly motions toward the pond. "Shall we?"

I clip the leash to Zoe's collar, and we walk in silence for a few minutes, the grounds around us emptying as students make their way to classes.

Neither of us wants to have this conversation with an audience.

Well, at least I don't, and Melly has the sense not to push things now, so same thing.

Instead, she bounces back to an old topic while we wait for privacy. "Let me guess." She puts a happy little hop into her words. "You invited me here because you changed your mind."

"Oh my god, no." I laugh. "I'm not going to be your local legacy. I'm not even local!"

She shrugs. "You live here. Locally. And your legacy is way cooler than anyone else I'm going to find."

"I told you, talk to Frank. Or Noel. Their families go back like a million generations here."

She side-eyes me. "You're not even a little bit fun, you know that?"

"I don't think we have the same definition of that word."

"Yeah, because yours is wrong."

I roll my eyes, but I know she's only teasing. One of her journalism courses this semester is a special-topics seminar called Beyond Bleeding Leads that focuses on finding the heart of smaller stories, the ones without sensational or violent hooks.

But because Melly is hardwired for high octane, she's still trying to find something with an edge.

It just can't be me.

She sighs. "Okay, fine. So what gives?"

I pull up the JodieL request on my phone and hand it to her without comment.

She swipes through and lets out a low whistle. "Big leagues now, baby. Right into the lions' den."

"Is she yours?"

"What? No way." She hands the phone back with a cheeky flourish. "I don't let mine screw up the username, boss."

"I'm not your boss." And I'm not. When Melly, a firm believer in asking forgiveness rather than permission, started recruiting targets on the dark web, it was one hundred percent of her own volition. The fact that it worked and was safe—thanks to a tech-wizard friend she had—was the only reason it was allowed to continue.

I push the phone back at her. "Look again, remembering the rules."

We stop walking so she can give it her full attention, and I wonder if I'm being paranoid.

When Melly peers at me through dark lashes, the look there tells me I'm not. Or if I am, she at least understands why.

Her face twists in uncertainty. "Have you replied?"

"Not yet. I mean, I know it's probably not, but if it is some kind of trap, then I don't want to engage. At all."

"Okay, let's think this through," Melly says, setting off again. "Because while I get your suspicions, I'm not convinced either. She did send photos."

"That have nothing identifiable. No face, no locations, nothing. For all we know, they're not even from the same person."

"The skin tone is consistent," she says, but must realize that's not conclusive. "Is there a chance this is like some kind of close-encounter-with-the-cop-kind PTSD thing from summer? I know it wasn't comfy having them so close, but that doesn't mean anyone suspected what you are."

"I don't know. Maybe?"

"I mean, what's more likely? Someone needs saving from an abusive cop or that those same cops are launching the softest fishing expedition in history?"

I sigh. "I know. But it's practically anonymous. What if they did get some kind of tip and they really are trying to confirm it?"

"Then I don't think they'd use their own men as bait," Melly says. "Why would they?"

"Fair point," I concede. "But it could also be like hiding in plain sight. They wouldn't think I'd suspect a trap if I was making a pie for a cop. And it would be easy for them to get the pictures too. They'd have them in evidence, right?"

"True." Melly is quiet for a few steps as she mulls it over. "What's your gut say?"

"My gut? The thing that likes pie and is prone to butterflies? I don't think it deserves a say in this."

"I'm serious." And to my surprise, she is. She isn't teasing, and she isn't trying to steamroll in with her own opinion. She's waiting. "You've been doing this long enough to have an instinct. What's it telling you?"

I begin slowly, the thoughts still solidifying. "It's telling me the statistics are in favor of this being a real request. It's also telling me—based on experience—that anonymous requests aren't to be trusted."

"Anything else?"

I swipe open the phone. "That I need more information."

She claps me on the shoulder. "There you go. Always trust your gut."

What she doesn't know is my gut is currently knotting itself up around the knowledge that Noel is not going to be happy about this. If I'm wrong and reaching out puts me in danger, it's not only my life that could be ruined. It's his too.

Chapter Five

When I reply to JodieL, I treat it like any other initial inquiry. I ask for details, confirmation of identity, and a full rundown of the target. I keep the wording as neutral as possible, and again, this isn't much of a departure from how I normally handle things. The only difference is that I don't include a contract yet. Not without establishing bona fides.

Including her referral source.

I also have Melly trolling the web, trying to see if there's any trace of our mystery woman on the forums such people might frequent. It seems unlikely that she'd find me that way without Melly acting as intermediary, but it's worth a try.

Every time my phone pings, I feel a jolt that reminds me more than a little of my encounter with my last anonymous client. That was bad in a stalking-and-blackmail sort of way, and I can only hope I'm not setting myself up for a repeat. At least this time I can count on Melly not going rogue.

I hope.

I know there's a part of her that will always be at least a little wild, but in the two years since we met, she's gone out of her way to use that energy for good.

That is, if matchmaking me with murder pie targets can be considered good. And I think it can. Maybe not by the strictest legal definition, but still.

What's legal and what's right aren't always the same thing, and I need no more reminder of that than the little pies cooling on the rack.

Each cutie pie—a cookie-sized pastry with sand dollar slits in the middle—is filled with simple, crowd-pleasing fillings. Tonight's are apple—from Noel's orchard, of course—chocolate, and raspberry, and they're brimming with as much strength, hope, and conviction as their little crusts can hold.

"Hey, pie pal, help me box these up," I say as I slide the trio of trays onto my worktop. There's a stash of prefolded pie boxes on top of the dry-storage rack, and I grab one while Ana drags her milk crate into place.

I show her how to stack the pies in overlapping rows of alternating flavors and leave her to it.

"Can I decorate the box when I'm done?" she asks.

"Go for it."

She gives a happy wiggle that reminds me more than a little of Zoe, and Juan plucks the Sharpie from the pocket on his sleeve to slide down the bench to her.

From the dining room, there's a low hum of activity, and when I stick my head out, I see there's still a decent crowd of mostly regulars lingering over their plates. Perfect.

I fetch a pair of pumpkin pies from the walk-in and get to slicing bite-size pieces that I arrange in pairs on saucers. Each gets a kiss of whipped cream—vanilla bean on the paler slices, coffee on the darker. I drop plates at Juan, Ana, and the dishie's stations and heft the tray one-handed, bracing it against my shoulder so I can grab a pile of forks with my free hand.

I almost lose it all when the swinging door to the dining room bursts open just as I'm about to go through.

Frank, all bristly white hair and bluster, takes one look at my tray and hustles me back into the kitchen.

"I'm not paying you to give my pie away," he snaps.

"You're not paying me at all," I say, a familiar refrain as I sidestep around him, skirt swishing as I nudge the door open with my hip.

"Definitely the chai," Juan calls, and I grin, ignoring Frank's incredulous sputters.

"Ooh, pies samples?" Amanda coos as she offers to take the tray from me. I tell her I've got it but insist she and her sidekick take a plate and report back.

I flit around the dining room like a pie fairy, dropping samples and requests for feedback. This is a frequent enough thing I do that I can trust people to be honest. No one, especially not one of Frank's regulars, is going to lie to spare my feelings. After all, they want pies they like on the menu, and sugarcoating the truth won't get them there.

When I first started this arrangement with Frank, it was simple: pies in exchange for parking rights and access to water and electricity. The pies were simple too: apple, cherry, chocolate cream. Nothing fancy.

Although to be fair, even my basics were fancy compared to the mass-produced abominations they'd been passing off as pie before I arrived.

Even the magic was simple, a quintessential blend of homey comfort and nostalgia that made you feel enveloped in a welcoming warmth. It was a much-needed antidote to Frank's brasher customer service style.

Over time, though, I've gotten a little more creative with the diner pies. Nothing major, not after the one time I added lavender to the lemon meringue and nearly gave Frank a stroke. But after my honey cream apple pie won the state's pie contest and landed me a spot on *Bake My Day*, enough of the diners wanted to branch out beyond the classics that Frank has begrudgingly allowed a specialty pie to be added to the standard rotation.

Hence the taste test.

Pumpkin is going into the fall lineup one way or another; the only question is whether it gets a feature spot.

The vanilla bean–topped pie is the Thanksgiving classic everyone expects, doctored up with nothing more than magic. The other one is special, and as I set a pair of plates in front of an older couple, I explain why.

"This one is pumpkin chai latte. It's spicier than the classic, with cardamom, star anise, and pepper to go with the standard cinnamon, clove, and nutmeg. There's also a touch of espresso in the crust and the whipped cream."

"Oh, that sounds right up my Cora's alley," one of the women says, watching her wife with the kind of affection usually seen on first dates. As I leave them to enjoy their pie, I realize that's not quite right. Hollywood wants us to believe in the swoony romance of new relationships, but there's something to be said for the kind of love that grows after a lifetime tended together. It's something I haven't considered much—I don't exactly have role models in that department, and when I first left home, I could barely imagine two days out, never mind two decades. A cozy marriage like those two have was never something I saw in my cards.

Still, I never saw settling down in one place for longer than a week in my cards either. Or sharing the secrets of my magic. Or, you know, dating at all.

And here we are.

So who knows.

Maybe someday.

Chapter Six

Delivering the dinosaur-bedecked box of cutie pies to Saint Stan's takes every mushy love feeling I had in the diner and rips them up, lights them on fire, and pees on their ash.

Romance is not a monolith. Relationships can save you and they can doom you in equal measure. I know that.

It's why Pie Before Guys exists and it's why I'm here, dressed in ripped jeans and an oversized hoodie.

The domestic violence support group meets twice a month in the church basement. I don't always stay. It can be hard to hear the stories and not act, but I can't make decisions for people, especially not the people here. The survivors here have had too many choices stripped from them already. I won't deny them the autonomy to save themselves the way they need to.

If, on occasion, that way includes taking a cast iron frying pan to a deadbeat's head, well, I'm not going to feel bad if my strength and conviction cutie pies helped galvanize that decision.

But that's the extent of my independent involvement.

As much as I may want to, I can't go after every monster who's sent someone to this group. Not unless I'm asked. That's a straight shot to Serial Killerville, population: me, and that's how things get bad.

I have rules in place to avoid that. I can't choose targets for personal gain. If it's personal, it creates a pattern, and patterns get you caught.

I won't accept money for murder pies. Ever. This isn't a pay-to-pie operation. Criteria must be met, and accepting orders is entirely at my discretion. The one person who tried to bypass this learned a very hard lesson.

I don't kill women or marginalized people, full stop. This may seem like an arbitrary boundary when there are plenty of women who abuse their kids or spouses, but it's my arbitrary boundary. These distinctions matter when you live on the knife's ethical edge.

For my own safety and that of my clients, I will not reveal myself as the face of Pies Before Guys or the identity of anyone seeking a pie.

And finally, I never get in too deep to get out. Everyone knows you have to put on your own oxygen mask before helping others.

You can't help if you're dead.

Or in jail.

And yet as I listen to the woman sharing her story, it's hard to keep those rules in mind.

"It got worse after the neighbors called the cops," she says. "It's my fault I didn't press charges. I know that. But James got to the door first and said I'd fallen down the stairs, that we were heading to the hospital just to make sure nothing was broken—" She breaks off, snorting a laugh at something so far from funny there's not an appropriate emotion for it. "My skull was broken. My *skull.*" She touches her brow bone. "Orbital fracture. At the hospital he told them I hit the finial on the landing. He didn't tell them it was because he slammed my head into it. I didn't contradict him, and after the surgery, it seemed too late and he was being so good, so attentive, that I thought maybe it had scared him too, that maybe it would get better." She trails off and shrugs. "It didn't. It never does."

There are murmurs of agreement around the room. Everyone here knows men like that don't change unless they're forced to.

My fingers twitch, wanting desperately to be in dough, to be pressing the kind of magic into butter and flour that would give him the kind of change he deserves.

"He knew he got away with it. If he could break my skull without consequence, he could do anything."

James.

And the woman introduced herself as Sarah—no last name per group norms. Common names and not a lot to go on, but between my databases and Melly's dark-web sleuthing, maybe it's enough.

I shake the thought away.

Rules.

"I had no support system. No friends, no money of my own." Her shoulders pull back, and her eyes come up now. "But I had words. I can write, so even though I had no business doing it, I applied to every creative nonfiction MFA I could find that offered housing, full funding, and the willingness to waive the application fee. The further from home the better. And here I am. I'm forty-three, living on campus with students young enough to be my children, but I'm free."

"And what about him?" The question comes from someone new, who doesn't know it's not the kind of thing to ask, but it doesn't matter.

A slow, satisfied smile sets Sarah's face alight. "He doesn't even know what's about to hit him."

And there it is.

The reason why the rules exist.

Not everyone needs a pie to right the wrongs done to them.

The group's host, an older Hispanic woman built for bear hugs, takes the floor. "Thank you for sharing, Sarah. I would like to bring the discussion around to something you said now, something we hear frequently in this circle. You said it was your fault you didn't press charges. Your fault you stayed silent." She casts her gaze around the room, giving each person a moment of complete attention. "Some of you here have said those same words. Some of you remain silent still, both at home and in this room. And that's okay. But I think it's important to remind everyone that silence is not complicity. Sometimes silence is survival. Sometimes it's safety. But it is never consent. It does not carry responsibility or blame."

She gives this plenty of space to sink in.

"We live in a society that likes to put the onus on victims—dress a certain way, act a certain way, say this, don't say that—when we really need to put the responsibility where it belongs: with the perpetrator. You are not responsible for the terrors done to you."

"Yeah, that's bullshit," someone agrees. "Like, sorry, sir, my outfit didn't make you a rapist. Your overinflated sense of entitlement and the fact that you're a fundamentally shitty human made you a rapist. That's on you, not me."

"And it's not like you can always count on help," another woman says. "Tell the cops? Pssssh. How many of us have tried that? 'Oh, he's stalking you? You're scared? Have you tried not leading him on?' Fuck out of here with that."

"There needs to be a better system," says a woman with a shaved head. She gestures around the room. "This is reactionary. Don't get me wrong, I'm glad it exists, but it's a Band-Aid. It doesn't address the problem; it tries to stop the bleeding. The cops are reactionary too. Like Mara said about stalking. They're not going to do anything until *after* you're physically attacked. How is that helpful?"

The leader settles the eruption of comments with a gentle patting of the air. "What would help?" She asks it in that way of hers, as if each word has its own gravity. She holds the silence that follows, indicating this is a question she wants real answers to.

"Men not being shitbirds," Mara offers.

"Beyond that. Specifically. We are not responsible for our abusers' behavior and it's not on us to change them, but we're in a position to at least imagine what a better world could look like. In what ways can we make things better, independent of our specific circumstances?"

I have a way. I don't say it out loud, of course, but I have a way.

"Consequences would be a nice start," Mara says at the same time someone else says, "Stronger safety nets."

As the conversation turns to what those would look like, I realize it isn't enough.

I deal in consequences every day, and this group still exists, along with thousands of others just like it across the country. Even if I burned my boundary list and pied every man who sent a woman to this meeting, it wouldn't change anything. Not really.

In my pocket, my phone vibrates. I ease it out enough to see a Pies Before Guys notification and mentally shake myself.

Okay, maybe I can't pie my way out of a world of toxic masculinity and the systemic bullshit that lets it flourish, but so what? That doesn't mean it's not worth trying.

My heart kicks up when I see who the message is from.

Jodie.

Chapter Seven

The message, like the first, doesn't follow the rules, but as I speed across town, I understand why.

The public library closes at eight, so I'm cutting it close, but all I'm hoping for is a glimpse, something to confirm she's real. I know there's a chance she walked out immediately after sending the email, but I'm counting on her lingering. It's what I would do if I were her. Just to keep up appearances.

Her response is a ramble, the forms disregarded in favor of straight text that I reread at every traffic light I hit.

I'm sorry for not including my referral but I can't risk putting her in danger. I'm writing this from the library because I think he's monitoring my phone and I don't know how long it's been going on. If he finds her, he can hurt her and I won't be responsible for that. If you can't help me without her name, I understand. I just didn't know where else to turn. There's no way I could've found you without the button she gave me so I hope the fact that I'm here is enough proof that I had a referral.

My name is Jodie Azaria (see attached) and I'm 23. I have no family and no one here who can help. Everyone trusts him. He works for Turnbridge PD and if I try to run, he'll find me. He has before.

The Last to Pie

*His name is Troy Sullivan. We live at 42 Meadowbrook Lane,
Turnbridge, MA. There are cameras everywhere but I was told the pies
are untraceable. Please. He doesn't have set days off and I volunteer
Tuesday and Thursday at the library, but you could deliver it any time.
Please. I know how it works. I can serve it to him.*

It has to be now.

*I'm pregnant. He told me he'd kill me if I had an abortion and
deprived him of a son, but I can't have this baby.*

I can't be tied to him forever.

I have to get away.

I need your help.

Please.

Attached is a photo of a driver's license bearing Jodie's information and a series of photos showing the same woman's face at
different angles, mottled bruising smudged from her ear to her
chin.

It could still be a trap. Jodie Azaria could be a real abuse victim
who went to the police, and they could be using her name and photos to lure me out.

But I don't think so.

The panic in her message feels too real, too unscripted. Surely if
it was a trap, they'd play by my rules to keep me unsuspecting. The
forms would be filled out with exactly what I wanted to see.

It's 7:54 when I pull into the rear parking lot of Turnbridge
Public Library. It's one of my regular places to park Penny in the
summer, when the library is bustling with families happy to bribe
rambunctious kids with curiosity-spiked pies in exchange for good
behavior.

I may have crossed paths with Jodie in this very parking lot without ever realizing she needed help.

A phrase from the Saint Stan's meeting pops into my head: *stronger safety nets.* Jodie could've walked by me a dozen times, but you can't help when you don't know the need exists.

I pull slowly past the designated staff area, wondering which of the three cars is hers. If she volunteers, I imagine she'll help close up, then walk out with the others.

I back my ancient pickup into an out-of-the-way spot and wait.

Two minutes pass. The straggling patrons are the first to leave, emptying the parking lot. Inside, lights flick off, darkening the windows in a cascade.

At the same time, the glare of headlights sweeps the parking lot as a black-and-white SUV pulls up to the main entrance.

Police.

Every instinct says to run, the same as it has since I struck out at seventeen. That instinct is the thing that has kept Zoe and I safe and together, but I tamp it down.

I wait.

The front door opens, and a tall Black man emerges. His locs are pulled into a thick bun, and I remember him from my summer visits and how much he liked the strawberry balsamic pies. The thick-framed glasses and cardigans he favors are so quintessentially librarian that I couldn't picture him in any other line of work. He exchanges a few words with the cop that I can't hear before moving the sidewalk sign back to the foyer, completely at ease.

Everyone trusts him.

The cop isn't here for me.

He's here for Jodie.

When she emerges, alone, all I can think of are the poor gazelles in nature shows and how you want to scream at them to go the other way, that the lion is just offscreen.

But as much as I can't stop the gazelles, I can't stop Jodie. Not like this, in the open, with no preparation and no pie to speak of.

And it's definitely Jodie.

The face before me matches the one from the license photo, with the same ash-brown hair falling past her shoulders. She's wearing leggings with a dusty-pink sweater that swallows her slim frame. I wonder if that's her normal style or if she's trying to hide in it.

The passenger door of the SUV swings open, and as the overhead light comes on, I get my first look at him.

Blond hair cropped close to a cinder block skull.

Wide shoulders.

And older than her by enough to be weird.

Huh.

Maybe this isn't him. Maybe it's a buddy sent to play chauffeur.

I can't decide whether that's better or worse.

She climbs into the SUV with no hesitation, like it's the most normal taxi in the world, darkening the interior with the thunk of her closing door.

I'm tempted to follow as they pull a tight U-turn and make their way onto the main road, but I don't.

There's reckless, then there's tailing-the-literal-cops reckless.

Baby steps.

Besides, thanks to Jodie's message, I know where they're going.

I send the contract before I even leave the library parking lot.

I don't think twice about it.

Chapter Eight

Waiting is always the hardest part.

The time between sending the contract and getting an official order can take minutes or it can take days. Sometimes the order never comes at all, the contract itself enough to solidify the reality of the client's situation.

Even when it's deserved, it's no easy thing to kill a man.

I'd like to think the orders that disappear do so not because of cold feet but because the clients have found a different path out. I have to believe that's true; otherwise the temptation to save them from themselves would be too strong.

Jodie makes me wait.

And wait.

I expected two days based on what she said about needing the library computers for communication, but her Tuesday and Thursday volunteer shifts pass without a word.

The silence makes me edgy in a way that other contacts haven't, and not solely because the pie is slated for a cop. No, it's because she's right in my backyard. I've seen her. Usually when orders come, the only direct contact I have with the women is when I deliver the pie, and sometimes not even then. Plenty of people order their pies to be delivered directly to the target and we never even cross paths. It's a good system. Safe.

But Jodie is the first client I've had who lives right in town, and it's hard not to watch for her when I'm out.

It's even worse with him.

When I got home, I hopped right online, once again forced to acknowledge that the database subscriptions I pay an arm and a leg for are indeed worth it. I confirmed that Troy is indeed the burly white dude I saw in the SUV picking Jodie up from the library. His ID photo was a little dated, but the craggy shape of his shaved head was a dead match.

The guy absolutely radiates smug cop, even in pictures.

I confirmed age and address and was icked out by both. Google Maps showed the house to be part of the soulless McMansion subdivision that had gone up when I first arrived, the one masquerading as a gated community, as if it hadn't been plunked on the outskirts of a hippie college town.

And his age? Too old by a good twelve years. I'm not saying age-gap romances never work, but given the already skewed power dynamic in this one, I very much doubted it hadn't been a deliberate choice on his part.

I violently disliked this guy, and I found myself doing more research than I should without a contract. I couldn't help it.

I dove into the Turnbridge PD's Facebook page, which had a staggering amount of followers and more photos than some influencer pages. I found Troy among the dozens of shots of officers in schools, talking to elementary-age students under the guise of normalizing police presence—as if kids needed to see more guns in classrooms.

No wonder Juan kept Ana at home.

I scrolled past all the K9 photos after establishing that Troy didn't seem to have been assigned one.

That was a plus. Delivering a pie to a guy with a trained attack dog would test even my skills.

There were toy drives and community notices and a holiday photo over a year old. The cops were all in uniform, but their plus-ones were in festive formal wear. I clicked to enlarge, and there was Jodie, Troy's arm tight around her waist, wearing a smile that didn't quite reach her eyes.

I scrolled until I found his hire announcement, part of a five-officer recruitment several years ago. I noted the names of the other four, just in case. Chances were he'd made friends with the guys he came in with and, if it turned out he was into anything worse than domestic violence, they would know about it.

* * *

The more that time passes, the more it bothers me.

Even Noel notices as we set up for the final Saturday farmers' market of the season, still in the side-by-side booths where we met. His has grown since then, the original plastic blue pop-up tent having been replaced with sleek brick-red canvas bearing the orchard's new logo.

The cidery does enough business that he doesn't need the market income anymore, but I like that he still comes anyway.

The October morning is chilly, and I have Zoe bundled in a pumpkin fleece that is already earning her plenty of coos as she investigates the other booths setting up nearby.

"Drink," Noel says, handing me a steaming paper cup of spiced goodness from one of the urns he brought.

I inhale the sweet warmth before I sip, letting the spice linger on my tongue. "Nutmeg, anise, cinnamon, and clove," I guess. It tastes like the apple version of my pumpkin chai pie.

"Bingo," he says. "Too much clove?"

I taste it again. "Nope. Orange too?"

"Peel," he confirms.

"Two thumbs up," I say, draining the rest.

He goes to take it back but instead catches my hands, his long fingers wrapping around mine. He's close enough that I have to tilt my head back to meet his gaze.

"You good?" he asks, warm brown eyes full of real concern.

"Of course." It's a lie, but I still haven't told him about Jodie's last message, so it feels like my only option. I don't want to bring her back up until I know she's placing an order. There's no reason to get back into it until then.

He kisses my forehead. "You haven't been around much this week. I miss you." He pulls back, searching my face. "I didn't freak you out with the kid thing, did I?"

I choke out a laugh, because with so much worrying me about Jodie's situation, I actually managed to put that conversation in a triple-locked box in the basement of my brain.

Noel drops my hands and runs his through his dark hair, the way he does when he's flustered. "I did, didn't I? I didn't mean to, I swear."

"I know," I assure him. "It's all good, really."

"And I didn't even necessarily mean, like, with me—"

I put a finger to his lips in what I hope is a playful and not panicked gesture. "Shh. It's okay. Promise. But I think we both have other things to focus on right now, yeah? Like farmers' market finale?"

"You're right."

The last market of the season always brings a big crowd, and this year is no different. The weather is perfect for it—bright-blue sky and the sun strong enough to burn off the morning chill. I see a lot of regulars, and Noel and I both have steady lines for most of the morning.

Still, I'm scanning the crowds, wondering if Jodie is a market person. The library has a booth near the gazebo selling used books, but I can't remember her ever manning it, and the pair of older ladies who run the table come to me often enough for cutie pies that I would've noticed.

What I do notice, more than usual today, is the TPD patrol car parked at the edge of the common. A sedan, not an SUV, but I don't know if that means anything. Do town cops change cars, or do they always keep the same one? That seems like something I should know.

I can't see the driver from here and scan the crowd, looking for a flash of blue among the shoppers.

When I spot it, it's not the navy of a uniform but a head of sapphire curls, which can only mean Melly's here.

She has her camera and stops often to capture faces, rarely seeming to ask permission. This is her new thing. It's technically called street photography, the capture of strangers' portraits in the wild, so to speak, but the Turnbridge common is so far from "the street" that it seems comical. Still, it's art for the sake of art, disconnected from her journalism program, and some of the shots she's taken have been pretty amazing.

I watch her cut a wide arc toward my booth, approaching from Noel's side. He has his head bent, his lean frame curved forward as he points out heirloom apple varieties on a diagram for an older man. There's a line behind him, but Noel doesn't rush him at all.

Melly raises the camera, and Noel is so engrossed that he never even notices.

She grins at me before disappearing around his truck, popping out in the gap between it and Penny.

"What's good, Pie Girl?" she asks, plunking herself down on the RV's metal step. She kicks her legs out and crosses her combat boot–clad feet at the ankle, making herself comfy.

"The pear and Gruyère," I say, offering her a cheese-crusted cutie pie. She tries to wave it off, but I insist.

Melly is one of those people who eats simply to keep herself alive and doesn't get the recreational aspect of it. It boggles my mind. Some things should be enjoyed, and this particular pie is one of them.

She nibbles the edge of the crust and nods. "It's like a fancy Cheez-It."

"I'll take that as a compliment."

She polishes the rest off in two bites. "Trust me, it was."

She sits there through another rush, content to people-watch while I sling pies and pass customers back and forth with Noel. This is why he comes back, I think. The banter and teamwork aspect that marked the beginning of our relationship is still very much part of our market routine. It's easy and fun, and no matter how big Hollow Hill Orchard gets, I hope it continues.

My run ends first, and I collapse on the step beside Melly.

"You're a busy bee," she says, plucking at the mustard-colored fabric of my skirt. It has a subtle hexagon pattern and tiny bees scattered around it.

"Always."

"So," she says, the word heavy with expectation. "Contract?"

I sigh. "Not yet."

"Do you think she chickened out?"

"It's not like that," I say, not wanting to get into the intricacies of why people can withdraw.

She shrugs. "Sometimes it is."

"Maybe. But it's their choice."

"You should message her again."

A shadow falls over us as Noel leans against Penny's pink side. "Message who?"

Before I can answer, Melly beats me to it. "The cop's chick."

Chapter Nine

When Noel's eyes meet mine, it's like an entire conversation passes unspoken between us.

There's an uncomfortable beat where Melly looks like she has no idea she just put her entire combat boot in her mouth.

"I thought you dropped that?" Noel says in a way that really isn't a question. He keeps his tone very, very neutral, and it somehow makes me feel worse than if he were angry. But instead, his face is full of concern and, yes, betrayal. I should've kept him in the loop from the beginning. He didn't have to be happy about it, but he didn't deserve to be in the dark.

"It was legit," I say, aware that there are only so many details we can get into in public.

He nods, once.

Melly pulls her legs up and claps her hands on her knees, pushing off the step. "Well, I came, I saw, I made it awkward, so that's my cue to bounce."

"You can stay," Noel says, retreating to his booth. "I have customers."

Melly grimaces. "Sorry. I didn't know it was a secret."

"It wasn't." I sigh. "He's just worried. With it being a cop and being local, you know?"

"So if it was the same situation but with a fireman in Bethesda, that would be okay?"

"You know it's not that simple."

"Isn't it? You help people who need it. She needs it. This sleaze-bag shouldn't get a free pass because he has a badge and a Turnbridge address."

She's not wrong.

But neither is Noel.

I do know that.

But I also know that, no matter the risk, I have to help.

* * *

When Thursday rolls around and I still haven't heard anything from Jodie, I lose whatever scrap of patience I still possess.

It doesn't matter that I know better, that I have rules for a reason.

I don't like that Troy's already restricted her communication to public library computers and that he appears to chauffeur her every-where. I can't confirm that, but there are no cars registered to Jodie and only one to him, a massive black pickup that I would bet my pie van she isn't allowed to touch.

She has no social media for me to stalk, and his is nothing but police pride flags and the kind of memes that would get you fired from other jobs. There's only so much online digging I can do before I start to go stir-crazy.

Which means time for recon.

I roll into the library an hour before closing, late enough for her to be there, early enough that I won't cross paths with Troy.

It feels reckless, even though she has no idea I'm the one behind Pies Before Guys. If she recognizes me, it will only be from parking Penny in the lot outside, and that's fine. I'm a Turnbridge resident; I have every right to be inside the library.

That's what I tell myself as I exchange a friendly nod with the geeky Black librarian at the desk. I wander, pretending to peruse the new releases on the first floor, all the while keeping an eye out for Jodie.

The library isn't huge, but like all libraries, the stacks of shelves offer plenty of places to hide. I hit the nonfiction section and get waylaid by the cookbooks. One in particular, *Piety*, catches my eye. It features elaborate crust art, the pastry equivalent of fondant cakes. Gorgeous, for sure, but not my jam. While I could work a heap of magic into all those fiddly bits, I can make a week's worth of Frank's pies in the time it would take to make one of these.

Still, the pictures are stunning, and I imagine an alternative life where I spend all day making a single pie for myself rather than the dozens I go through daily. I slide the book back into place, not even able to fathom such a thing, and let out a peep of surprise when I see what's next to it. I sneak a glance through the shelves, expecting to be shushed before remembering we don't live in a fifties stereotype.

Temporarily forgetting my real mission, I pull the heavy book out and prop it open on an empty bit of shelf to snap a few pictures. *Tough Cookie* is stamped across the cover in blocky black-and-yellow capitals above a picture of Vic Rossi, her muscled forearms crossed over a flour-dusted apron. A black tank top proudly displays the tattoos scrolling over her shoulders, and it's no wonder she's turned into a full-blown badass baking icon.

I open the *Bake My Day* group chat and upload the picture. Since the show—and all the subsequent drama—wrapped, most of us have stayed in touch, and like my life in Turnbridge, it's something I wouldn't have imagined for myself, this group of friends spread across the country. Derek, Vic, and Freddie are all up in New York, close enough to visit, with Nell back in Ohio, happily chained to her doughnut shop. We get the occasional update from Gemma in

44

Paris, the baby of our group, who is poised to blow us all out of the culinary waters.

I make sure my phone is on silent before the replies start and continue my wander.

Vic was the second of our group to take the show's cookbook offer, encouraged by Tony's positive experience. Courchesne has one in the works too, but she's more focused on filming the second season of *The Real Ace of Cakes* for Netflix, the queer and quirky baking show that has become an unexpected hit.

Unexpected to Netflix, that is. Not to us. We all knew she was gonna kill it.

It's a thought that would make me laugh if I weren't trying to be library quiet, because if I did a cookbook, wouldn't killing it be my theme? I can see it now: *Mango Mojito Murder Pie, ingredients mango, mint, and manslaughter. If you can't make your own magic, store-bought is fine.*

I shake my head, grinning, and head upstairs. No, a cookbook will not be in my future. I've had more than my share of the public eye thanks to the show.

Upstairs, a bank of computers is sparsely populated with a few people clicking away, and a reference librarian—not Jodie—is busy at her desk. Stacks of shelves fan out in rows on both sides of the space, and I start in fiction, thinking Jodie might be shelving returned books. That seems like a volunteer-y thing to do.

But no. There's an older Asian man browsing mysteries and a teenage girl in sci-fi, but no Jodie.

I check nonfiction, abandoning my guise of casual perusal.

She's not up here.

I trot back downstairs, skirt billowing around me as I go. I bypass the desk and go into the common area, where a notice board announces upcoming programs and tables are arranged for reading or quiet conversation. The food pantry room is open but empty, and I continue into the youth section.

It's a whole new world over here, almost chaotic, with dozens of nooks and subsections. A trio of almost identical toddlers are parked on a race car carpet, surrounded by board books and coloring pages, while a fourth raids the toy bin in the corner. The woman supervising them looks like a parent, definitely not Jodie. I wonder if all the kids are hers and feel a flash of sympathy. I know Ana can be enough on her own, and she's only one objectively awesome seven-year-old. I can't imagine having a pack of four all under that age.

I suppress a shudder and move farther into the room. There's a lone kid on the computers, headphones barely muffling the sounds of his game, and a woman straightening bins of picture books. I peer down shelves of middle-grades fiction with no luck, but as I reach the young adult section at the back, I catch a glimpse of movement. A small woman, her leggings and cream sweater just visible through the gaps of the shelves.

My heart kicks up. I haven't thought this through. I mostly wanted to confirm she was okay, but now that I'm here, do I say something? I duck into a YA aisle, knowing I can't exactly march up and offer my hand and a cheery *Let me help you kill your boyfriend.*

Can I?

No.

But maybe I can be subtle about it.

It wouldn't be my first time directly interacting with a potential client, after all. A few years back, at the Saint Stan's meeting, there was another woman who wasn't quite ready to change her situation, and something about her called to me, drove me to interfere. I offered her the button that has become the official Pies Before Guys calling card, a kitschy slice of cherry pie with a banner bearing the PBG name and my contact info on the back. I didn't tell her I was the piemaker, of course, but I let her know options existed. Options she hadn't considered.

But I'm not prepared for that tonight. My button stash is back in the van, and while there might be one or two squirreled away in the truck, they're not helping me now.

Something else, then.

My mind flashes back to the notice board in the lobby, all the flyers tacked up there. I go back out, careful to appear nonchalant. I don't want to draw attention to myself right now. I scan the board, and yes, there. A light-blue notice with little strips cut along the bottom, several torn away to leave gaps like broken teeth. The remaining tabs are emblazoned with the logo and number of a national domestic violence hotline. I pull one off and return to the youth room. If she's still in the back, it will be easy to sidle up and leave the slip. Just something to remind her she has options.

Then I can go. I can wait, and if she decides to get back in touch with me, great. If she decides to use the hotline, also great.

I just want to remind her there are ways out.

She's sitting on the floor when I get there, a curtain of shiny hair cascading from her tipped head as she examines the manga on the bottom shelf. I must make some noise, because she turns to look up at me, and I drop the number, the little blue paper fluttering to the floor.

The teenager in the cream sweater plucks it off the floor and holds it up. "Here, you dropped this."

Chapter Ten

I'm so flustered by the girl not being Jodie that I throw stealth straight out the window.

I take the paper back and pocket it. "Thanks."

She smiles and goes back to her book search, and I go right out to nerdy library guy.

He looks up as I approach, face open and ready to help.

Poor guy.

I plaster what I hope is an equally friendly expression on my own face. I don't want to set off any alarm bells, but the ones ringing in my head are loud enough that I can't let this be a wasted trip.

"No Jodie tonight?" I ask, as if it's a given that I know her schedule, that I know her.

His dark-brown eyes fill with sympathy behind his thick-rimmed glasses. "She'll be gone for a while, I'm afraid. Is there something I can help you with?"

Every nerve in my body goes into alert mode. "Where is she?"

He cocks his head ever so slightly, weighing me up. "Are you a friend?"

"Yeah, from school," I lie. It comes out easy. "We haven't hung out in ages, but I thought she said she was in on Tuesdays and Thursdays and wanted to surprise her. No worries, though; I'll just text her."

48

It must be convincing enough, because he says, "She emailed yesterday. Her mom passed, and she went back home to see to things. Said she didn't know how long she'd be gone."

My hand goes to my mouth, and I shake my head. "Oh, how awful."

"I know. I asked if there was an address to send flowers, but she hasn't gotten back, which is understandable. I'm sure she's overwhelmed."

My mind races as I try to visualize her last message. *No family, no one who can help.* I know she said she had no family. But this guy is so sincere that I'm starting to doubt my recall.

"If you talk to her, please tell her we're all thinking about her here," he says.

"I will, of course. Thanks for letting me know."

"She's so private, but we love having her around." He shakes his head sadly. "She was finally starting to come out of her shell, and now this. Poor girl."

I can see that he means it, that he genuinely cares for her, and I feel awful deceiving him, but right now he's my best source of information.

So I milk it.

"I wish we hadn't lost touch for so long." I sigh. "It sounds like she's happy here, though, with this job and her boyfriend, right? Seems like they're pretty serious, from what she told me."

There's a slight hesitation, a flash of something barely perceptible that makes me want to push, but I don't. I wait.

He shrugs one shoulder. "Like I said, she's pretty private. Comes in, helps with shelf reading and such, and goes home. We've tried to get her to come out with us a few times after work, but no dice. I guess she's digging the housewife life, you know?"

There's a note at the end of the question, like it's a challenge rather than an observation.

Like I'm not the only one fishing here.

I lean into it, because why not. "I guess. Honeymoon phase and all that, right?" When he doesn't give me so much as a nod, I continue. "I haven't even met him yet—that's how long it's been since we hung out—but he sounds nice, from what she's told me. He's a cop, right?"

"That he is." It's neutral, noncommittal, but the warmth he had in his eyes when he spoke about Jodie is gone.

"One of the good ones?" This is not neutral and I know it. I don't mean it to be.

There's another flicker of something across his face, shut down as soon as it appears. This guy must interact with dozens of people each day and he's good at schooling his emotions, but not perfect. Not when I've made it my job to notice the things people try to hide.

"He seems nice enough."

"You've met him, then?"

"Only to say hi. He drops her off and picks her up."

That confirms what I already thought. She doesn't get to drive that pickup he has, and she certainly can't touch his squad car. She's completely reliant on him to get around. Sure, Turnbridge has a better-than-average bus service thanks to the local colleges, but I doubt it ventures out to Troy and Jodie's swanky subdivision. I wonder about grocery trips, the regular running around that so often falls to women in straight relationships. Does he chauffeur her there too? Does she Uber? And what about doctor's appointments? The pharmacy? She clearly doesn't want to go through with this pregnancy, but without a car, without a phone she can trust to be private, the logistics of sorting it out in secret are almost impossible.

No wonder she needs me.

"What's your impression of him?" I ask. "As a person?"

There's a beat of silence long enough to make me think he won't answer, but he says, "Look, I might be a nerd, but I'm a Black nerd. He's a white cop. I'm polite, but I keep it moving, you know?" He levels his gaze at me, and I get the feeling he might be as good at reading people as I am, that he's been doing the same calculations about me this whole time. Interesting. "If there's something you want to ask me about your friend, just ask. We don't have to dance around it."

"Is he good to her? Does she seem happy?" I know she's not, but I want to know how well she's been keeping it hidden.

He sighs. "She says she is. And I don't know why she'd stay this long if she wasn't, but I don't know. She's smart and she's funny, when she lets herself be—like she'll make up wild backstories for patrons based on what they're reading, but it's like as soon as she catches herself having fun, she shuts down. When it's not busy, we all shoot the shit, talk about what we're up to outside of here, but she never has anything. It's like she comes here two days a week, then she's home. I don't think she has hobbies or anything she does that isn't about him. It's not normal."

As he speaks, my heart breaks a little for Jodie. Her message was so desperate, she seemed so convinced that there was no one in her life who could help her, but she was wrong. This guy? This guy would've been on her side.

"I'd miss her if she left," he says, "But part of me hopes this going-home thing is permanent. That she stays. It might be better for her."

"Maybe," I agree. If there was a home to go. If there was family waiting. But her message made it sound like there wasn't, so I have to wonder where she really is.

"I'm Heath, by the way," the librarian says. "Like I said, if you talk to her, please let her know we're thinking about her. That I hope she's all right."

"I hope she is too," I say, with way more honesty than I mean to.

* * *

When I get back to Penny, the first thing I want to do is go into research mode, but a certain pit bull has other ideas. I clip Zoe's leash on, and she bursts out of the RV, thrilled to be out in the crisp fall night. As we walk, I use the time to sort out everything else I need to do.

First, I need to finish Frank's diner pies for the weekend. That's a given, but an easy one.

I also know I should update Noel on Jodie, which is decidedly less easy. I know he's worried, but I can't in good conscience let this one go, especially after talking to Heath. There's more to this story than even her message conveyed, and if I'm the one who can help her sort it out, I have to. It's that simple.

What won't be simple is figuring out how. I don't have a contract from her, which means she's technically not a client. I can make her a pie, sure, but at this point that would be my choice, not hers. Not officially. Her message made it clear it was what she wanted, but only the contract can finalize it. It's an emergency-exit step, a chance for people who don't want to go through with it to jump ship before anything is final.

There's a chance, of course, that that's exactly what's happened here. That Jodie decided she'd figure it out a different way or that, in the aftermath of her mother's death, she couldn't deal with it right now.

Her mother.

That's top on my list. Determining if a mom even exists, and if so, in what capacity.

My phone vibrates in my pocket, and I pull it out.

Noel. *See you tonight?*

I waver, tempted, for the first time, to simply ignore him. I don't want to argue about Jodie. I don't want to have to justify why I do what I do.

He sends me a photo, the scarred wooden dining table already set for two, then one of a ball of dough nestled in a metal bowl. *Pizza date?*

I can't help but grin. It was the first thing he ever made me, and it was spectacular.

I text him back. *Need to do Frank's pies first, but I'll bring dessert.*

I'll also be bringing my laptop, but I don't mention that. I can research after he's asleep.

Chapter Eleven

The pizza is, once again, spectacular.

Noel has perfected his crust so it's the ideal combination of crispy bottom and pillowy insides, and he's topped this one with a tangy local goat cheese, caramelized onions, and sweet pears.

Zoe is tucked under the table, happily feasting on crust scraps, her favorite part of pizza night.

I tip my bottle of fizzy maple cider at him. "Compliments to the chef."

He clinks his bottle to mine, looking adorably pleased with himself.

"You should really do pizzas for the cidery," I say, slicing the last piece in half and taking the side with extra onions. "You could build a brick oven and everything."

He grimaces. "I don't know. It's one thing making them for us, but for customers? In large quantities?"

"You could totally do it. These are top-notch, seriously. People would pay good money, especially with toppings like this that pair with the ciders." I stab a crust in his direction for emphasis before dropping it for Zoe. "C'mon. I wouldn't lie to you about food."

"I know."

"So stop doubting yourself. You wouldn't have to go in all at once. It doesn't have to be pizzapalooza every day. Maybe offer it as a special, see how it goes. We could probably even rent a pizza oven. I can talk to Juan—I bet he knows someone."

The more I talk, the more cautious excitement blooms in Noel's eyes.

Hollow Hill has rapidly become a Turnbridge fixture, and thanks to features in several foodie news outlets, it's even turned into a destination spot for New Englanders. Noel even had to hire a small staff after it became clear the popularity was more than he could manage as a solo operator.

"Maybe we could do it in November," he says. "Post pumpkins."

I laugh. "If there's even such a thing as post-pumpkin."

"I didn't think they'd grow like that," he protests. "It was my first time!"

In addition to apple picking, Noel added a pumpkin patch to this year's family-friendly festivities, but he had failed to predict just how well the pumpkins would take to the orchard soil. Not only did he end up with about a million of the things, but they're all absolutely enormous.

"Well, you've established yourself as the pumpkin king of Turnbridge, that's for sure."

"There are worse things to be."

"Indeed."

As we clean up the detritus of dinner, we brainstorm pizza ideas and baking timelines. It's fun and easy, exactly the way things with Noel always are, and in the end, I decide research can wait until morning.

* * *

I work during the lulls between rushes. There's a predictable ebb and flow to campus days, with the lines dwindling to the occasional straggler while classes are in session.

I prop my laptop on the narrow counter below the serving window so I can keep an eye on things, but most of my attention is on the information spooling out in front of me.

There is a staggering amount of easy-to-find data about most people online. It's disturbingly easy, actually, what a simple search with the right combination of factors can pull up, even for the average user. This is especially true the more online the subject is, thanks to living in a world that encourages people to post the most mundane minutiae of their day for public consumption.

Throw in the private investigator services I'm subscribed to and it's even easier.

But it's not magic, and right now I would kill to have the kind of power that could produce answers with the flick of a whisk.

Instead, I scroll.

My known-relation search on Jodie is coming up blank enough that I wonder if she's using an assumed name. If she changed it legally, I should see a record of that somewhere, but it's bothering me that I can't find a single familial connection. I mean, someone gave birth to this girl at some point, somewhere. I just need to find her.

I open the search up nationwide, knowing it will take longer to slog through all the possible Jodie Azaria connections, but I have to try. I need her mother's name and, preferably, a death notice. I'll take an obituary, a coroner's report, anything.

I'm lost enough in thought that I don't even notice someone is at my window until they ask, "Whatcha doing?" loud enough to make me jump.

"Having a heart attack, apparently," I say, hand on my racing heart. At my feet, Zoe lifts her head as if she can't believe I disturbed her nap like that.

Neither can I.

"Anything exciting?" Melly asks, going up on her tiptoes as if it will be enough to give her a glimpse of my screen.

I sigh. "Mixed bag so far."

Without waiting for an invitation, Melly spins away from the serving window and lets herself into the RV. She doesn't bother dragging a stool over, just hops on the short side of the L-shaped counter behind me, planting her elbows on denim-clad knees and leaning forward to peer at the laptop.

"Hey, I cook there," I say, swatting at her legs.

"And now my butt's here." She shrugs, then waggles her eyebrows at me. "And it's not even naked."

"Something for which both I and the health inspector are grateful."

"You never know," Melly says cheekily. "You might like it."

"I might be in a relationship already," I remind her in the same easy way I always remind Frank he's not paying me.

"You're no fun." She pouts, but she doesn't mean it and immediately shifts gears. "So, what do we got?"

"I think your lack of impulse control may be rubbing off on me." I fill her in on my impromptu library trip and how it left me with more questions than answers.

"But some answers," Melly says. "You know she's had a set routine that's now disrupted. That's out of character. And you know there's something about this cop that even had library boy's Spidey sense tingling, not that he did anything about it."

"That's not fair. It didn't sound like they were really close. You know how hard it can be to talk to people about their personal lives, never mind abusive relationships. I think he was trying to respect her boundaries."

She shrugs. "I don't think it's hard to talk to people about that shit."

"Of course you don't. But you also have a lack of tact that borders on sociopathic."

"Does it, though?"

I laugh. "Anyway. I'm working on confirming the dead-mother story."

"Was that an example of tact, oh sensitive one?"

"You know what I mean. You saw the message—she said she had no family." I gesture at the laptop. "So far that seems true."

"So do we know anything about her other than that she's dating a uniformed shitbag?"

"I have academic records, three semesters at a community college in Colorado, but as far as I can see, she's never been a student in Massachusetts. Given her age and our unusually high concentration of colleges in spitting distance of town, that's weird, right? And she doesn't work. At least not above the table. Just the volunteer gig twice a week."

Wrinkles of disdain crease Melly's forehead. "So she's what, like an unmarried housewife? At twenty-three?"

"That's what Heath thought, and right now, he's the one who knows her best."

"That's fucking weird," she says.

I sigh. "Not if he's going all in on the isolation. It's practically Abuser 101. She doesn't seem to have friends, she doesn't have family. No job. Nothing that isn't connected to him."

"Why let her volunteer at the library, then?"

"I don't know." It's something I've been wondering too. "It could be an image thing, like *Ooh, look at my girl's little volunteer job she has so she can feel useful.* Or it could be some kind of test. Or a reward. I don't know. But he doesn't keep her hidden, I know that. There are pictures of them at police events online, and Heath said her social life pretty much revolved around him. They might have couples friends, but at the end of the day, they're going to be his people, not hers. Everything is on his terms, including the library."

"Fucking bastard," Melly mutters.

"Yup. Hold the thought." I close the laptop and shift back into Pie Girl mode to greet a pair of professors who want to order pies.

When they're gone, I turn to find Melly sitting cross-legged on the counter, chin propped on her fist. There's an intensity to her face that I know all too well now.

"What?" I ask warily.

"You're overthinking it," she declares, waving at the laptop. "All of it. You have the address and you have the order. Make the damn pie. It doesn't matter if her mom is dead. You can still sort this shit out right now."

"I don't have a contract. You know how this works."

And she does, even if she's too focused on action to admit it. Despite almost blowing up the entire business when I first met her, she is the only person besides Noel who knows exactly what I am. And she gets it. One hundred percent. I could've written her off for what she did back then, but I didn't, and she's proven dedicated to the PBG cause. If I were a more cunning kind of killer, I would appreciate her solely for her usefulness, her recently acquired ability to suss out clients from the darkest corners of the internet, but it's more than that. I simply like her, even when she's lobbying hard for the devil on my shoulder.

She lets out a frustrated growl that I understand in my soul. "It shouldn't be a crime to help people who won't help themselves."

"That's what I do. And it technically *is* a crime, regardless of the enthusiasm of the recipient," I remind her. "Which is why I'm not storming the castle."

As soon as the words leave my lips, though, I realize that's exactly what I need to do.

I don't need to dredge the internet looking for evidence that Jodie is at her mother's.

I can simply go see if she's home.

Chapter Twelve

I'll need to bring a pie, because of course I do.

The world could end and I would be there, pie box in hand.

I spend a lot of time working out what to make, longer than I normally would. It's not a murder pie, much to Melly's disappointment, but it is magic.

I start with the crust, a gingerbread crumb base made from scratch cookies. It's a good, stiff dough, and along with spices, I mix in the same blend of strength and conviction that goes into the support group pies. It's potent but fairly neutral, a bolstering sort of magic, the strength focused on finding safety and stability rather than physical force. I know there's as good a chance that Troy will eat this pie too, and I can't risk something that will enhance his baser impulses.

Ana helps me roll out the dough, giddy with the chance to use her dinosaur cookie cutters to stamp out a herd of stegosauruses and T. rexes.

While they bake, I whip up a big batch of basic icing and divide it into small bowls for her to color. While part of me wonders at the wisdom of giving an already opinionated seven-year-old magic that could intensify that, I'm not denying the kid a chance to decorate dino cookies.

I'm a murderer, not a monster.

When the first batch comes out of the oven, it's all I can do to keep her little hands off them. "They need to cool first," I remind her. "Or your frosting will melt. Here, let's do some piping bags."

We scrape the colored icing into bags fitted with an array of tips while Juan looks on from his station at the flat-top. "You're gonna regret that," he says, a knowing grin creasing his face.

For a second I think he means the magic, but I wave him off. "She's got this."

"Yeah?"

I look down and see a rope of neon-pink icing coiling like a snake on the stainless-steel bench and laugh, taking the bag from Ana. "Watch," I say, twisting the top and wrapping it with a rubber band. I take her small hands and position them, one at the band and one near the nozzle. "Squeeze like this—" I close my hands around hers, and we scrawl a legible, if not pretty, *Ana* across the bench. She giggles. "And when you're done, loosen your grip and it will stop. Yeah?"

"Yeah!" She does a pass of writing her name on her own, giving the final *A* a swirly flourish.

Juan laughs and shakes his head before going back to his order.

Ana and I clean the bench and lay out a batch of dinosaurs that will keep her occupied and well out of the way of the molten sugar I need.

The filling is a twist on classic banoffee flavors, but instead of tinned dulce de leche, the base will be a thick salted cinnamon caramel.

And if there's one thing caramel doesn't need, it's little arms in close range, because there are very few things worse than sugar burns.

Before long, the sweet smell of spicy caramel suffuses the kitchen, edging out the ever-present scent of fryer oil and fat.

The sounds around me—Juan's singing, the dish machine, and Ana's quiet narration of her task—fall away as I stir slowly, concentrating on channeling clarity into the caramel with each stroke.

The mechanics of the magic have always been a bit of a mystery, much in the same way walking is if you think too hard about *exactly* how it works, all the tiny factors that go into moving a single foot. It's such an automatic part of me that it's impossible to precisely break down all the steps to it.

With the right ingredients—focus and food—it just happens.

When the sauce has thickened with both magic and heat, I turn off the flame and hit it with a finishing drizzle of cream and a heap of softened, salty butter. It's from a dairy in town, and coarse flakes of salt sparkle in it like stars.

I coat the back of a spoon and let it cool for a minute before tasting.

Perfect.

I set it aside to thicken so it will be almost spreadable when it goes into the crust.

At her station, Ana has frosted all of her cookies, herself, and most of the bench.

"Told ya," Juan says with a smirk, and I laugh.

"Fair enough. You would know."

"I've had to seriously redefine what a clean house means since this one came along." He shakes his head with an affection that makes it clear he wouldn't have it any other way.

"Okay, pie pal, let's shift gears," I say. We gather the frosted cookies onto a sheet pan and stick them on the cooling rack. They'll be easier to box up once the frosting has had a chance to harden a bit. After another wipe-down of the bench, Ana hops up on her milk crate, wielding my French rolling pin like a weapon.

"Can I make the crumbs?" she asks hopefully.

"Of course." I dump the other sheet of unfrosted dinos—plus all the misshapen scrap pieces we baked off—into a big bowl.

Taking the rolling pin vertically in both hands, Ana stabs it down into the bowl, using the blunt end to bludgeon the pile of dinosaurs to dust.

"Die, dinos, die!" she chants, and in that moment, for a brief flash, I can see the appeal of this having-a-kid thing.

The fact that it's this moment probably says more about me than it should.

"Ana," Juan chastises. "You love dinosaurs. Be nice."

"It's the circle of life," she says merrily, not pausing her pummeling.

"At least she's learning something," I say, laughing as I grab the edge of the bowl to keep it from skittering off the table beneath the onslaught.

"Yeah, from *The Lion King*."

Just then, the swinging door to the dining room flies open and a scowling Frank stalks in. "What is this racket?"

"Extinction event!" Ana crows, and the look of confusion on Frank's face as she demolishes the cookies is priceless.

"Goddamn women," he mutters. "I let the pair of you into my kitchen and it's constant chaos, all the time."

"You love it," I tease.

He harrumphs and takes the plate Juan is finishing. For someone who claims to be a crotchety misanthrope, he spends a lot of time running food and interacting with customers. I think his grumpy-old-man act encourages people to tip their servers more, because they're so much nicer than him.

I also think he's very aware of this.

When he's gone, I still Ana's assault and check the results. "Looks good."

"Like a crumble-saurus," she says.

"Exactly." I grab her a box and set her on the other side of the bench with her cookies. "Why don't you pack these up while I finish the pie?"

She agrees and I set to work on my crust, holding some of the crumbs back to use as garnish and stirring melted butter into the rest. It goes in the oven for eight minutes while I slice a trio of small bananas, the only magic-free element of the crust. I can work intention into things that need assembly but not stand-alone ingredients.

When the pie is finished, it's a delight of warmly spiced crust, salty caramel, bananas, and vanilla bean whipped cream.

I spike the cream with a bit of bravery, just for good measure.

* * *

The gate at the entrance of Jodie's subdivision is open, and the uniformed white guy in the booth doesn't even glance up when I drive through. There's a conspicuous camera mounted on the stone column abutting the gate that makes me think he might have a bank of security monitors in there.

One of the selling points of the Meadowbrook development is supposed to be its state-of-the-art security systems, and Jodie's message did say there were cameras *everywhere*. Personally, I don't get the appeal of living in these cookie-cutter houses under constant surveillance, but to each their own. I stick precisely to the posted ten-mile-per-hour speed limit and find number forty-two easily. Like all the other houses, it's set far back from the street on a sprawling expanse of green lawn, its borders marked with neatly trimmed hedges. They must have an entire army of gardeners who do nothing but keep those bushes in shape.

The driveway is empty, all the doors of the three-bay garage closed, and I pull in, wondering if I'm about to deliver a pie to an empty house.

Still, the SUV isn't here, and I take that as a good sign.

I park and get out, shaking out the fox-patterned skirt of my dress so it's not sticking to my tights, and fetch the pie.

When I ring the bell, I can't help noticing the small glowing light above it. A camera, again, and not a surprise. It seems most houses have them these days, and I don't let it bother me. This is nothing but a normal delivery on a normal day.

There's movement from inside, and I plaster on my best Pie Girl smile as the door opens partway to reveal the last thing I wanted to see.

Troy.

Managing to look both suspicious and superior, he jams the toe of one scuffed white sneaker behind the door like I might try to force it the rest of the way open.

Behind him, I can see the edge of a coatrack above a bench and a neat row of women's shoes tucked below. Somehow I know Jodie doesn't wear her shoes in the house, the same way I know she's the one who has to wash the floor when he does. I remind myself that I have bigger things to sort out than their gender-role bullshit and up the wattage of my smile.

"Hi, I'm the Pie Girl." I hold the box out. "Jodie Azaria is this week's winner of our free giveaway. Is she in?"

He doesn't take the box.

"Wrong address," he says, closing the door. "No one by that name lives here."

Chapter Thirteen

S he doesn't *live* there?

I drive back to the diner with the question on repeat. He didn't hesitate, simply spoke the words like truth.

But they're not true.

I know they're not.

I know from her message and from talking to Heath.

Plus, I know what I saw in that entryway. A long, blush-pink cashmere coat. Women's shoes.

Certainly not the kind of things Troy would wear.

He's lying. I know he's lying, but what I don't know is why, and I don't like that.

When I get back to Penny, I park and pull up Jodie's message before I even get out of the truck, needing to be sure. And yes, there it is: *We live at 42 Meadowbrook Lane.*

We.

I send a follow-up message, the kind of nudge I rarely make. I keep as innocuous as possible, letting her know she missed delivery of her free pie but she'll be reentered for the next raffle and asking her to please get in touch if she still wants a custom order.

Even though I know better, I wait, phone in hand, hoping a reply will ping right back.

No such luck.

I let the facts of the day filter through my brain while I walk Zoe, trying to work out the best angle.

The way I see it, I have two problems now. I have a girl who needs a pie but hasn't completed her request, and I have a target who is very likely the reason she hasn't been able to do so.

I know what Melly's answer would be—just make the pie—and as I let myself back into Penny, part of me is tempted. I put the kettle on and retrieve the sunny-yellow teapot that's usually too big for one person, but something tells me I'm going to need it.

My phone vibrates with a text that I hope is somehow Jodie, but it's only Noel sharing a picture of the cidery's crowded tasting room. I heart it and switch back to the PBG account, just to check if I missed a reply.

Nothing.

In addition to my laptop, I fetch a stack of the index cards I usually reserve for writing out new pie recipes. Sometimes notes need to be scratched out longhand.

It starts with doodles while my tea steeps, a series of overlapping cubes as I play out the idea of making the pie. I could do it, sure, and now that I've met him, it would be all the more potent, but he wouldn't even take the pie I had today. I think Jodie was right in saying she should be the one to serve it, but even beyond that, a murder pie today doesn't get me the answers I need.

I jot down my questions on a green card: (1) *Why did he lie about her not living there? (2) Where is she?*

I flip it over and start listing possible answers to the first one.

He meant to say she was out of town.

They broke up/she left him.

I want the answer to be that one, but my gut says no. If she left, she would've taken that coat with her. You don't leave nice winter stuff behind when you live in New England, not if you can help it. But she wouldn't need a coat if she wasn't going outside.

He has her trapped inside.

It's possible. He wouldn't even open the door all the way. But why lie? Because I was a stranger and it didn't matter? Or because it's actually true? With a chill, I realize she might *not* live there, or anywhere anymore.

He killed her.

The panic in her message was palpable. It was real. It was why I was willing to upset Noel, who cares more about me than anyone in the world, just to help her. She feared for her safety.

Her photos proved she was right to.

My stomach knots, rebelling against the usually soothing tea. If Jodie is dead, it's my fault. I knew she needed help and I waited. I waited and I followed my stupid rules, and for what? For things to get so bad she physically couldn't complete her order?

Fuck.

A potent mix of guilt and edgy desperation snakes around my chest, constricting my lungs and making my heart flail. It's the kind of panic I haven't felt in years, not since high school when I made that first murder pie, when I didn't know what I was capable of. The aftermath—that death, an accident—felt like this.

It's one thing to target people who deserve it, who can't be stopped in any other way. It's righteous, a way to protect the world from monsters. But this?

This is wrong.

This feels like murder.

I let the monster win, and an innocent person paid the price of my inaction.

It's inexcusable.

The pain in my chest worsens as my breathing gets faster.

I let her die.

I might as well have killed her myself.

A high-pitched whine fills the RV, and a weight drops onto my lap.

Zoe.

Her blocky head presses hard into my legs as she makes concerned keening sounds that instantly bring me out of the spiral.

"Shh, it's okay," I tell her, petting her velvety ears. "It's okay."

And after a few shaky breaths, it is.

I'm getting ahead of myself, and I know better.

I pour another cup of tea and pull up the contacts on my phone. My thumb wavers over two names before dropping down.

Melly picks up on the first ring. "Are you in trouble?"

I snort. "I haven't even said anything yet."

"Yeah, that's what concerns me. We're not phone call friends. You realize we've never had a phone conversation that wasn't preceded by a text, right? At least not one that wasn't part of some kind of crisis. So yeah, you pop up on my screen and I think trouble."

"Fair enough." I sigh. "I need a sounding board. Can you talk?"

"Sure." There's a rustle on her end and the sound of a door closing. "Do you want me to come to you?"

"No, this is fine." I catch her up on my aborted delivery attempt.

"And he just lied to your face?"

"I'm trying to work out why. And where she might be."

"Shit, do you think he killed her?" She sounds aghast and I try to laugh off her bluntness, but the knot of worry has tightened back around my chest and I can't seem to muster enough air.

"Thank you, tact queen. It's not like I haven't been having a complete panic attack about exactly that or anything." I force a deep breath that doesn't quite fill my lungs and exhale hard.

"Wait, seriously?"

"Seriously. That's why I called. I keep thinking if he killed her, it's my fault—" She starts to interrupt, but I cut her off. "Which I know is stupid. If he did kill her, he's the only one at fault, I know that. But it doesn't *feel* like that, and I can't think clearly if I'm too busy feeling stupid feelings."

"So you called me," she repeats slowly, a note of something I can't identify in her voice.

"Yes. Because you don't do stupid feelings and I need to figure out what I'm dealing with here." I run down the other options on my *why he lied* list for her. "Anything else you can think of?"

She *hmm*s for a bit, then says, "He wanted you to think he was single so he could hit on you?"

"Then he would've taken the pie and invited me in."

"Good point," she says. "Okay, I've got nothing."

"Right. So the real question is, where is she? Whether she's alive or not—" I try not to get stuck on the *not* and only mostly succeed. I clear my throat to cover it. "Alive or dead, she's somewhere. I want to know where."

"In a broad sense, you have two options," Melly says. "She's in the house or she's not. Shit—Daisy? Hold on, I'm going to lose you."

The call drops, and I write *house* on the top of an index card labeled *Where?* while I wait for Melly to call back. Below it I write *hidden*. Then I write *grave* and try to ignore the buzzing in my head.

I trace over the word, spooling out the possibilities as objectively as possible. Troy's a cop. If he killed her, he would be too smart to bury her on the property, especially with the overenthusiastic security systems.

If she's dead, she might not even be buried at all.

I'm trying to figure out how to put that on my list, because all I can think of is *disposed* and that's not a word I want associated with someone I was supposed to save, when a pounding knock rattles

Penny's door and makes me jump. Zoe's deep bark echoes in the RV and I shush her, sure it's going to be Frank, who categorically refuses to bother with phones when he knows right where to find me.

But when I open the door, it isn't Frank standing there but Melly, holding up a white paper bag.

"Froyo," she says, handing the bag to me. "It has all the shit on it. Caramel and brownies and candy and whipped cream and like six kinds of sprinkles. I didn't know what you liked, so I got all of it."

It's so unexpected that I temporarily lose all sense of words. "What? How? I said you didn't have to come. So you brought froyo?"

"Yes. Have you ever actually been to the froyo place in town? It's like a rainbow threw up an ice cream van on a unicorn. It's horrible."

I laugh, because that's about as far from Melly's aesthetic as anything could possibly be and yet here I am, holding the spoils of her sacrifice. "But why?"

She shrugs and looks at her combat boots, then back up at me. "Because it sounded like you needed it." There's something on her face I haven't seen before, but before I can puzzle it out, she's brushing past me up the steps. "Come on. It's going to melt and we have work to do."

Chapter Fourteen

It takes longer than I want it to, but in the end, surrounded by the detritus of froyo and the late-night falafel order we demolished hours ago, I find Jodie's mother.

"Holy shit," I mutter. Neither Melly nor Zoe raises their head from where they're sleeping, Zoe on the bed, barely visible in the midnight gloom, and Melly beside me, head on folded arms. In the soft glow of a single under-cabinet light, she looks peaceful enough that I almost don't want to disturb her, but only almost. I nudge her stool and she jolts up, a flash of confusion crossing her face before her brows knit together in a scowl.

"Easy there," I say. "I have news, and not just that you're a cranky waker-upper."

"I wasn't sleeping," she snaps.

"Yeah, obviously." I have to force myself not to grin at the absurdity, but I know it's unfair. I've been wide awake, focused on getting at least this one answer, and watching someone troll through public records isn't exactly thrilling entertainment. I give her a minute to fully join the waking world before ambushing her with information.

"I'm not cranky either," she grumbles.

"Course you're not." This time I can't stop the smirk, but I quickly smother it, both for fear of my own safety and because, well, what I've discovered isn't really a laughing matter.

Melly rolls her head, cracking her neck on both sides then shaking in a way not unlike Zoe after a bath. "Okay. I'm good. What do we got?"

I spin the laptop to give her a full view of the screen.

"A death certificate?"

"For one Ann-Marie Cordace, also known as Jodie's mom."

"So the library dude was telling the truth? Why didn't Troy just say that when you were there, then?"

She's awake, but not fully. I tap the computer. "Check the date."

She squints at the screen. "Holy shit."

"My thought exactly."

"This was five years ago."

"Yup. There's no way she's out of town seeing to her dead mother's affairs if those affairs were settled when she was eighteen."

Melly takes this in, tapping a finger to her full lips. "So library dude is lying and Troy is lying."

"Maybe."

"Maybe?" she echoes. "I'd say obviously."

"I mean, yeah, obviously, outright lies are still on the table, but I believed Heath when I talked to him, and he has no reason to lie about Jodie's whereabouts. He clearly and genuinely believed she went home to grieve."

Melly looks back at the laptop. "To where, Colorado?"

"He didn't say where home was, just that it's what her email said."

"And we have no proof that email was real," Melly says. "Right. So not a lie if he believes it's true."

"Exactly."

"And Troy?"

"Might be lying, but I don't think so." The thought doesn't choke me like it did earlier. I've had time to adjust. To get angry. "If he killed her, she technically doesn't live anywhere, does she?"

The RV is dim, illuminated only by the blue tint of the laptop screen and the cabinet lighting, but it's enough for me to see my own fire reflected in Melly's eyes.

"He thinks he can get away with murder. We're not going to let him."

"You're making the pie?" Her blue eyes widen but don't waver, a current of understanding thrumming like electricity. She knows what an unordered pie means for me, the lines it would cross.

We both do.

I shake my head, not breaking eye contact. "Not yet. First, we're going to find her. We're going to prove he did this. Publicly."

"He'll get off. Cops always do." Her words are soft, like she doesn't want to break the spell I'm casting.

"I don't care. The world will know what he did. And he'll know that, at least on some level, no one will ever hear his name without associating it with scum. We'll do that." The rage simmers, magic thickening like jam, but when I step over the line, it is with deadly, perfect calm. "Then he's going to get the kind of murder pie that will make him wish he was never born."

* * *

In the light of morning, the mission should seem absurd, overblown, but it doesn't.

It feels right.

I may have gotten this girl killed through lack of action, but I won't let that go unpunished.

Justice will be served.

With pie.

I let Zoe out, and we're greeted by the overwhelming scent of bacon wafting through the open back door of the diner. It always seems to travel farther on cold air. From inside, the cacophony of the Sunday morning rush provides a familiar soundtrack as I give Zoe a lap of the back lot.

I'm already building the to-do list in my head, feeling some sort of way at once again being on the solving end of a murder. It's not territory I'm comfortable with, even after the practice run at *Bake My Day*, and this time I'm not trying to dodge the police, I'm investigating them.

A bunch of celebrity chefs and star bakers were nothing compared to this.

I'm so absorbed in my plotting that I almost don't see Juan pop out behind the diner, empty plastic oil jugs in each hand, until Zoe starts hauling me his way. Fifty pounds of excited pit bull has no regard for her own strength, and I remind her to be easy, making her wait as he lobs the jugs into the dumpster. I wave, ready to release Zoe for pets if he has a second to spare, but he doesn't see me.

His gaze is caught on Penny, and the look that crosses his face tells me exactly what he's seeing even as Melly emerges, curls still mussed with sleep and leather jacket slung over her shoulder.

Juan looks between her and me, then straight at me. Through me, it seems, as understanding passes over his face. I shake my head furiously, because he's not understanding. He's very much, radically, and violently misunderstanding, but Melly saunters over before I can explain.

"Christ, I'm wrecked. You sure know how to give a girl a good time," she says, oblivious to the scrutiny. "I gotta grab my bike, but we'll catch up later, yeah?"

I groan, torn between shushing her and telling Juan it's not what it sounds like, but he's already back inside, the screen door banging in his wake.

She follows my gaze. "Unless you want breakfast first?"

"No, go. Sorry I kept you all night."

She pins me with a stare that manages to be serious and sleepy all at once. "Please. We both know that's not true and that I wouldn't have been there if it wasn't exactly where I wanted to be."

For a tiny moment, the space of a blink and no more, this almost feels exactly like what Juan so clearly thought it was, but I shake it off. "I can drive you to your bike if you want."

"The walk'll wake me up," she says, flashing that trademark grin.

I don't remind her that she spent much of the night passed out on the counter.

I also don't tell her how much it meant that she was there, how just having someone at my side kept things from getting too dark. Part of me wants to tell her, but even if I had the words, there are some things that shouldn't be said in the back lot of a diner.

Plus, she'd never let me live it down.

There's a pause where it seems like we might hug, or what? Cheek kisses? A fist bump? But Melly breezes past, giving me a clap on the arm that sorts the whole thing out. "Keep me posted," she says over her shoulder, then disappears around the diner.

"Will do," I say to her retreating back, then sigh. "Okay Zo, time for damage control."

I leave Zoe in the RV with breakfast, then make the short trek to the kitchen, feeling unpleasantly like I'm on a walk of shame.

Inside, things are in full swing, with Frank barking orders at Juan and Alex, the assistant cook, as if they've never worked a shift before, and servers scuttling in and out. The swinging door to the dining room barely pauses on its hinges.

"Pie Girl, you pitching in?" Frank calls as soon as I step in.

"What do you need? More pie?"

"A pair of goddamn hands," he says, foisting a tray laden with plates at me. "Amanda dropped a whole pot of coffee and is having a cry about it like some kind of rookie. Table four."

I take the tray because there is clearly no option not to, but I catch Juan's sidelong glance as I do. I should've known better than to think there'd be any chance of private conversation in here on a Sunday morning.

I put on my best Pie Girl smile as I push through the door, barely dodging the busser coming through the other side, and find that the smile turns genuine. There's an adrenaline to days like this, when the kitchen is busy and the dining room overflowing, that is pure and somehow fun.

As I round the counter, I nod hellos at the regulars sitting along its Formica edge and spin out into the dining room proper, skirt swishing.

"Frank's finally put you to work?" one of the old guys asks as I go.

"And still not paying me," I chirp.

"Stingy bastard."

I laugh. "You know it."

I pause, orienting myself to the room. Table four is Amanda's, so right side, in the window. I weave my way through the crowded space, careful to keep my tray high and steady. Unlike the servers who can carry six plates balanced on their arms, no tray necessary, I lack that grace. Give me a couple of pie boxes to heft, great, I can do it with my eyes closed. But plates heaped with steaming food? That requires attention. The kind of complete focus that stops me from actually noticing the occupants of my destination table until I'm upon it.

Cops.

Four of them.

Two in uniform and two who might as well be, given how obvious their occupation is.

"Well, you're certainly an upgrade," the one closest to the door says when he clocks me. "Hell, you could throw the coffee at us and I wouldn't even care. Might even be into it." He winks in a way that he clearly believes is charming, and his buddies laugh.

The one with his back to me has blond stubble coating his bare head and the roll of skin above his too-tight collar. The tray wobbles, and I come close to one-upping Amanda's coffee fiasco.

It can't be.

Seriously?

His seat gives him a clear view of the sidewalk outside and me a clear view of his reflection in the plate glass, enough to confirm what the sinking in my stomach already knew.

Troy.

In the flesh.

I do the only thing I can.

I ignore him.

"Okay, folks," I say, cheery as can be. "Who has the bacon Benedict?"

The plainclothes guy near the door claims it, and I go around the rest of the table delivering dishes. Troy is last—eggs with extra bacon, sausage, and hash—and when I set the plate in front of him, he finally acknowledges me. What starts as a perfunctory thanks morphs into confusion when he registers my dress. I've never wished for a more basic fashion sense than I do now. If I were in black pants and a diner shirt, like everyone else serving, he probably wouldn't have even noticed. But no. I need to have a collared green dress bedecked with cheery squirrels chasing fat acorns around the full

79

skirt. It doesn't exactly go unnoticed, and if there's anyone I don't want noticing me right now, it's this scum sack.

"I know you?" he asks.

"I'm here a lot," I say, refusing to let the smile falter. Refusing to show how much I wish I could turn his breakfast into murder pancakes. Not yet. And definitely not here. "Is there anything else I can get you guys?"

The rest of the table tucks into their food, but Troy continues to stare. I see the moment it clicks, a subtle hardening of his eyes. "You tried to give me a pie."

I feign surprise. "Oh my god, you're right." I laugh. "It's the uniform. Didn't even recognize you. I'm sorry again for getting the wrong house."

"So you're a waitress who gives away pies?" He sounds skeptical and more than a little condescending.

"I run a pie business and also bake for the diner." I hoist my empty tray to my shoulder with a wide smile to bury my irritation. "I try to leave the serving to the professionals."

"Don't know if I'd call that last one professional," the other uniformed cop says, and I want to ask exactly how professional it is to be going out to breakfast when you're supposed to be on duty, but I don't. I can't get into it with them, any of them. Not even to defend Amanda's honor.

I need to get away from this table.

"Well, you give a shout if you need anything," I say, turning to go and hoping fervently that they don't, at least not until Amanda is back on the floor.

I don't get two full steps away when a voice pins me to the spot.

"Did you ever find her?" Troy asks.

There's a rushing in my ears like the sound in an empty shell, and it's like the entire dining room falls away. I close my eyes for the briefest of moments before spinning with a lightness belying my rage.

He's craned around in his chair so he can see me, and when I meet his eyes, there's a mirth there that reminds me of little boys who pull the legs off spiders.

I think it's the first true glimpse of him I've seen.

"Not this time," I say. "But she still has a chance to win."

Chapter Fifteen

I keep the cool facade intact all the way back to the kitchen, but the rage is building like bubbles in an overboiled pot.

I sling the tray onto the rack just in time to see Amanda emerge from the walk-in, eyes red with shed tears and also something else.

A flicker of the same fury boiling in me.

I beeline toward her, and she gives me a panicked look that I wave off. "I took your table; they're fine. What happened?"

"Thanks," she says. "Is Frank pissed?"

"No more than usual. What happened?"

"I dropped the coffeepot."

"I know that part. Tell me why."

Amanda's eyes narrow. She's a sophomore at Turnbridge, working on dual degrees in biology and philosophy. There's not a stupid bone in her body, and she knows I already have a guess. Her lip curls with the kind of disgust usually reserved for stepping barefoot in roadkill.

"He grabbed my ass." She says it like she can't really believe it. "Like my literal cheek. In his hand."

"Which one?"

"Buzz cut. Facing the street."

Of course it was. I swallow the info like whiskey, holding on to the burn in my belly. Let him keep giving me reasons. Every infraction is going into that pie. He's going to pay for them all. "And you dropped the coffee?" Part of me wants to hear she threw it at him, but she's nicer than that.

"I was just so surprised. It's like a cliché, right? This isn't some fifties truck stop. It's a college town. And they're cops." She shakes her head. "And then one of the other ones started saying shit when I was picking it up, and I just, I don't know. Lost it." She looks embarrassed now that the anger has fought off some of the adrenaline, but she's still rattled.

"I don't blame you. No one does."

"Don't tell Frank? I don't want it to be a thing."

Part of me wants to do exactly that, because despite the bluster, I know Frank would back his staff over the customers any day of the week. To him, there's an endless line of people who will eat at the diner but a far shorter list of folks he'd like working there. He fights for the ones he has. But I respect her choice.

"I won't. And I'll finish their service, or one of the others can. There's no reason to give them the satisfaction of seeing you again."

Relief brightens her face. "Thanks. You're a lifesaver."

"I try."

*　*　*

It takes until the end of the breakfast rush for me to get Juan's mostly undivided attention, something I rarely have to fight for. He's one of the best friends I have here, and even though I tell myself it's the fault of the busy morning, I know it's not that simple.

He's avoiding me.

I wait until he's giving the flat-top a quick clean before the next wave comes and sidle over, tiny pie in hand. It's still warm, made with dough I had in the walk-in and a doctored-up fig filling. It was quick, but it's also perfectly fresh and full of the feelings I have for him, for this place. It's like the diner blend on steroids.

"I come bearing pie," I say, holding out the peace offering.

He eyes me but takes it, polishing it off in two bites. "Tasty."

He resumes scraping at the dark surface of the flat-top with the spatula, pooling the oily breakfast scraps along the edge. It's not the ideal soundtrack for a serious conversation, but such is life.

"That," I say, gesturing to the back door, where Penny is parked just beyond, "wasn't what you thought."

"I think it's probably not my business," he says evenly.

"No, it is. Because I know what you're thinking and how it's making you look at me, and I would never do that. I'm not a cheater. And hell, even if I was, don't you think I'd be stealthier than letting her waltz out bright and early in front of you guys? I would never involve you in something like that. You're family." The words tumble out like I'd been the one to ingest the magic, but that's not how it works. I can wield the magic, but I can't be affected by it. This is simply naked honesty.

And it works.

Juan pauses his cleaning and looks at me, brows knit over dark eyes. "Yeah?"

"Obviously." I realize this is something I should've been saying before now. Sure, he knows. He must. And Frank too, but that doesn't mean I shouldn't be stating it outright every now and then. Maybe not on the tail end of a Sunday rush while defending myself from infidelity accusations, but sometimes. I sigh. "Look. Feelings are hard for me. Talking about them. But I love you guys. You and Frank and Ana and Eric. But you especially. And how you see me matters, and I don't want you thinking the worst of me."

His face softens, and he props the spatula on the edge of the flat-top and grabs a quart container with a straw poked through the lid from the shelf above. He uses it to gesture at the back door, and I nod, following him out.

He kicks the milk crates away from the wall and drops onto one, propping his elbows on his spread knees. I follow, tucking my skirt around my legs to keep the breeze from re-creating a Marilyn Monroe display.

The crisp fall air feels almost arctic after the heat of the kitchen, and for a moment we soak it in, the only sound the occasional rattle of ice from Juan's drink as he spins it in his hands. I don't rush him.

He sets the quart container between his feet and looks up, face serious. He raises a finger. "One, I don't think the worst of you." He stalls my interruption with a second finger. "Two, I love you too. Obviously. Do you know the hole there'd be if you weren't here?" He shakes his head, a smile twitching at the corners of his mouth. "Shit, for one, me and Frank would've probably killed each other for sure. You changed the mix when you showed up, and it was for the better. But anyway, three." He raises a third finger and holds my gaze. "I also like Noel. A whole hell of a lot. He's the real deal." My heart twists because he feels he has to tell me this, like I don't already know it. He adds a fourth finger. "Last, it's none of my business. Seriously. What you do in your private life is private. That's on you. And I admit I'm a little biased when it comes to this particular area."

"My turn?" I ask when he doesn't add any more fingers to the list.

He raises his eyebrows in a silent *Go on.*

"I'm not cheating on Noel." I look hard into his eyes as I say this, like I can laser-beam the truth from my brain to his. "I know that's what it looked like, but I swear, it's not. Trust me, if I wanted to be dating Melly, I'd be dating Melly. I know that option is on the table. But it's not what I chose. I chose Noel."

He nods, and I think the laser beam of truth has worked when he asks, "So what was it, then?"

"Just friends, I swear."

He cocks his head, and I know he's seeing her coming out of the RV again, sleepy and disheveled. I put myself in his shoes. In Noel's, if he had seen what Juan had. And I get it. It looks bad. I sigh and tip my head back like I might find an answer in the clear blue sky, but there aren't even clouds.

I can't tell him the truth—that we were up all night trying to figure out if a cop was a killer and how I was going to kill him for it. It's bad enough that Noel and Melly know about Pies Before Guys. I can't tell Juan the whole truth, but I can tell him some.

"I had a stupid panic attack," I say. "And yes, Noel should've been my first choice of emotional support animal, but you know what Saturday nights are like at the orchard. I couldn't ask him to step away from that. So I called Melly. She brought froyo, and we stayed up talking. That's all."

Concern floods his face. "Are you okay?"

I wave it off. "Yeah. It happens sometimes. It's been a long time, though. All good now."

"Good," he echoes. "Shit. I'm sorry. I should've known better than to think—"

"No, it's fair," I say. "Really. But it was nothing like that. So maybe don't rat me out to Noel just yet?"

"I won't." He shrugs one shoulder, a sharp spasm that seems subconscious. "It's a shitty position I thought I was in, though, had I been right, you know? I don't know if I could've lied to him, even for you. He'd want to know. He'd deserve to know. I did."

My eyes snap back to his, and there's hurt there that has nothing to do with our present conversation. "It wasn't Eric, was it?" I ask, not sure I want the answer.

"God no. Before him, though. And it was bad. I was young and I thought he was going to marry me, but it turns out what I thought was love and support was really more like Stockholm syndrome and

financial abuse." He shakes his head like he can't believe his own stupidity, and my heart breaks for him. "I was financing his entire life, including the affairs. Even after I found out, I didn't stop, not at first, like I could prove I was worth choosing if I just did enough for him. Earned more money, tried harder."

"Jesus, Juan," I whisper. "You didn't deserve that."

"Oh, I know that now, trust me. Hell, on some level I knew it then, but love, man." He shakes his head.

"I get it." And I do. Without love and its twisted permutations, Pies Before Guys wouldn't exist.

"No one deserves that," he says. "Hence the knee-jerk reaction earlier." He stands and holds out a hand, giving me a smile that's pure Juan. "Forgive me for being a judgmental dick?"

I take his hand, and he pulls me to my feet and straight into a bear hug.

"Already have."

Chapter Sixteen

I know that before I can throw myself headlong into this mission, there's one more thing I have to get squared away.

My stomach is in knots on the short drive to the orchard. Sunday afternoons at the cidery have been good for me, both from a business standpoint and personally. Beyond the pie sales, getting to see Noel thrive in the joyous chaos of running a business he loves always brightens my day.

I try to channel that as I navigate the maze of tightly packed cars. One of the fields has been set aside for parking, but without the spots being clearly marked, it gets pretty haphazard on busy days, and as usual, this is a busy Sunday.

I wave to Kai, the new barback, who gives me a cheery chin tilt in exchange, both hands occupied with kegs of cider. Bright fiddle music filters from the barn–turned–tasting room, the Irish melody foot-stompingly infectious.

It's a normal weekend and I'm a normal piemaker, doing what I do best. What Noel knows I do. It will be fine.

It has to be.

I set up and barely have my window open when the line forms, and for the next few hours I'm too busy to think about anything except the pies in front of me. Zoe is in her element, zipping around the familiar orchard and visiting with the many dogs accompanying their cider-head owners.

To look at the bustling crowds, you would never know that a few years ago this place was in a state of near neglect, thanks to Noel's uncle fighting him every step of the way on property rights after they inherited it from Noel's grandfather. To think his uncle wanted to sell it blew my mind even then, when it was just a bunch of ramshackle buildings and acres of trees. But now? This place is Noel's legacy. The orchard is in him the same way he's all over it. There isn't a single facet that he hasn't lovingly pored over, planned, and turned into reality. I can't picture him anywhere else in the world, doing anything except exactly this.

From the RV I can catch glimpses of him as he pours flights of ciders, chatting easily with the clientele. He's come a long way from the sweet, slightly unsure farm boy I first met at the market so many Saturdays ago.

I'm brought back to the present by a piercing shriek. "Ahh, you're here!"

It takes a moment to register who's standing at my window, the Hollywood-handsome Black man and short round white girl with the cat-eye glasses so very out of context here, at the orchard.

Without warning.

Then all at once, I'm shrieking right back, rushing out of the van to crash into a group hug.

"What are you two doing here?" I ask. "Why didn't you tell me?"

"Just passing through," Derek says, flashing the megawatt smile that caused half the country to fall in love with him during his brief stint on *Bake My Day*. Vic had predicted on day one that he'd be the show's villain thanks to his high-finance bank job, but he was far too sweet for it to stick.

"We saw you were on the schedule for Sundays here and wanted to surprise you."

"Mission accomplished," I laugh. "I'm surprised. The best kind of surprised. It's so good to see you! How is everything?"

"It's good," Nell says. "The shop has been doing great. I love it. We need to get everyone back together and have a doughnut fest."

"For sure. Every time you post new pictures, I'm ready to get on a plane."

"They're worth it," Derek says, but the way he's looking at Nell makes it clear the doughnuts aren't the reason he's making regular trips to Ohio.

"And you guys?" I ask, unable to keep the grin off my face. They were adorable back then, and away from the camera, it's even better.

"Still long distance," Nell says.

"But not for long," Derek finishes. "I'm working out a hybrid option at work. I should be able to work remotely three weeks a month and only have to fly into the city for the fourth."

I give an impressed whistle. "Look at you, fancy pants."

He laughs. "It pays the bills, and I like numbers."

"And fancy suits," Nell teases.

"And fancy suits," he agrees. "And doughnut shops."

"That's all me these days," she says, preening under both his gaze and her own success. The confidence is a good look on her.

"It is," Derek says. "Seriously. People are traveling from all over for this one."

"We definitely have to do a reunion trip," I say. "I don't care if we have to kidnap Courchesne and Freddie from Netflix. It's happening."

"They'll probably try to bring Netflix," Nell says.

Derek laughs. "You can't blame them. They have a good thing going."

I shake my head. "They can have it."

"Seriously, though, we'll figure something out," Derek says, unable to suppress the sparkle in his eye. "I'm sure there will be something soon to celebrate."

Nell flushes, and I look between them, feeling a step behind. Almost shyly, Nell holds her left hand up, and I don't even know how I could've missed that much sparkle. Derek's salary easily could've afforded the kind of ostentatious diamond that screams *Notice my obscene wealth,* but this is understated, a band of alternating pale-pink and white stones set flush into a platinum channel. It's the kind of ring that wouldn't rip the nitrile gloves Nell wears while dipping doughnuts. The thoughtfulness of that would impress me if it weren't exactly what I've come to expect from Derek. He's that good, all the time.

"I'm so happy for you! When's the big day?"

"We're still working that out," Nell says, putting a hand on her stomach. "And it's maybe not the only thing we're planning."

My eyes go wide. "No. Really?"

She grins. "It's not the timing we talked about, but . . ."

Derek beams at her. "We're not complaining."

"It's still early, so we're not telling a ton of people yet," Nell says. "But so far so good."

"It's actually why we're here," Derek says. "We're going to see my parents in Boston to give them the news but figured if we flew into Hartford and drove, we could also drop in on you too."

"I'm so glad you—"

Before I finish the thought, a bearded white guy carrying a kid piggyback butts in. "Excuse me? Are you still doing pies?"

"Yes, sorry, one minute," I say, flustered.

"We should be hitting the road anyway," Derek says.

"Wait, let me pack you up some pies to bring." I scurry back into the RV, telling the guy at the window I'll be right with him, and assemble a heaping box of cutie pies for them. I hop back down the steps, handing the box to Derek. "And go see Noel inside. He'd love to say hi and foist some cider on you."

"I wouldn't say no to that," Derek says.

"Get nonalcoholic ones too," I tell Nell. "They're so good. Ahh, you guys!" I crush Nell in a hug and then Derek, jostling the pie box but not caring. "Congratulations on all the things."

"Thanks. We'll obviously be sharing with the group soon, so—" Derek mimes zipping his lips, and I nod.

"Of course. Secret's safe."

We say goodbyes, and I go inside to deal with the impatient guy at my window, thoughts still completely taken up by the whirlwind of this weekend. "What can I get you?"

He orders, and I give him his cranberry cutie pie and chicken pot pie without charge. "To make up for the wait," I say with a smile, and he leaves content, but not before dropping a five in my tip jar.

Later, I catch the white-blonde of Nell's hair as she walks, tucked beneath Derek's arm, through the parking field, and something in my heart swells for them.

Engaged, with a baby on the way, and radiating the kind of happiness people dream of.

Love, when it goes wrong, may be the reason Pies Before Guys exists, but that's the exception.

Love usually gets it right.

I slide my window shut and flip the sign to CLOSED. I have loves of my own I need to track down.

* * *

I find them together, Zoe fast asleep beneath the bar Noel is wiping down. The crowd has thinned, families needing to get home to their Sunday evenings.

"Hey, you," I say, sliding onto a stool.

Noel leans across the counter and kisses me. "Hey, you."

He tastes like apples and everything comforting about fall. "Busy day."

"Another one." He can't keep the pride off his face. "It was good to see Derek and Nell."

"It was. We're going to have to make the trek to Ohio at some point. We really need to check out the shop."

"You know I'm not going to say no to a road trip, especially when there's snacks at the end." He grins, something soft in his face. "We should try to go soon, before they have their hands full. With the baby."

I'm a little taken aback but try to keep it hidden. "They told you?"

So much for their stealth mode.

"Derek said they might as well, since we're a package deal. Said it wasn't fair to expect one partner to keep secrets from the other." He gives the counter a final polish and slings the rag over his shoulder. "I think he missed the class where bankers learn to be bastards."

I laugh. "He really did. It's probably the only thing he's ever failed."

"You staying over tonight?" Noel asks. "We could do pizza testing. I have lots of dough prepped."

"Of course," I say, with an easiness that belies the sinking in my stomach.

"Good. If you want to head up, you can pull a couple rounds, let it rest at room temp. I probably have an hour left down here."

"Sounds good." I nudge Zoe with my toe to wake her, and she stretches with a tongue-curling yawn before clambering to her feet. "Oh, tough day of being cute, huh?"

"Always," Noel says, a cheeky grin splitting his face.

I roll my eyes. "That was awful."

"But true."

"You're terrible."

He grins. "You love me."

"I do."

I really do.

Chapter Seventeen

As I putter around Noel's kitchen, I turn over in my head Derek's words to him about secrets.

He's right. I don't want him to be right, but he is.

Privacy is one thing. All relationships need a certain amount of privacy, but secrets can easily turn into lies. Sometimes they're necessary, sure, but Derek was right. The difference is partners. It's one thing for me not to tell the world my plans, but I know I have to tell Noel. He knows so much already that not telling him is tantamount to lying.

I'm better than that.

We're better than that.

I don't ambush him with it, because I'm not a monster. There's no reason we can't have a nice dinner and showers and be comfortable for uncomfortable conversations.

Noel is on the couch when I come out of the shower, his lanky legs propped on the roughhewn wood coffee table, a notebook on his lap. He chews the end of a pen as he considers whatever is on the page.

Zoe is curled like a brown-and-white bagel on the ancient armchair in the corner that she has officially claimed as her own since we made a habit of coming inside.

At least I'm only about to disturb one of them.

I tuck myself into the corner of the couch, legs beneath me, and throw myself off the cliff. "I've been trying to think of a way to say we need to talk that doesn't sound as ominous as *We need to talk*, but I'm stuck."

He looks up from his notes, the concern looking a whole lot like the concentration of moments before. "Well, you're excelling at ominous, if that makes you feel better."

I huff a little half laugh, because even when things are serious, this sweet and sincere farm boy can make me smile. "It doesn't, but thanks." I take a breath that wooshes out in a hard rush of anxiety. "Okay, so it's about the cop case."

He sets his notebook on the table and drops his feet to the floor, turning to face me. It feels like there's an ocean of sofa between us.

"You're doing it anyway." He says it like a statement, not a question. He knows me.

"It's more than that." I sigh. "The girl is gone. Missing. Maybe dead." I give him the rundown, refusing to cave to the panic spiral. It's easier to keep it at bay now because this is all old news. I've moved past the initial gut punch of guilt and am back on the familiar ground of justice, where I'm comfortable. I can do things there.

Noel doesn't interrupt, not once. He's good like that, but I can see him processing, the way his eyes narrow and his jaw goes hard. He's not happy, but I knew he wouldn't be.

"I don't want to lie to you," I say. "Ever. I know you think I should leave it alone, but I need to see this through. I needed to when I got the order, but I hesitated. I waited a whole week to get back to her, and now she's gone. That week might've mattered."

"You can't blame yourself for this," Noel says, and that, right there, is what I love about him. Even though he's upset, his caring shines through. He is the very opposite of every man I've ever pied.

"No, I blame Troy. But I also know I could've stopped it. And I didn't."

"Because I convinced you not to," Noel says slowly, his tone unusually flat.

I meet his eyes, hard. "No, don't do that. This isn't your fault either. You raised valid points. And I can't do what I do from jail, and I was worried it might be a trap. Me. The hesitation was all mine. And that's why I need to set this right."

"Why don't you go to the police? Report her missing?"

"Go to the police and say what? *Hey, guys, one of your buds in blue killed his girlfriend and you should arrest him, even though I don't have a body or any proof yet?*" I scoff. "You know how that would go over."

"Okay, what about the FBI? Bypass the cops altogether."

I shake my head. "Killing your girlfriend isn't a federal crime. Not unless he took her across state lines to do it, and even then, it's not the murder that makes it federal but the kidnapping. It's not like TV. The FBI won't swoop in on their jet to save the day."

Noel exhales and drags a hand through his damp hair. "I don't know. State police? Internal affairs? There has to be something."

"There is. Me."

"Something else. This isn't okay. It was bad enough when you were going to murder-pie an actual cop, but now you're going to investigate the very same cop for a murder you think he committed? You're a private citizen and a serial killer." His words are fast and shrill, but even he looks startled by that last bit. "I'm sorry, I didn't—"

"No, it's true," I say. "I am. Technically. But I only have to be because guys like Troy don't do their jobs. That's why I can't let him get away with this. The cops already don't protect the people who need it most. I can't condone one committing outright murder."

"You're playing with fire on this," he says, eyes pleading. "Don't you even care?"

"Of course I care. That's why I'm doing it."

"About us, I mean. Or at least about yourself."

It's a low blow, and we both know it. "That's not fair."

"Isn't it?" The words aren't angry, just sad. "When you were on the show and everything went down, you were so concerned about having the cops around. Why is this so different?"

"Because I had actively planned to kill that guy," I remind him. "I had a pie ready to go and everything. So, no, I wasn't thrilled to have police all up in my business. But the difference this time is I didn't fail to kill a guy, I failed to save someone who needed me. Right now, I'm the only one who knows something is even wrong."

"Because you're not telling anyone," he says, desperation creeping into his voice.

"Noel. Listen to me." I scoot across the expanse of the couch so I'm in front of him. I take his hands in mine and they tense, but he doesn't pull away. "I showed up at his door as a stranger, and he looked me in the eye and said no one named Jodie even lived there. Her coworkers believe she's at her mother's funeral, but her mother has been dead for almost six years. I think Troy sent that email to keep them from questioning her absence. He has layers of deception on this thing and a head start. He has the professional knowledge to get away with this and a team of comrades who will absolutely take his side over mine. If I'm going public with this, it has to be with an absolute avalanche of evidence. That's how it'll be safe. When there's no doubt."

He doesn't say anything for a long moment, but there's a flicker of movement and his thumb starts rubbing tiny circles on my finger.

When I continue, it's softer. "She was twenty-three. She liked books and making up stories about people. She wanted to leave, to have her own life. Her own story. He can't get away with making her disappear."

Noel studies our joined hands. "What about her family? Can't they do something? Make a report?"

"There's no one. From what I've learned so far, she had him and the library staff, that's it. And she wasn't close to anyone at the library. They didn't know what she was going through."

He sighs. "Why didn't she tell someone?"

I squeeze his hands. "She did."

"Someone other than you. Before it got to that point."

"Because it's not that simple." He knows that. Especially after spending so much time with me and grappling with what I do, he knows, but he still can't help asking. I know he's not victim blaming, that he just wishes he could wave a wand and make this someone else's problem, but it's the same question everyone wants answered when things get this bad. They don't understand how hard getting help can be, that it's not simply a matter of making an announcement.

When the perpetrator is part of the very force that should be protecting you, well, then it's even harder.

And that's why I'm here.

"This is who I am," I whisper. "I'm the thing that stops the monsters."

He exhales, the air ragged as it leaves his lungs. "I just don't want to lose you."

"You won't."

"You can't promise that."

"Can't I?" I squeeze his hands and try to smile, wanting to bring him back from the things he's scared of.

"You can't. You could stir this up, and you might be the one who takes the fall. I don't want that. Not now."

"But maybe before?" I joke.

"Not ever. But especially not now." He looks around the room, at Zoe snoring softly on the armchair, the fire burning, and the windows beyond which the literal fruits of his labor lie. "We have so much going for us. Our whole future is right here, spread out and waiting. I don't want to risk that. Not for anything."

I absorb the enormity of that as the couch seems to sway beneath me. I sink back into the soft cushion and let the vertigo pass.

"I mean, this is what you want, right?" Noel asks. "A life here, with me?"

"Of course it is." I close my eyes. Not long ago, the mere thought of staying in any one town longer than a week or two made my skin crawl, but that changed when I hit Turnbridge. It still takes me by surprise sometimes, how settled I've become, but somehow that doesn't make staring down the barrel of forever any less monumental.

"Then you need to be safe," Noel says, as if we've settled something.

"And I will be. But I also have to be *me*. And that means seeing this through." I meet his eyes. "Safely. I swear."

He searches my eyes, and I wonder what he's seeing that causes the shift. He sighs, drops my hands, and drags both of his through his hair.

From the chair, Zoe lifts her head to regard us sleepily.

Noel scrunches up his face, and when he opens his eyes, there's a stolid resolve in their brown depths. "Fine. You're right. I can't build a future with you if I can't accept all of you, murder, danger, and all. What can I do to help?"

Chapter Eighteen

M onday dawns without any of the clichéd angst associated with the start of a week.

I know what it cost Noel to get on board last night, the fear he had to set aside, and while I know he would be happier if I abandoned the whole thing, I feel better knowing I'm not sneaking around.

I leave him snuggled in bed and return to Frank's, Penny in tow.

I want to get well ahead on diner pies for the week, and Monday mornings are the best time to take over the kitchen, since it's Juan's day off and I won't be in his way. I have less concern for the new cook, who needs to learn to share space.

The fact that it's Ana who greets me at the back door makes me wonder if I slept through all of Monday and that's why it doesn't feel like one.

"Hey, pie pal," I say, spotting a frazzle-faced Juan at his usual spot, flipping pancakes with a bit more force than usual. "What are you guys doing here?"

"Skipping school," she singsongs.

"Well, lucky you," I say, tying an apron around my waist.

"Can we make pies?"

"We're gonna make *all* the pies," I promise.

I send her to collect bowls, just to give her something to do, and sidle up to Juan. "So how's it going?"

"Oh, you know," he says, slapping a pancake onto the plate without ceremony. "Alex called out yet again and Eric got sent on another conference, and I'm not sure how I'm supposed to be homeschooling that monster if we're never actually at home." He emphasizes each point by adding another pancake to the stack.

"Okay, first—" I take the plate after he adds a pile of hash browns on it and put it on the pass-through for the morning server to grab. "We can kill Alex. It might take time, but if it'll improve your morning, I'll go find him and make him regret ever calling out."

"I'd pay to see that," he says, a bit of the normal Juan spark returning. "I bet you could do it too."

"Damn right. And so what if Ana's getting a jump on her culinary education? Plenty of people go to school specifically to study cooking."

"In high school or college. Not when they haven't even learned to tell time."

"You're being too hard on yourself," I say. "She's happy. She knows she's loved, she's learning things that excite her, and she's never once had to do an active-shooter drill, so she's got that going for her."

"You're right." He sighs. "I just feel like I have so many balls in the air and today they're all made of shit and fire."

"Thank you for the sparkling imagery." I laugh. "See, you could be teaching that."

"Yes, because that's exactly what my kid needs, my kitchen vocabulary." He shudders at the thought.

"Tell you what. I'll keep Ana with me, and we'll make it educational. We can talk about fractions and weights and, I don't know, pie charts."

"You don't mind?"

"Course not," I say. "You do know you have other homeschool options than winging it, right? There's co-op groups where people rotate who has the pack of kids for the day. That way they can lean into their teaching strengths and the kids get to socialize more. Just a thought."

Juan raises an eyebrow, and I don't tell him that I only know about such things because I once delivered a pie to a woman whose kid was part of one and needed me to come when he was out of the house.

I shrug. "You don't have to do it all on your own is all I'm saying."

"But I want to."

"I know. Because you're awesome. But the world won't end if you get some help, at least while you and Eric both have less-than-ideal schedules."

"Maybe you're right."

"Often am," I quip, and spin away to get started on the first of many pies.

* * *

By the afternoon, Ana and I are surrounded by enough pies to make Frank concerned.

"Lotta damn pies for the beginning of the week," he grumbles. "You got something you need to tell me? You leaving?"

"No, of course not." Ana slots the last unbaked apple pie onto the freezer-bound sheet pan, and I heft the tray with both hands. "Just getting ahead." I pause as Ana scurries to open the walk-in door, then the freezer door beyond. I add the tray to the rack already laden with similarly prepped cherry pies. They can bake from frozen and no one will ever know the difference.

"So what is it, then?" Frank asks when I emerge. "You moon-lighting somewhere else? At that damn cidery? Because we talked about that."

"I'm not moonlighting." I laugh. "And you're at Hollow Hill every Thursday night, so I don't think you can judge me for supporting my own boyfriend's business."

Frank harrumphs. "I like the band he gets in there, that's all."

"I'm not leaving," I promise. "I just have a busy week and wanted to make sure I didn't fall behind."

After some grumbling, Frank gives in. "'Preciate that. You know how these people get about their pie."

"I do. But there's plenty here, and I'm still going to be in and out. Just trying to stay organized."

"Some people could learn from that," he says in Juan's direction.

"I'm the one who's here on my day off," Juan reminds him.

"Right, right. Damn kid," he mutters, shaking his head. I figure Alex has one more chance before he's fired, if that.

I pull my apron off and sling it over my shoulder. It's one of my grandmother's creations, frilly and pink and not something I would ever send through the diner's laundry service. The seams are stitched with her special blend of cozy love and optimism, and while the magic can certainly survive washing, I couldn't survive it getting lost.

"Okay, I'm off." I say goodbye to Juan, hating to leave when he can't, but at least Ana is happily parked in a box she's nested with clean aprons, book in hand and slice of pie within reach.

I take Zoe for a quick walk, using the time to switch my brain from diner pies to murder pies. Murder is too much at this stage when I still need so many answers, but even though I have other magic at my disposal, I've already tried to deliver a pie to Troy's house once. I won't get a second chance, not without drawing attention to myself.

Even if I could force-feed him a pie, the magic isn't infallible. It works on what's already in a person, drawing out emotions and action based on what I put in. With murder pies, it's not actual murder that goes in but the loudest, most emphatic urge to *stop*. It's why I need the details of what the target has done, so I can tailor the magic to specifically what it is that needs stopping. On occasion, a pie is enough to set the change in motion without killing them. Sometimes a single slice shifts something in them enough that they see the error of their ways and never hurt anyone again.

But it's rare.

For most of these men, they're wired in a way that the only thing that will stop them is death. So that's what happens.

That's why things like honesty magic can be tricky too. It's not a targeted truth serum. Sure, it primes the eater to loosen their lips, but what comes out isn't always what you're looking for.

There is someone such a pie might be good for, though, with that general blend of *Share your thoughts*, and I add making it to my to-do list.

First, though, research.

I take my laptop to my bed, where I can sprawl out with Zoe and get to work.

I start with Troy's social media. I don't expect to find confessionals or anything, but the fact that he keeps up a pattern of posting multiple obnoxious memes a day means he isn't troubled enough by anything going on in his life to change even that unnecessary behavior.

He has his personal email address displayed on Facebook, and I copy it into a separate search to see what else it's associated with.

I find inactive accounts on several older platforms, plus a locked one on Patriot Social that doesn't surprise me at all. Given what he's posting on the public account the town and his employer can see, I can only imagine how much worse it is on the cesspool that is Patriot.

The one thing I don't see, which somewhat surprises me, is a single dating app. Even though he was in a relationship with Jodie, my gut says he's not the kind of guy to let that stop him from at least looking.

There must be another email, then.

I enter his police department address on the off chance he really is that stupid, but it comes back clean.

I set up a thought-dump file and type in *other emails* and move on. Right now I'm in gather mode, hoarding bits of info like a magpie, and I don't want to get bogged down by what's missing.

Switching to one of the paid databases, I plug in Troy's name and address and am rewarded with an image of his current license. Perfect.

I run the history and find only records for registration fees paid and a single Massachusetts license renewal.

Huh.

So he's not from here.

Without his social security number, all I have is his name, but it will be enough. I open my parameters nationwide and wait while options filter in.

There are far too many Troy Sullivans walking around this country.

Sorting by birth year, I scroll until I find mine.

Colorado.

Bingo.

I run the Colorado number, and this time I get all the hits, everything from speeding tickets and accidents to the more harmless expired registration fines. They're clustered tightly around his late teens and early twenties, when he apparently went through a reckless streak that makes me wonder what made him decide to switch from getting tickets to writing them.

Something nags at me, and I'm scrolling back through the list of offenses when it clicks.

It's not an offense he committed that I'm looking for.

It's one he worked.

Shit.

I start with Google, hoping to get lucky. I plug in Jodie's mother's name plus *car accident*.

A *Reddington Register* link is the top hit with the headline *Victims Identified in Deadly Crash*. I click the link and get a short article six years out of date. I scan, confirming details I already know. Lincoln Azaria and Ann-Marie Cordace died in a single-vehicle crash on Larkmont Road; a third passenger was left in serious condition. A link at the bottom says *This is an update of a developing story*.

I click and get the previous article, this one topped with a photo of police examining a crumpled car that stirs memories out of hiding to punch me in the chest.

I wasn't there and I didn't have to see the aftermath, but I can imagine my mother in a car just like this, wrapped around a tree. My father was driving.

He walked away from that crash, but as I look at the photo on my screen, it's hard for me to believe anyone could've survived this one.

I refocus on the present and search the article for names, but everything is phrased in general terms. *Police are investigating*, *an officer at the scene confirmed*, and so on. Nothing helpful.

Nothing but the photo.

I click to enlarge it, but it was taken far enough back to make it impossible to distinguish faces. Still, I can automatically discount the Black officer and both of the women. One of the white men has his back to the camera but a head full of dark hair. The last guy is near the car, peering at something inside, face partly obscured. But he's broad, with massive shoulders. There are plenty of white guys built like that on football fields across the country, but I don't think it's a coincidence that this one is here. In Colorado, at the scene of his young girlfriend's nightmares.

Chapter Nineteen

I barely notice it's gotten dark until Zoe whines to go out.

My eyes burn from too much screen time, and the deepening twilight is the perfect balm. People always complain about how early night comes after daylight savings, but I like it. There's a cozy, closed-in feeling from the dark that makes soup and sweaters impossibly appealing.

But cozy isn't on the agenda tonight.

I have a mountain of notifications begging for attention on my phone, and I know at least some of them are going to be from Noel. I've been down a rabbit hole all afternoon and I know I shouldn't leave him in the dark, but I also know he doesn't want to know the ins and outs of what I found. His offer of help was more of the moral-support-and-not-breaking-up variety than anything hands-on. And I respect that. It's one thing to know what I'm doing and look the other way, but it's a whole other thing to get involved.

Which is why Melly's the one I call when Zoe and I get back to the RV.

"News?" she asks straightaway.

"Lots. You busy?"

"Don't have to be."

"I need to see Noel tonight, but if you want to swing by, I'll catch you up."

"Give me ten."

She hangs up and I begin sorting through my phone, starting with a text to Noel. *Hey you. Busy day, but I'm free later if you want me?*

He responds immediately. *Always.*

I switch to email, respond to a bride inquiring about wedding pies and someone else wondering when Thanksgiving orders will be available, and then pull up the account that really matters.

A new message sits in the Pies Before Guys inbox, and my heart kicks up even though I register right away that it's not from Jodie.

Carol01930 has written to tell me about her husband, Al, whose abuse has reached the point that she fears for her daughter's life. And it's not for lack of trying on Carol's part. He's already tracked them to three shelters, which got them permanently banned from the last for the scene he caused, but not before someone slipped her my info.

The photos make it a no-brainer.

I send her the contract and refresh the account a couple of times, hoping for an immediate reply, but it doesn't come. They rarely do, but no matter. She'll have her pie the day she responds.

No one is waiting anymore.

The roar of a motorcycle fills the air, and I put the phone away, making sure notification sounds are back on for Pies Before Guys stuff. I don't want to miss anything.

Melly knocks but doesn't bother waiting for an invitation before throwing the door open and marching inside.

"You'd make a shitty vampire," I say.

"I was invited inside long ago. In vampire terms that's like a lifetime pass." She straddles a stool like it's the saddle of her bike. "So what do we got?"

I lead with the bombshell. "Troy was in Colorado when Jodie's parents died. There was a car crash, and he was on the force there at the time."

I don't bother telling her how long it took me to confirm this. If there's a database that stores detailed employment history, it's not one I have but one I definitely wish existed. It took a mix of cybersleuthing and a phone call that could possibly get me arrested for impersonating a police officer, or at least a police department's human resource office.

"What, and they've been together the whole time?"

I swallow a ball of disgust. "She was eighteen when her parents were killed."

Melly balls a fist and flexes her fingers. "How does a cop twelve years her senior start dating a girl that young when her parents just died? Nope. Wait. That answered itself. She never would've if they'd been alive."

"It's more than that. She was in the crash. Judging by the photos I could dig up, he was one of the responding officers. He very well could've been the one who pulled her out of the back seat."

"Her white knight," Melly says.

"Yup."

"Christ. She never had a chance."

"I don't think so."

"How'd they end up all the way across the country, though, if they both lived there?"

"That I haven't worked out yet," I admit. "But we know they did end up here and that he kept her incredibly isolated. It's a classic abuse tactic, but the cross-country move makes it even more extreme. It could've been as easy that, moving her for the sake of isolation."

"Her parents are her only family?"

I nod. "Only child, and the only grandparent I could track down is in an assisted-living facility for dementia patients."

"Shit."

"She wasn't isolated there, though," I say. "It took an obscene amount of scrolling, but I found the comment threads about the accident on Facebook. The town page is very active, and the out-pouring of support for her was overwhelming. A lot of the posts were from classmates. She lost her parents, but she did have friends there. A support system. They organized a GoFundMe for her hospital bills, and the school even postponed their graduation ceremony so she could participate after she was released. There was an article about it, how she had to overcome so much to walk across that stage."

"And then what? He sweeps her across the country?"

"It wasn't that fast. There was almost a year between the accident and his hire here."

"Were they living together?"

I shake my head. "Not officially, but who knows. Her license only ever showed her parents' address and he had his own house, but she could've been staying with him." It was hard to imagine her returning to her own empty house after the accident to deal with her injuries on top of the ghosts of her parents in every room. She was practically still a kid.

Melly exhales a puff of air. "Okay, so that's all background. I'm not saying it's useless, but how does it help us right here and now? I mean, I doubt he up and smuggled her body back to Colorado."

"No, but information matters. If we know where he came from—not just physically, but mentally, behavior-wise—it can maybe help us figure out how he's thinking now. Nothing predicts the future like the past."

One side of her mouth quirks up in a teasing smirk. "Okay, Aristotle."

I roll my eyes. "I'm serious. It's a thing."

"History repeats itself, yeah, I know. But unless this guy has covered up a murder in the past and left detailed notes about how, I'm not sure it helps us right now."

"It's just a start. I'm not a pro at this," I remind her. "I wanted a foundation to build on before I start throwing ideas around all willy-nilly."

She raises an eyebrow, letting her silence judge my word choice.

"You know what I mean. There's no such thing as too much information."

"That's true," she says, a thoughtful look on her face. "We need to do more digging into who he is now. I'm going to help."

It's phrased as a statement of fact, not an offer, and I know it's useless to argue. "Be careful. This doesn't work if we just roll up to his door demanding answers."

"Are you implying I can't be subtle?"

Now it's my turn to raise an eyebrow, which I'm sure doesn't look quite as arch on me as it did on her. Some people are just born with superior brow control.

"I can be subtle," she assures me. "And like you said, it's only background right now."

"Okay. Report back anything interesting?"

"Obviously." She hops off the stool and pauses before going. "You know, we could plan to meet up tomorrow and swap info, then? In person? We could do falafel again?"

"Are you trying turn our investigation into a date?"

"Hey, murder mystery dinners are totally a thing." She grins widely as she backs toward the door. "That's a yes? Seven?"

I laugh. "Sure, it's a yes."

"It's a date."

"But not really."

The door rattles as it swings shut, but not before her response filters in.

"Tomato, tamahto."

Chapter Twenty

Carol01930 replies to me that night, and I tell her I can have the pie in her hands by tomorrow afternoon.

She's on the North Shore, so the drive alone will take the better part of the day, but I'm not making her wait.

I call Noel and tell him an order came up and that I'm staying in to bake. Even though he says it's fine, I can hear the disappointment.

"It's not the cop case," I tell him, as if it will help. "It's another one. A mom and her kid are—"

"I don't want details," he interrupts. "If that's okay."

I choke back the rest of the sentence. "No, of course. No one wants details of these things."

"It's not that I don't care—"

"I know. But you don't need the graphics."

"That's bad, right?" He sounds genuinely bothered by his unwillingness to hear more.

"It's understandable," I say gently. Just because I can't look away doesn't mean I should expect others to bear similar witness.

"I just . . . I don't know. It's like—I don't look at roadkill either, even when I know it's there. Not looking doesn't make it disappear, but it lets me stay focused on the better parts of the world, you know?

Oh god, not that I'm comparing abused women to roadkill. That's not what I mean at all."

I laugh; I can't help it. "I know it's not. And I really do get it. It's fine."

"I feel like I should be better at handling the things you deal with every day. So you're not doing it alone."

"I did this alone for a long time," I remind him. "It's only recently that I let anyone into this world. It's enough that you accept it. And me. You don't need to wallow in it."

"You don't think less of me for it?"

"Of course I don't."

He sighs. "You're the strongest person I've ever met. I don't know anyone who could see the things you do and still have faith in humanity."

"Faith in humanity is why I do it. I can't let the worst of humanity define the whole of it." The conversation has taken a more serious turn than I anticipated when I called, and I feel like I owe it to Noel to lighten things back up before we say goodbye. "I mean, some people plant flowers on traffic islands; I kill trash. Everyone can brighten up the world in their own way."

He laughs. "I love you. Even if you're a psychopath."

"I love you too. And I'm not. Just so you know."

We say good-night, and even though it was a throwaway line, not even enough to be called a joke, *psychopath* rolls around my head as I assemble what I need for the pies. I figure if I'm already pulling ingredients, I might as well kill two birds with one baking sheet.

The thing is, I don't think I'm a psychopath. I'm pretty sure Noel doesn't either, not really, but from the outside, if anyone knew exactly how this flour and butter were about to be wielded, it wouldn't be such a stretch to believe I were.

When my gift first went off the rails, I did go through a phase of wondering if I was evil, if that was why my magic had turned out the way it did.

All the other Ellery women who had the power used it purely for good. Most of them worked tiny, small-scale acts along the lines of my diner pies. Even my mom, who spent most of her time styling her magic into the hair of the elderly and infirm, never did more than invoke comfort and light and love. And that's not a criticism. I spent many hours in Penny back when she was a mobile salon, and I saw how those women left after having their hair done. Their heads were higher, their steps lighter, and their hearts a little fuller. That mattered.

But she never cured them. Not of what really ailed them.

When I asked her why, she said it was because she couldn't, that the magic could only enhance what was there, not alter the fabric of reality.

I believed her, right up until I was faced with my first dead body.

I tried to reconcile the two opposing facts while I was on the run. How could I use my magic to end a life but she couldn't use hers to alter the fabric of reality? Killing someone sure felt like a massive alteration. The kind that tears reality's fabric to tatters and makes confetti from its threads.

Somewhere in the boonies of upstate New York, I concluded I must be the problem. If my magic went haywire, it must've been because something was already haywire inside me.

I didn't feel evil, but even then, I doubted any villain ever did.

Now, after repeatedly confronting some of the worst men the country has to offer, I know that's true. They feel entitled to their actions, like they're right and it's everyone else's fault they have to do the things they do. They don't see their actions as specifically evil, though, simply as consequences to other people's existence.

But at seventeen, I didn't have that proof. I also didn't grasp the absolute callous disregard for other people that comes from the truly evil. Had I experienced that, I would've saved myself a lot of mental anguish, because I don't have the capacity for that kind of cruelty. Not even a little bit.

I do the things I do because I *care*. That alone is plenty to keep me out of the psychopath category.

I even care enough to give the targets of my murder pies an out. If they can find it in themselves to do better, on a cellular or synaptic or whatever microscopic level a scrap of decency might be found, then they can live. It's that simple. If they die, it's because they deserve to, because it's the only way to make them better people.

And if that sounds like a whole lot of justification on my end, then so be it.

But I believe you can be a serial killer without being a psychopath too.

We contain multitudes.

*   *   *

I start with Carol's pie because I don't want to rush it.

She asked for a classic double-crust apple pie, her husband's favorite.

I review the details of her situation, taking plenty of time to commit every detail of every photo to memory. Echoes of them will stay with me forever, but absorbing the horror is key to tailoring the magic.

The dough needs to be made first, so it can rest before rolling. I portion out two and a half cups of flour, then add hefty dashes of sugar and salt. I never measure those, because even though baking is science, sometimes it's instinct too. I chunk up half a pound of butter, the good high-fat European stuff that I reserve for special occasions. And what's more special than the last thing you'll ever eat?

Calling up the worst of Al's atrocities, I press my hands into the flour, working the butter in until I have even flakes throughout. Every press and squeeze imbues a plea to *stop*, stop hurting your wife, stop terrorizing your daughter.

He will taste the pain he has caused, and he will have a chance to change.

If the dough could talk, it would be screaming.

I stir in a drizzle of Hollow Hill's cider vinegar and enough cold water to bring it all together. I turn the ball of dough out onto the counter and cut it in two, pressing each half flat and wrapping it in Saran to go in the fridge. The magic will meld as the dough rests, suffusing every strand of gluten and molecule of fat with power.

The filling is next, and as I chop the apples, it's like everything else drops a little further away with each pass of the knife. I'm not thinking about Jodie, or Noel, or anything that isn't making sure Al sees the error of his ways.

If he won't change, he's at least going to know exactly why he has to die.

The apples go in my biggest sauté pan with butter, cinnamon, and a hefty sprinkle of roasted sugar. I am a firm believer in a cooked-fruit filling for pies, especially murder pies. The more time I can spend hands-on with the ingredients, the more potent things will be.

When it's in the oven, the crust egg-washed and fluted, the world starts to come back. There's no changing things now. The magic is set. One way or another, Carol's life will get better very soon.

Chapter
Twenty-One

I drop Zoe at Juan's first thing, knowing it's going to be a long day and that she'll be happy hanging with his pack.

His mother, Magdalena, is bustling around the kitchen making oatmeal for Ana, and I apologize for adding one more charge to her day. Juan has three dogs of his own and a huge fenced-in backyard they can access through the doggy door, so even though I know Zoe won't be a bother, it's already a pretty full house.

"Zoe is always welcome," Magdalena says, pressing a cup of coffee I don't have time for—but can't refuse—into my hands.

"We're doing weather today," Ana says. "Zoe can be in the class."

"Very exciting," I say, polishing off the coffee and thanking Magdalena. "I should be back midafternoon."

"You don't rush yourself," she says, taking my cup. "The more the merrier here."

I leave a little bit jealous that Zoe gets to spend the day being doted on and start my long drive east.

Carol requested that the pie be delivered when her husband was out, an arrangement that accounts for over half of my orders. Even though the women aren't making the pies themselves, they know what's in them, and a lot of them want to be the ones to serve it up.

I don't blame them.

I make good time, following GPS to an older but well-kept neighborhood. Carol's house is in the middle of the street, a yellow Cape exactly like the ones surrounding it. The burnished sunset of mums in window boxes gives the house a cheerfulness at odds with what I know goes on inside.

I park and retrieve the pie box from the footwell, thinking of her and her daughter fleeing this little house for shelters and being pursued by the monster from within, and I'm glad she'll get to keep it.

Despite the darkness, this house has hope.

She will make it a proper home.

She has a neat stone walkway leading to the front steps, and the door opens before I reach the top one.

"You came," she says, wonder and relief mixing in her voice. "I almost felt like I made the whole thing up."

"Pies Before Guys is always happy to help," I say, not wanting to take direct credit. Even though I do the deliveries, I keep up the pretense that PBG is more than a one-woman operation.

Although, in some ways, I suppose it isn't anymore.

"Is that it?" she asks, eyes fixed on the box.

"Indeed." I lift the lid so she can see. "Freshly baked and ready to eat."

"It looks so ordinary."

I close the box. "It is. You and your daughter can eat it and be perfectly fine. The only person it will affect is your husband."

I hold the box out, but instead of taking it, she steps aside, holding the door open. "Come in?" she asks, like I might refuse, like she feels she should know better than to make a request of someone's time.

I cross the threshold into a comfortably furnished living room. While it's clean, the decor is a few decades out of date for the forty-something woman in front of me.

"It was my grandmother's house," she says when she sees me notice. "I still like it this way. It feels safe." She snorts. "That's so stupid, given, you know." She flaps a hand to encompass everything that has gone so wrong in her life.

"No, I understand." And I do. It's the same tug I feel to stay in Penny, even though I know how happy it would make Noel for me to move in with him and how much sense it would make. Walls can contain entire legacies, and that's no easy thing to give up.

Inside, with the door safely closing out the rest of the world, she takes the pie from me.

She seems on the verge of saying something she can't find the words for, so I give her the same out I give everyone. "You can change your mind at any time. All you have to do is throw it out or give it away. The pie is simply an option."

"Oh, I'm doing it," she says, eyes turning to steel. "That's not it."

I wait, not wanting to rush her. Even when it's justified, murder is never a simple thing.

"What's it like?" she eventually asks. "When it happens?"

"It's very peaceful." In fact, it's almost ironic how gentle the final moments are, when kindness is the last thing these cretins deserve. "It usually happens very fast. He'll eat, then start to feel sleepy, maybe act a little loopy. If you can get him to lay down, it will be easier for everyone."

"It's not like cyanide or anything? He won't fight it? I'm just wondering if I need to find somewhere for Sophia to go. I don't want her to be traumatized, but I don't want to throw off our routine and upset him, risk him not eating it."

My heart goes out to her, because I know exactly what it will be like for her daughter to see her father die this way. Even though he deserves it, it won't be easy. "That's a decision only you can make. But it isn't a violent death. There's no gore, nothing dramatic. It's like falling asleep."

She nods. "I think she can handle that. After everything he's inflicted on us, she can handle this one last bit."

I don't tell her how many daughters have ordered pies for their fathers and chose to be the ones to serve them. Maybe not eight-year-olds, but still, kids. Teenagers. They're tougher than they get credit for.

"After tonight, you'll be able to heal," I tell her. "Both of you, from all of it."

She meets my eyes, and hers are the kind of tired built from too many years of being on guard. I hope that, after this, she can rest.

"Thank you," she says. "For saving our lives."

* * *

I drive back across the state with her thanks ringing in my ears.

What I do is terrible, but it's also necessary.

It matters.

But even though I know that, the praise feels unearned when I think of Jodie. She had every right to be saved, same as Carol, but I hesitated out of a selfish fear for my own well-being, as if mine mattered more than hers.

As if I had a right to prioritize suffering.

The dissonance of helping Carol and failing Jodie is enough to drown out any voice of reason whispering that my next stop is a bad idea, a dangerous one.

And besides, I have the other pies made and ready to go.

The box of cutie pies is tied with pink twine and stamped with my steaming-pie logo.

I know I'm going to be seen for this one, so I figure the best way I can hide is in plain sight.

I pull up to the entrance of Meadowbrook, and like the last time, the gates are wide open, the guard less interested in my arrival than whatever has his attention inside the booth.

Perfect.

I park inside the gates and get out. I adjust my dress, fluffing the skirt and pulling the sweetheart bodice down a bit, tying the cardigan tighter around my waist to emphasize the curves I owe to far too many pies and Juan's generosity with the fries.

There is no part of me above using them to my advantage.

Pasting a cheery smile in place, I fetch the box and march over to the booth. I knock twice on the door at the back and wait.

The guard, a white guy in his early thirties, looks wary when he opens it, no doubt wondering why I didn't approach the window instead.

"Help you?" he asks, eyeing me. From his vantage point above, I know he's seeing a fair bit of cleavage, and while it should probably make me feel like less of a feminist, it mostly makes me feel bad about how easy this is going to be.

I up the wattage of the smile and hold the box out. "Hi there. I'm the Pie Girl, and Meadowbrook Properties thought you guys deserved a special treat for all your hard work." I lean into the *treat*, just enough to make sure his interest is firmly piqued.

And realize it's overkill, because his face has lit up in surprise at the mere mention of rewards. "No way," he says. "Sweet. No one ever cares we're here half the time."

I capitalize on his obvious pleasure and step up into the booth with him, opening the box as I go. "Here, let me show you what we've got."

I run him through the flavors—apple, chocolate spice, and raspberry—all while taking in the booth. It's small but not cramped, and as I suspected, there's a bank of monitors on the desk, each screen split into a grid of squares displaying different parts of the development. A handheld gaming console glows beside a charging phone, the screen paused on a Pokémon battle.

He pushes it aside to make room for the box, not remotely embarrassed about being caught off task while receiving a gift from his supposed employer, and I set it down.

"The chocolate one is new," I say, offering him one. "I would love to hear what you think."

He bites into it, and crumbs shatter around the fudgy dark-chocolate filling, raining onto his desk like confetti. "That's banging," he says. "Is that jalapeño?"

I grin. "Close. Guajillos. And a bit of cinnamon."

"Sweet." He finishes the rest in a single bite and picks up a raspberry. It's halfway to his mouth when he freezes. "Am I supposed to share these with John?"

I assume John is the guy coming in after him, but I don't want to ask. Instead I give him a cheeky grin. "I won't tell."

"Right on." He crunches into the next pie, moaning in pleasure. "These are so good. Are you local? I would pay money for these."

"I am." I tell him some of my regular spots, leaving out Frank's, because something tells me he's the kind of guy who could get a little too enthusiastic about things. I take my time with it. While the magic starts to work, I let human nature get a head start, giving him lots of smiles and accidental-on-purpose touches, which isn't hard given the space we're sharing. I want him primed to help me because he likes the attention he's getting. I want him ready for when the magic kicks in.

After I finished Carol's pie the night before, I got to work on these. I could've made things easier with a single flavor, but I wanted to increase the chances of him eating more than one, hence the variety.

It's the magic that matters more than the flavors.

Mixed into each filling is a variant of honesty magic, a blend that should inspire him to be helpful and willing to share what he knows. There's a tiny dash of recklessness in there for good measure, to encourage him to abandon any attachment he may have to the rules, but the fact that he's already so receptive is enough for me to know it wasn't necessary.

As he eats, the monitors behind him cycle through their images. Most are static shots of quiet streets, which makes sense. This is the kind of neighborhood that requires a steady income to maintain, so most of the occupants should be at work or school.

"How are you liking it here?" I ask, just to start loosening him up.

"It's boring," he says around a mouthful of crumbs. He seems to realize this is rude, because he grabs the Mountain Dew off the desk and chugs half before wiping his mouth with the back of his hand. "Sorry, but yeah, it's super dead. I can't complain, though. The pay's good, and no one cares if I game all day."

"You don't have to monitor things?"

"It monitors itself." He points to one of the screens, where a car is pulling out of a driveway. "Everyone's cars are tagged with trackers. The system logs them automatically. I only have to keep an eye out if there's a nontagged vehicle in the area."

"Aren't there a lot? I mean, people must have guests and deliveries all the time."

He shrugs. "Yeah, but it's just a ding when they pass a camera. I hardly have to look up. Honestly, it's kind of pointless. It's not like this is a high-crime place. The worst thing we've caught was an Amazon truck hitting a mailbox." He makes a mock-terrified face, then rolls his eyes. "All this was an add-on Meadowbrook did so they can jack the price. It makes the yuppies feel like they're getting their money's worth or that it's more exclusive or something."

"The houses all have monitoring too, right?"

He shakes his head. "That's separate. They have full access to their home systems, and it outsources monitoring directly to the security company. I don't have residence access, thank God. Last thing I need is to see what these people get up to in private."

I laugh to cover my frustration. That's exactly what I was hoping to see. And he would've handed access over, no problem. I have zero doubt about that. The pies and the novelty of having company are more than enough incentive.

I can't waste this chance.

Chapter Twenty-Two

I consider the bank of monitors one more time, knowing that what I need is a big ask, bigger than access to a single specific feed.

The ethics are the same, but it will be significantly time consuming, and the half-life of magic is unpredictable at best.

Still, I can't let this be a wasted trip.

"Do you store footage here?"

"For street and common area cams, yup."

I swallow the sigh of relief and put on my best puppy-dog eyes. "I don't suppose I could ask you a huge favor?"

He doesn't even hesitate, bless his himbo heart. "What's that?"

"I want to try to look for someone." I'm suddenly unsure how to phrase the request in a way that doesn't make me sound like a stalker, but his face is so open and ready to help that I can do nothing but trust the magic to do its job. "Jodie Azaria?"

"Jodie, Jodie," he says, trying to place her. "Troy's Jodie?"

My heart picks up. "That's the one."

"Why do you need to track her?"

Again, I put my faith in the magic. "Just because. And I need this to stay between us. Is there a way to find her in the footage you have?"

He rubs the scruff on his chin and thinks. "Not easily. And I don't think she has a car registered."

"Troy does."

He shoots me finger guns. "Yes, he does. We can definitely track that."

I exhale, relieved to hear the clacking of his keyboard and not any more questions.

"Okay," he says, more to himself than me as he clicks around one of the screens. "I can narrow by comings and goings, filter by dates. What's helpful?"

"You are," I say, and he beams. I would almost feel bad about how well this magic is working if I weren't so desperate for a scrap of information. "Let's focus on leavings to start."

I want the window narrow, so I give him the dates between the last time I messaged Jodie and when I showed up with the pie.

"You got it." He clicks around and gestures at me to take his chair. "They'll run through automatically, but you can adjust the speed. Date and time stamp is down here, and click these if you want to go forward or back."

I scoot in close to the monitor as the recordings start. The angle of the camera makes it easy to see into the front seat of the big pickup as it exits the gate and gives a quick glimpse of the bed too. I speed up the playback, not really knowing what I'm looking for. Troy knows this gate is monitored, so it's not like he'd throw Jodie in the back with a big map pointing to a dump site.

I remind myself this isn't his only vehicle either and that the department SUV probably isn't being tracked by Meadowbrook security.

I'm about to ask what I'd need to do to get the footage from the houses when I freeze.

She's there.

Then she's gone as fast as she appeared, the recording automatically moving to the next frame.

I click back and pause.

Jodie.

On the screen and very much alive.

The shot is clear enough that I can see her mouth open midword, her eyes fixed on Troy. She doesn't look happy, but neither is she panicked. She's safe here.

She's alive.

I check the time stamp: 10:24 AM two days after her last message to me.

I click through the rest of the frames, heart hammering, but she doesn't reappear.

"Can I see arrivals? Through today?"

"Sure." He leans over me, and in two clicks I have a view of the truck returning. I fast-forward to the day Jodie left and then let the footage play through.

She doesn't return.

It doesn't mean she didn't come back in the SUV, though. I can't discount that. "What about arrivals for all nonregistered vehicles?"

"No problem."

I ask him to narrow the date range and click through quickly, knowing the SUV will be easy to spot. And it is. It makes regular appearances, but Troy is always alone.

Until he isn't.

Hope shocks my heart, but no, the passenger is clearly male and clearly a fellow cop.

I keep clicking, fingers rigid on the mouse, but Jodie doesn't appear.

The small booth seems to shrink around me.

She left this community two days after she sent me her last message. She was with Troy and she was alive.

Now she's gone.

* * *

The security guard was bummed to see me go, but he was blissfully unaware of my change of mood, even inviting me to stop by again.

I told him I might, but I doubt I'll have a reason to.

Before I left, I returned to the frame with Jodie and used my phone to take a picture, just in case. It was already seared on my brain, but I wanted a proper copy.

Right now it's the closest thing I have to evidence.

The sun is dipping when I pull out of Meadowbrook, and I can't help being hyperaware of the camera capturing my exit as I make the same turn Jodie did.

They could've gone anywhere from here.

The possibilities multiply as I drive to pick up Zoe, each street I pass leading to dozens more. And that's only Turnbridge. What if he took her out of town? Out of state?

The options threaten to overwhelm me, and I force myself to focus on the task at hand. I have to get Zoe and I have to get home.

Only that.

Everything else can wait.

Part of me wants to cancel my dinner plans with Melly and let home really be the final thing on today's to-do list, but I don't. For one, it's easier to talk in person, and as much as I don't want to admit it, I'll feel better getting this afternoon out of my head.

A burden shared and all that.

She arrives at seven on the dot, the punctuality so out of character that I realize she's as invested in getting to the bottom of this as I am, and it's a relief to have someone in my corner.

It was one thing to solve a murder I had nothing to do with on *Bake My Day*, but this one, that I let happen?

I'm not above wanting an emotional support sidekick.

Over fragrant plates of falafel, I tell Melly about my visit to the security shack.

"Was that smart?" she asks, pulling a piece of pickled turnip from her wrap and popping it in her mouth.

"It was necessary. And it was safe. I had a reason to be there, I wasn't hiding, it's all aboveboard."

She raises a skeptical brow. "You have a loose definition of all those words. I like it."

I roll my eyes. "There were no cameras in the booth itself, so there's no recording of what we actually did. Like I said, perfectly safe."

"And you don't think he's going to tell? If I had the most boring job in the world and you showed up dressed like that, with free pie, on a secret-agent mission, you can bet your ass I'd be rubbing that story in the faces of all my coworkers."

"He won't tell." I hope. "The magic is good. It was worth it anyway, because now we know that she was alive on that Thursday. The last time the library saw her was Tuesday. Wednesday they got the email that she was 'going home,' and Thursday morning she left that house with Troy and never came back. I checked all the footage. She does not come back through those gates."

Melly lets out a low whistle. "That's a lot of days for him to make her disappear."

"I know." I don't bother recounting the spiral that very thought caused on my drive home, because I'm past it now. "But here's the thing. They left on Thursday. I have him reentering the development alone that night and leaving again the next morning—Friday—dressed for work in the SUV. I was back there Saturday morning to deliver pie, and he was home. It's a lot of days if we take it from that last sighting to today, but far less if we look at his actual movements. Wherever they went, it took less than a day to get there and back."

A look of admiration crosses Melly's face. "Nice deduction, Sherlock."

"Right now it's a timeline, that's all. But it's a start."

"It is." She picks through her wrap, sampling bits of veggie as she thinks. I don't know why she bothers getting wraps only to deconstruct them, but at least she's enjoying it. "Do you know what time he returned that night?"

"Nine-oh-seven."

"So roughly twelve hours, round trip," she muses.

"Oh, wait a second." I jump up, barely containing an actual *aha*, and fetch my laptop. "We can figure this out. Right now."

I'm winging this, but it's going to work, I know it. It would feel more dramatic if I had a paper map and a marker, maybe one of those whiteboards TV detectives get, but I'm not one to look a technological gift horse in the digital teeth.

My search for *driving radius map* delivers a handful of promising options, but the best is at the top. The Time It Takes app is exactly what we need. I hurriedly set up a free-trial account linked to a burner email and plug in Troy's address, set the travel parameter to six hours, just to cover the possibility that he drove straight out and back to wherever he went, and wait.

On the screen, the map zooms in to his address, then back out, an overlay of blue steadily expanding across the areas he could reach in a six-hour drive.

"Man, I love technology," Melly says.

When it stops, we have a ragged blob covering all or part of nine states.

Melly groans. "I take it back."

"No, it's okay." This is the closest thing I've had to a proper lead, and I refuse to be disheartened. I shrink the distance slider down to five hours, and we lose two states from the radius. "I think we can assume a smaller zone, because he probably didn't drive somewhere and immediately turn around. I mean, it would take time. Whatever he did." The air in the RV seems to thicken at the thought of what exactly that might've been. "I mean, he took her out of there alive. It's not like he was just dumping a body."

Melly purses her lips, jaw going on hard. "Right. And even if he was dumping her, he probably wouldn't do it on the side of the road. That would take time."

"If he buried her, it would've taken a couple hours." I move the distance slider back a bit more, shrinking the range and ignoring Melly's sidelong look. "Trust me. It would've."

She nods. "That's still a lot of ground."

"Killing her would also take time." I keep the words matter-of-fact. I have to. I drop a little more time off the slider.

"Not if he shot her. He's a cop. It's not like he doesn't have guns."

"He wouldn't use a gun. It would be too impersonal, too quick. He would want his hands on her." Tendrils of rage snake through me as I imagine what he could've done. "And like you said, he's a cop. He wouldn't risk the ballistics if he didn't have to."

"True."

We both study the updated map, all the places they could've gone.

"There has to be a way to narrow it down further," I say, knowing there's no way the two of us can cover this much ground.

"What about a tracker?" Melly asks. "Don't a lot of killers return to the scene of the crime? Like to gloat?"

"Sometimes, but if he's really trying to get away with it, I don't think he will. He would know that gets people caught."

"You still haven't discounted the tracker, though," she points out.

"If he's not going back, a tracker wouldn't help," I say slowly, an alternative already forming.

"But you know what would?" she prompts.

"His route has already been tracked. By his phone, for sure, and maybe by a separate GPS in the truck. It won't be easy to get that information, though, not as civilians. But resident vehicles are also tagged for the security company. It's how we could filter comings and goings. I wonder if those tags are GPS enabled or if they're just designed to trigger the cameras like the toll transponders." I'm thinking out loud, grasping at threads of ideas. "GPS makes more sense, though. It's a security thing. If a vehicle was stolen, the company could locate it, right?"

"Maybe you need to visit your new friend again?"

"Maybe." I kick myself for not thinking of this earlier. "In the meantime, we at least have a radius. We know she left alive and that she didn't come back. She's out there somewhere. And we're going to find her."

Chapter
Twenty-Three

I t feels too risky to go back to the security booth so soon, so I do
the next best thing.

I lie my ass off.

Twenty minutes on the phone with Select Security, under the
guise of a scorned wife, and I've learned the company that services
Meadowbrook is headquartered in Alston with private servers boasting
top-notch encryption to ensure that all data is meticulously
protected. When I explain, sniffling, that I know my philandering
husband is cheating on me and that I need to use GPS to prove it,
they're polite, confirming that vehicle location is indeed a service
offered in case of theft, but that they're sorry, they don't store driving
histories. Before I hang up, they remind me that they take discretion
and their clients' privacy very seriously.

Bastards.

I pace Penny's tiny kitchen, fuming. They can track, but they
don't store. It feels like a lie. I bet that data exists and they don't even
do anything with it. I wonder about the logistics of pieing my way
into the headquarters, going so far as to pull them up online to try
to get a feel of how many people would stand between me and the
person with answers. Several, for sure, and probably separate security
guards guarding the security firm.

I let out a growl of frustration that makes Zoe raise her head from her paws to give me a tilted look of confusion.

"Someone knows where he went," I say, like she might be able to tell me.

She only sighs and lowers her head, drifting back into a peaceful doggy dream world.

Oh, to have the life of a spoiled pup.

The map is still open on my laptop, and I try to figure out how to narrow it down without GPS data.

There are things I didn't want to work out in front of Melly, because even though she's established that she's solidly team murder pie, there's a difference between supporting and doing.

I know about doing murder.

I also know about covering it up.

I figure if he drove her somewhere, it's somewhere remote. That nixes all the cities, the bigger towns within the radius.

The problem with New England is the sheer number of places that are ideal for body hiding.

I assume, for nothing more than the sake of efficiency, that he killed her at the same place he left her, meaning somewhere properly remote.

She was already afraid of him. When push came to shove, she would've fought. She wanted to get away, to have a life without him, and she would've scratched and clawed and screamed her way to safety if she could've.

So he had to bring her somewhere where that wasn't an option.

I put the kettle on, contemplating how I would do it if I were him.

It would have to be somewhere familiar, somewhere I knew was safe. I couldn't pick a random patch of woods to drag her into, hoping that hunters or hikers wouldn't stumble across us midmurder.

It would have to be somewhere I could count on for privacy.

Somewhere I'd been.

And I realize exactly how I'm going to find her.

Connections get you caught. It's why the most successful serial killers choose victims they don't know, and it's why I left home when I was seventeen and never looked back.

There's a connection, that inescapable need for the familiar, that is going to be Troy's undoing. And I am going to turn over every scrap of his life until I find it.

* * *

It is a truth universally acknowledged that confidence and a clipboard will get you anywhere.

In my case, confidence, a clipboard, and a navy polo shirt.

The school uniform shop one town over was able to outfit me in a shirt and khakis that made me look exactly like my security guard friend. Sure, I was missing the logo on the chest, but from a distance? Aces.

I added a navy baseball hat and was relieved when the clerk rang me out without asking questions.

There were a million things I should've been doing instead of this—like seeing Noel or selling pies—but after getting off the phone with the security company, sitting still felt impossible.

And there's nothing quite like edgy restlessness to inspire bad decisions.

I used my map app to survey the area around the development. Sure, I could walk right in the front, but there's confidence and then there's carelessness. While Troy has no reason to even ask to see the gate footage, I don't want to leave any traces if I don't have to. Not for this trip, when I don't have a valid cover story.

With privacy being such a selling point, it's no surprise to find much of the development is bordered by woodlands.

Which is perfect.

I locate Troy's house and the adjoining woods and figure I can hike it.

Sure, I'm not exactly the most outdoorsy of people, but needs must, and I'm not afraid of getting dirty.

The thing I learn about maps and woods is that it's not as straightforward as getting directions across town. Even toggling to walking directions doesn't help, as it tries to take me the long way, out of the woods and back down the road. All I wanted was a ballpark estimation of how long the trek would take, but that was apparently asking too much, and fifteen minutes in, I'm starting to wonder if this was such a great idea after all.

Still, I'm far enough into the woods that I can no longer see the road, and the little dot on the map that is supposedly me looks closer to the houses than to the road, so I push on.

Ten minutes later, the trees end in an abrupt line, dumping me into a backyard. Not knowing the extent of the surveillance, I step from the woods completely in character, acting as if I'm inspecting an imagined perimeter. I keep my phone on the clipboard so if anyone sees me it appears I'm doing something official, but really I'm using the map to orient myself within the neighborhood.

All things considered, I planned the hike damn near perfectly. I'm only two houses down from Troy's and on a trajectory that will let me arrive from the back.

Not bad at all.

Tugging my hat a little lower, I continue on through still and empty yards. The hedges that mark property lines are tall enough for privacy, but they only border the sides, not the back where the woods are, so I have unobstructed views of each yard and house as I pass.

I maintain my steady pace, occasionally checking my clipboard, and carry on right past Troy's house as if there's nothing special

there. I have to, just to be safe. I haven't nailed down his work schedule, so there is a chance he's home, but I figured it was a chance
worth taking.

Luckily, all is quiet, no signs of life to be seen. I double back,
bolder now.

The backyard is mowed and clear of leaves, something I'm sure is
paid for rather than done by Troy, since the other yards are equally
spotless. The grass is completely unblemished. It's not that I expected
to find a freshly dug grave, but still, I had to confirm. I'll make my
way back to the truck using the woods directly behind his house, but
I don't expect to find Jodie here. I think wherever he brought her on
Thursday is where she's been the whole time.

I just need to figure out where that might be.

The backyard tells me nothing about Troy. There's a raised patio
identical to the neighbor's, a covered grill the size of Penny's kitchen
set to one side of the sliding doors.

Those doors are impossibly tempting, and I'm up the stairs before
I can talk myself out of it.

I don't see a camera, but I'm not stupid enough to think that means
anything. I take a minute with my clipboard and then deliberately inspect
the door. If I'm on camera, I want to look like a security tech doing
something thorough. I run a hand over the frame, testing the door, and
find it stubbornly locked. I carry on as if unbothered, using the time to
peer beyond the door into the bowels of the house. It's open-planned,
which seems at odds with the whole focus on privacy but works in my
favor. The kitchen backs right onto the patio, and it's clear that whatever
upkeep is paid for by the development doesn't extend inside. The sink is
filled with dishes, the large granite island littered with coffee cups, pizza
boxes, and more filth than I'd bet was allowed when Jodie was here.

The dining area to the right is cleaner, save for a uniform shirt
slung across a chair, and in the living room beyond, a giant TV hangs

above a fireplace with an armchair positioned in front of it, a game controller balanced on the arm. It looks out of sync with the rest of the furniture, like it didn't always go there, and I wonder if this is his version of success or squalor.

He got away with murder and is what? Making the house a man cave, a den of takeout and video games? Is he living his frat-boy dream, or is this a descent into something more chaotic? Is the mess a sign of stress, the toll of his actions on his conscience? I wish I had a baseline, something to judge this against.

What I don't see is a single sign of Jodie. From this angle I can't see the foyer, the coatrack or the shoes, but from here, no one would know a woman was ever here.

And that worries me.

If he got rid of her, it would stand to reason he had to get rid of her stuff too, and I make my way around the house on the garage side, stopping where the bins are tucked behind a latticed wall, because God forbid people can see them from the street. I peek inside, knowing there's no way to pretend this is official security business, and find a mountain of beer cans in recycling and a single bag in the garbage side. I wonder how much evidence is sitting in a landfill right now.

But no. The bins aren't big enough to fit an entire life into, and Jodie has lived here for years. Getting rid of a body takes effort, but so does erasing every trace of her from a house. A single trash day wouldn't cut it.

To the left of the bins is a door, because, again, God forbid the neighbors see the trash going out.

My fingers hesitate above the knob as my heart speeds up. There's no telltale video doorbell like I saw on the front door. I check the frame above, the roofline, searching for any sign of surveillance. The front of the house is covered. I know that for certain. I wouldn't be surprised if the patio was too. But the bins? They might not be.

Either way, there's no way my security company cover story will hold with what I do next.

I try the knob.

It turns easily, and I'm so surprised I freeze, waiting for alarms to sound, lights to flash, something to indicate that I've breached the perimeter and that someone knows.

Nothing comes.

I step inside, warily, knowing full well that if I'm caught right now, I can be arrested. There is no reason for a security tech to be inside without the property owner, but that's something that can be dealt with later, if there's footage and if it's watched.

There's no alarm panel on either side of the door, and I relax a little. I'm inside. I'm not going to waste this.

The garage, unlike the house, is tidy to the point of obsession. Rubber totes hang in tracts above the empty bay, and an array of bicycles are mounted on individual wall racks beside a pegboard of tools and equipment I can only half identify. A rainbow of fishing poles line the other wall, and I know in my bones Troy is the kind of guy who would include fish in his dating profile pictures, as if the size of a fish remotely correlates to the size of anything else.

The hulking pickup completely fills the other side of the garage like a sleeping beast. I try the door and am shocked when it opens.

I climb up on the running board and peer inside, almost overwhelmed by that nauseating new-car scent. I scan for a GPS unit or anything that would give me a clue of where he took Jodie, but the only clutter is an empty phone holder with a charging cord draped over it. The interior is spotless.

The kind of spotless that could be the result of trying to remove DNA evidence, for example.

I know it could also be the kind of spotless that's the result of a certain kind of guy thinking his car is his kingdom, and judging by the garage, Troy is that guy.

But the two aren't mutually exclusive.

I rifle through the glove compartment, which offers only a folder of documents and what looks like the truck's original manual. It's a far cry from my own glove box, with its abundance of air fresheners, lotion bottles, and spare hand sanitizers.

I expect equally spartan contents in the center console and am correct. A spare charging cord, some coins, and a multitool. I curse car-obsessed men. This should've been a gold mine of information; instead, it looks like it just left the showroom.

And that's why the glint of silver stands out.

Wedged in the gap between the seat and the console is something smooth and shiny, out of place.

An iPad.

One of the small ones, with a third of a charge and locked with a passcode.

But not a fingerprint.

My heart kicks up. Taking it with me would be theft, no question. It moves my breaking and entering firmly into burglary territory.

Which is still less than murder. I secure the iPad facedown to my clipboard, not wanting to damage the screen.

I can decide what to do with it before I leave. For now, I have to keep moving.

Beyond the truck is another door that leads into the house, and my breath catches.

It's one thing to be in the garage, the truck, but it's another thing entirely to go inside.

I tell myself it's probably locked, and even if it isn't, surely it will be alarmed.

My fingers hover above the knob.

The problem with video security being so widespread is there are so many ways to configure it. I had a taste of that back when I needed a system for Penny because I was having an issue with break-ins. The doorbells triggers a notification, every time. It's why I have no intention of going near the front of the house today.

But the interior cameras? Plenty of people set up for passive monitoring. After all, who wants their phone pinging every time their dog goes to get a drink or their kid is running laps around the house?

The security guard said the footage was stored remotely but that homeowners had access. Troy is a cop, sure, but how often does he really watch the footage from his own house?

Then I remember what Jodie's message said. *There are cameras everywhere.*

He watched her.

Probably all the time.

But now that she's not here, does he still review them? Every day?

It seems like overkill to me, the kind of hypervigilance that's impossible to maintain.

Or maybe that's just me talking myself into a bad decision.

Doesn't matter.

I try the knob.

Chapter
Twenty-Four

As soon as I do, a whirring sound fills the garage and I freeze, unsure what I triggered.

The answer comes to me on a wave of pure panic.

It's the garage door.

Opening.

I release the knob, prepared to bolt, but I don't have time. There's nowhere to go. The gap is already growing, a shaft of sunlight slicing across the floor. I'll never make it. Not across the whole garage, not to the side door.

For a split second I consider going inside, consequences be damned, but no. Even if that knob turns, I can't trap myself inside with him, not knowing what alarms or sensors might be triggered. It would be one thing if he didn't have the cameras on his side, but without knowing their configuration, I can't risk it.

In the spotless garage, my options are limited.

The door creeps higher.

I run.

Keeping the clipboard clutched to my chest, I duck in front of the pickup, near the front tire.

Light climbs the wall as the door continues its steady rise, and I pray he's going inside, not switching vehicles. If he moves this truck, there's no way he won't see me.

He backs the SUV into the other spot, and it's all I can do to keep still, crouched where I am when every instinct screams to flee.

But I'm not fast. I'm not familiar with the territory.

He is both.

So I breathe as quietly as possible and I wait.

The car door opens. I hear feet hit the ground, followed by the thunk of the door closing. There's the muffled sound of a distant voice, and I realize he's on the phone, listening to someone.

Distracted.

I risk a glance beneath the truck. My next move depends on whether his path to the door takes him in front of the truck or behind it. I pray for behind. Behind makes more sense.

He goes behind.

I almost collapse in relief, but I can't.

Collapsing would make noise.

Instead, I scrabble along the front of the truck, shifting my hiding spot to the driver's side, farther from the door.

There's a pause and a tinkling jangle of keys.

So it wouldn't have opened anyway.

That makes me feel slightly better about my aborted mission.

When Troy speaks, his voice detonates like a bomb in the silence of the garage, and even though I know he's on the phone, there's a jolt of leg-shaking panic when I think it's me he's shouting at.

"I don't care," he barks. "I have my own shit I'm sorting out. I don't have time to cover your ass. I told you not to trust him. He's too fresh, and you don't have shit on him." He jams the key in the lock, and I can't make out the other person's words, but they sound agitated. "For fuck's sake, Kenny. It's not a bonding activity. It's you and me and Tommy having each other's backs. You don't bring the new guy into that. Not like this, not now. No, I don't care how hot she was. It's not just your ass on the line, it's—"

The door slams, plunging the garage back into silence, save for the almost audible slamming of my heart.

As much as I want to know what it is they were discussing, if the *she* in question was Jodie, I don't hesitate.

I'm on my feet and out the side door before I can think.

I hit the bins and freeze. I can either go straight out the back, through the woods like I planned, or I can go through the hedge to the neighbor's yard and go that way.

I think of Troy's house, what I saw through the sliders. His kitchen backs onto the patio. If he goes there, he has a full view of the yard. I would be easy to spot, and my presence might be enough to make him check his security footage, if it hasn't already been triggered.

The hedge is thick and taller than I have any hope of leaping. Through is the shortest route to freedom, but at what cost?

I inhale deeply, steeling myself.

Out the front it is.

I tug my baseball hat lower and move the clipboard into official position. If I'm caught, I'll play it off. I can do this. Sticking close to the hedge, I remind myself that all I need to do is get back to my truck and I'm good.

I'm far enough from Troy's front doors to know I won't trigger the bell camera, so I focus on looking confident and busy.

I have a reason to be here.

It's on my clipboard.

I pause in front of the neighbor's yard, glancing between the clipboard and house as if checking something official but really looking for signs of movement. Nothing.

Adrenaline urges me to run, but my brain and the watery feeling in my knees argue caution. I stroll through the yard, occasionally pretending to check something off, in case I'm being watched. An eruption of barking almost does me in, but I keep my steady pace, ignoring the fluffy white dog losing its mind behind the patio sliders.

Nothing to see here, pup.

I hit the woods without incident and trek a good way in before cutting over. As much as I don't want to risk being seen, I also can't risk missing something in the woods behind Troy's house.

While I don't think he'd bury her so close to home, it would be stupid not to check.

Graves, proper graves, aren't small, and they're not easy to conceal. Sure, you can pile leaves and brush over them, but if you're looking for it? In a limited area? You'll see it.

But I don't. Nothing about the ground back here is disturbed except by my trampling. There are no paths where a body might've been dragged, no mounds of dirt suggesting fresh digging, nothing.

I remind myself that the absence of evidence can still be evidence. She's not here, which confirms that we need to focus the search elsewhere.

That's something.

I emerge from the woods feeling like I've survived one of those wilderness races people like to torture themselves with and am desperate for a nice long shower. Or even better, a hot bath in Noel's claw-foot tub.

I can almost smell the bubbles when I realize I'm not where I should be.

My ancient pickup is nowhere to be seen.

But how can that be? Even if I drifted, came out farther down the road than I expected, I should still see it.

It should still be here.

Adrenaline makes an encore appearance.

Did someone seriously steal my truck? *My* truck?

The thing was already a couple county lines past decrepit when I borrowed it permanently from my father. These days it's barely running on luck and duct tape.

No one wants my truck.

And yet someone has it.

Someone who isn't me.

Fuck.

I call Melly, because there's no way I can tell Noel my car was stolen while I was breaking into a cop's house. He'd have a literal aneurysm, and I like him far too much to inflict that kind of stress on him.

She answers on the first ring, like always.

"I need your help."

Chapter
Twenty-Five

S he arrives less like a white knight on horseback and more like a leather-clad demon on wheels, tires kicking up a spray of gravel as she brakes in front of me.

She flips up the face shield of her helmet to reveal a huge grin splitting her face. She tosses me a second helmet. "Your chariot, madam." Her expression falters as I fumble it, barely keeping it and my clipboard from hitting the ground. "Wait. Why are you dressed like a phone salesman?"

I pull off the baseball hat and jam the helmet on in its place. "I'll explain later." Unlike Melly's, this one is open-faced and covered in stickers. I buckle the strap, praying I'm not going to have to test its durability.

"Hop on," she says, eyes sparkling.

I swing a leg over, grateful for the ugly khakis. There's no way this would go well in a dress. The seat vibrates like something alive, and I'm hit with the sense this isn't going to go well anyway. "If you kill me—"

"You'll what, kill me back?" She laughs. "You're perfectly safe. But you do need to hold on."

I wrap my arms around her waist, the clipboard with its all-important iPad sandwiched tight between us.

"Ready?"

"As I'll ever be."

She flips her face shield down and revs the engine. My arms tighten automatically around her, and everything about her feels firm and strong. Like maybe she won't get me killed.

"If I lean, you lean," she calls, voice muffled. "We stay in sync."

And with that single bit of instruction, she pulls into the road and hits the throttle.

I yelp in surprise, ducking my face into her shoulder, and the wind bites my face. The leather of her jacket is soft and warm from the sunlight, and after a few minutes that feel like hours, I relax a tiny bit. We're flying, no doubt about it, but she holds the bike steady, with none of the slaloms or antics I know she's capable of. I keep my death grip around her middle, the hard lines of the clipboard digging into my front, and if I ignore the fact of my own mortality, I can sort of see the appeal.

This is nothing like driving.

The closest I can equate it to is riding a horse, but even that isn't really accurate. At least a horse has a sense of self-preservation. You can go as fast as you want, but a horse usually isn't going to be on board with something truly dangerous.

The motorcycle is more an extension of Melly's own body. It's not a horse, with a separate brain and opinions. It's only her. It's her whims and wants, a machine completely at her mercy.

We come into town fast, and she's forced to slow as traffic thickens. Cars I know she would swerve around without a passenger become obstacles to be endured, and I appreciate the self-restraint.

She takes the turn into the diner wide, letting the bike stay as upright as possible, and pulls around to park by Penny.

When she cuts the engine, the world seems weirdly muted, but the ground feels electric as my legs continue to buzz with the bike's vibrations.

"Okay, what is your deal with that clipboard?" Melly says when both helmets are stashed. "I swear it's tattooed on my back."

I breathe deep, relishing being safe at home, even if the air back here smells like fryer oil and eau de dumpster. "I need five minutes, then I'll explain. Everything."

"Like where your car went?"

"Maybe everything but that. Can you take Zoe out while I change?"

She looks uneasy but agrees. Melly is many things, but a natural animal lover is not one of them. Still, Zoe knows the routine and takes Melly on a circuit of the back lot as I trade the polo and khakis for the softest dress I own. The cotton is almost velvety with age, and as I do up the buttons, I relish the freedom of the full skirt, so much less constricting than pants. I top it with a cozy cardigan and have tea steeping by the time Melly returns.

"Okay, now you look like you," she says, unclipping Zoe's lead and hanging it by the door. Zoe trots up the steps and plants herself at my feet for pets, and I happily oblige her.

Melly follows her in and hops up on the counter, giving one of the mugs an idle stir. "So where are we starting? Maybe with your stolen car? Your fashion crisis? Because I have to tell you, I can't figure out what connects those dots."

I look up at her, how nonplussed she seems by the apparent weirdness, and decide to start at the beginning. I don't get far.

"And you didn't invite me?" she asks. "Or at least tell me? Do you think there's any planet where I don't want to be part of breaking and entering?"

"It just kind of happened," I say, leaving Zoe to settle onto a stool.

"It just happened?" She scoffs. "It just happened that you got a whole disguise, hid your car, and committed crimes. It just happened."

"You know what I mean. I didn't really plan it. But I had to see what I could find out."

"And?"

I slide the iPad over. "This was in the truck."

She raises an eyebrow. "You do know those can be tracked, right? Like, it's a feature? Find My Device?" My face must convey exactly how much that didn't cross my mind, because she laughs. "For someone with your kill count, you're not exactly a criminal mastermind."

"There was adrenaline," I protest. "In vast, vast quantities. But I thought maybe if he used GPS to get somewhere on his phone, the app might sync data here."

"Okay, yeah. That was clever. But you need to get this out of here as soon as possible." She taps the screen to life and sees the passcode lock. "Any luck?"

"I tried his birthday and Jodie's, but no. I'm not sure how many tries until it locks me out."

She types something into her phone and says, "Six. You have four left. What about the date of the accident? When they met?"

"Oh, maybe." I type it in, and the prompt shakes in error. "Badge number?"

"Do you know it?"

"No."

"Hold on, maybe we can find it." She goes back to her phone, and in the quiet I put myself in Troy's shoes.

I'm a cop. An abuser. I'm so entitled I prey on young, traumatized girls without a second thought. They exist for my pleasure.

On a whim, I type 696969.

It opens.

The display shows the same grid layout as every Apple product, but it feels overlayed with a ticking clock, the knowledge that it can be tracked to this exact spot adding a layer of peril this situation doesn't need.

"I'm in," I say, almost not believing it.

"Seriously? Shit. You're fucking amazing," Melly says, leaning over to see. "I thought for sure I was going to have to pull some tech strings."

I brush off the praise, chest tight as I open the Maps app. I scan the location history, disappointment radiating through me as I see a list of businesses, some city addresses that I street view to see if they might be dump sites, but nothing that screams isolation, safety, or guilt.

Melly takes a picture of the list with her phone anyway, just in case.

"He knows where he went," I say. "It's somewhere he doesn't need directions to."

"That could be anywhere."

Like I need reminding of that.

I'm about to close the app when something about the map view prompts a thought. "Wait, there's got to be a way to disable the location tracking, right?" I'm already toggling to settings, searching for what must be an option, and yes, it's there. My finger hovers over the option to disable location sharing. "Do you think this triggers a notification? Like, will he know when it's turned off?"

She taps at her phone and shakes her head. "Nope, you're good."

I slide the switch, and it's like a weight lifts.

"I mean, this location might show up in the history," she clarifies, "but it won't show active locations anymore."

I shake it away. Some privacy is better than nothing. At least when it's my privacy.

I care less about Troy's and don't even hesitate to open the Select Security app. Hell, maybe while I'm here I can delete any footage of myself from earlier.

The app opens to a menu, asking me to select a feed, and for a second I think that's excessive. Would you really want to have

153

separate accounts for every single camera in your house? But when I click the drop-down arrow, I realize that's not what it means.

There are only two options.

Home.

Cabin.

My chest tightens and I reach out on autopilot, grabbing Melly's wrist.

Then I click on Cabin.

A grid fills the screen, each square offering a view of a different room. It's exactly like the monitors in the guard booth, but interior shots. All the angles are high, like the cameras are mounted on the ceiling.

Even the bathroom is displayed, the toilet, sink, and shower crammed together in the small space.

It's definitely a cabin, the furnishings rustic and utilitarian, the only decor an array of taxidermied fish mounted on plaques.

Everything is so still that when the movement comes, it's like a horror movie monster bursting into the frame.

I squeeze Melly's wrist.

Neither of us breathes.

In the bedroom, the blanket on the bed is thrown back and a woman staggers up from its depths.

It's Jodie.

She's alive.

Chapter
Twenty-Six

"Holy shit," Melly says.

We watch as Jodie stumbles to the bathroom, and I remember the pregnancy, the morning sickness that would come with it. I avert my eyes, even though she has no idea we're witnessing her vulnerability.

The time stamp in the corner ticks on, confirming that this is a live feed.

When Jodie returns to the bed, I can see she's trembling as she climbs back under the covers, bundling them tight around herself and flipping the top one over her head. She disappears from sight, like she was never there at all.

Melly and I both stare at each other, dumbstruck.

Then I launch into action.

I leave the feed, even though it kills me to, and tear through the app, hunting for a location. I click every clickable thing, but the only address I get is for the house. It's almost like the app thinks the cabin is an extension of the house, and I wonder if that was deliberate—either a way to hide its existence or to dodge paying for a second account. Either way, it doesn't help me.

It enrages me.

I switch back to the feeds, turning a clinical eye on them. Years of making murder pies have taught me the value of background details. When clients send me photos, I can learn as much from them as from what they tell me, sometimes more.

I start with the main room feed, enlarging it to fill the screen. If it weren't for the rolling time stamp, I could be staring at a photo. On one side there's a sagging couch with a plaid blanket crumpled in the corner, a wide coffee table littered with fishing magazines placed before it. On the other side is the kitchen, if you can call it that. A refrigerator dominates the space, and I wonder how the cabin sources electricity. If it's as remote as I expect, it would have to be on a generator. I wonder how long it's fueled for, how often Troy is making trips to see her.

Or if he is at all.

The rest of the kitchen consists of a short stretch of counter, an induction burner, and a coffeepot.

It's barely functional, but I suppose if you were a group of guys roughing it on a fishing trip, it would be enough.

There are dishes in the sink, a single bowl and glass, and a window above it that's been covered over from the outside with plywood.

I switch to the bedroom feed and find Jodie still hidden in her nest of blankets.

I wonder if she knows he's recording her 24/7 and figure she must.

He was at home too.

I turn suddenly to Melly. "I bet he recorded what he did to her. Wait a second."

I swipe back out of the feed to the main menu, and this time I do find what I want. The cabin feed is set to seven-day storage, but the home feed is on the sixty-day default. There are fifty-eight days available for viewing.

"He hit her. More than once. I had photos," I say, an idea brewing. "Do you think he stopped to turn the cameras off? In the heat of the moment?"

Melly cringes. "God, how do people live like that?"

"I don't know, but right now, I'm glad this guy does." I drag the slider back through time and am rewarded with a full screenshot of my own stupid self on the patio, bold as day, which I bypass quickly, but not without a longing glance at the Delete Archive button at the top of the screen. That's not what I'm here for, not now.

I scroll back further, not wanting to see what I know is there but needing to.

It doesn't take long.

There's no sound, and I'm grateful. I remember Noel not wanting to hear the details about Carol's pie, and I feel a flash of empathy.

It's one thing to see fight scenes on TV, when you know they're scripted and choreographed within an inch of their life.

It's another thing to see this, Troy's left hand wrapped in Jodie's long hair, the other shoving a pink-cased phone hard into her face.

I keep going back, and the frequency of incidents is enough to turn my stomach.

"He fucking recorded himself."

"It's evidence," Melly reminds me. "We'll need that."

"It's evidence obtained illegally. That we want to use against a cop."

"It's still evidence. Fuck it. Fuck the cops. We put that shit online, let public opinion sort him out."

"It's not that simple. You know that." We both do, but I also understand her desire to do it, to shine a light on exactly what kind of cockroach he is. "It's not time for that."

Melly growls in frustration.

"I know," I say. "But she's alive. If we tip our hand too early, if he knows we're onto him, he might escalate. He's already kidnapped her."

"Why would he bother? Why not keep her at home?"

I think back to her message, the panic pouring out of it. "The baby," I finally say. It feels right. "She wanted an abortion. He didn't."

"Because it gives him another way to control her." Melly sneers, and I know if she were in the same room as Troy, he would already be bloody. "He doesn't give her a say over her own safety; why would he give her a say over this?"

"It might be the only thing keeping her alive right now."

"I hate men," Melly says. "I hate cops and I hate this country and that women have less rights than guns and that you and me are sitting in a fucking kitchen trying to solve this because we can't trust the cops to do the right thing because hey, why change now?" Her breath comes hard and fast, and there's fire in her eyes that I feel in my belly.

"If you want something done right, you do it yourself," I say. "And we're going to do this right."

Using my phone, I record every scene of violence on the iPad, videos of videos that may not be legally admissible but are still important.

Then I tap Delete Archive.

Sure, Troy may wonder why his footage archive was purged two days early, but maybe he won't. Maybe he won't even notice. What he for sure won't notice is me peeking in his slider doors.

I get up and stretch, needing a minute away from what I've just seen.

My fingers itch to start baking, to work a magic I can force down Troy's throat until he gives me her location, but I can't. Not this time.

We're not going to beat Troy with brute strength, not when he's built like the poster boy for steroid abuse.

We have to be smart.

I go back to the cabin feed.

Jodie hasn't moved, is barely an outline under the blankets, and I survey the rest of the room. Beside the bed is a nightstand with a lamp and a facedown paperback. It doesn't change anything, but I wonder if it's something she brought or something she found. There's a bifold door leading to what is probably a closet, the same kind of door used on the bathroom. Nothing that locks.

Like the kitchen window, the window in the bedroom has been secured from the outside, but a narrow gap has been left at the top to allow some natural light to filter through.

The things this man probably thinks are a kindness.

I switch to the bathroom to confirm, and yes, that window is also covered.

There is a single door in the main room that must be locked from the outside; otherwise she would've walked right out.

I think of how she trembled on the way back to bed, but weakness wouldn't have stopped her. She would've found help, no matter how far she had to go.

And then I realize I missed something.

The shaking.

I do one more sweep of the cabin, wanting more than anything to be wrong.

He granted her a bit of light. What a hero.

What he didn't give her was a heat source.

"We're going to kill him, right? After we find her?" Melly asks, voice low and throaty.

"Yes we are."

Chapter
Twenty-Seven

It's nearly impossible to power down the iPad when the temptation to keep an eye on Jodie is so strong, but we do.

Even though the location tracking is off, it seems somehow risky to keep it on, like Troy will know we're watching him in real time.

Plus, neither of us has the right charger, and after all the video we watched, the battery has dwindled to a measly eighteen percent. I make a mental note to pick one up, because there's no way we're giving up this kind of access, but first, I have to find my car.

I know the fastest way to do that would probably be to call the police, but I'm not ready to do that yet. Not when the images of one of their own's abuse are so fresh in my brain.

"I'm thinking it got towed, not stolen," I tell Melly. "Who would steal it? On that road? Who would even see it to be tempted?"

"Yeah, but it's not a crime to park on the shoulder. Hunters do it all the time." Melly gives me a look, forestalling protest. "I certainly don't want to involve the cops either, but you have to admit stolen is an option."

"Only after I've exhausted the more likely one." I pull up a list of Turnbridge tow shops on my phone and start calling. There are four in town, and by the third one, I luck out.

"The blue Ford that was abandoned on Crocker Street?" the gruff voice asks. "Yeah, we got that in a couple hours ago."

"What? It wasn't abandoned. It wasn't even there for an hour."

"I didn't write the ticket, sweetheart, just picked it up," he says. "We're here till five if you want to get it today, or tomorrow we open at eight. It'll be a hundred and forty-three due at pickup."

"Seriously?" I swallow my irritation with a muffled groan. "Fine. That's fine. I'm on my way."

I hang up, seething. "So apparently I have to pay a hundred and forty bucks to spring it from car jail, and I have a ticket on top of that for vehicle abandonment."

"You can fight that," Melly says, fired up. "Like you said, it was less than an hour."

I heave a sigh. "I can't fight a ticket. I don't need that kind of attention. I've got to pay it." I'm already calculating where the unexpected fees will come from. The pie business keeps me comfortable but not rich. If the ticket is going to be another hundred on top of the impound, that's going to hurt. "I don't suppose I could hitch a ride across town?"

"At your service." Melly fishes the motorcycle key out of a tight front pocket and grins. "I think you're getting a taste for it."

"Hardly."

"It's okay to admit it," she says as I give Zoe a goodbye pet. "No one can resist the feel of that much beauty between their legs."

I don't dignify that with a response, but I have to concede—silently—that it does feel more natural this time. I'm less surprised by the accelerations and don't feel the need to grip Melly's waist quite so tightly. Which is a massive relief, because my skirt absolutely does not want to stay tucked around my legs and I resort to bunching the ends up in my fist to keep from flashing everyone or getting it tangled in the wheel. I find both options equally terrifying and am glad when we reach the garage unscathed.

In addition to towing, the shop does inspections and bodywork, and it takes me a minute to find my truck among the sea of vehicles.

That's because it's not out front. It's parked forlornly behind a chain-link fence, and the sight is enough to reignite my fury.

This is very much not my best day ever.

After paying the ransom, I'm allowed behind the fence to retrieve my truck, and I thank Melly for being my chauffeur for the afternoon.

"Like I'd leave you stranded," she scoffs. "So what now?"

"Now I go home, whip up some extra pies to pay for this fiasco, then I have to go see Noel before he breaks up with me." I deliberately don't mention Jodie or the case, not while we're standing in the middle of a tow shop. Just because I can't see anyone doesn't mean they're not obscured by parked cars. And if that sounds paranoid, well, that's better than overheard.

Melly purses her lips, seeming to understand, and strides back to her bike. "I'll meet you back at yours," she says without looking back, giving me no chance to protest.

I unlock the truck and climb in. I know it's stupid, but I can tell someone has been inside, and I'm not unaware of the hypocrisy of being bothered by it.

A piece of paper flutters over the dashboard air vents when I turn the key, and I steel myself, already dreading its contents.

As expected, it's the ticket.

What's not expected is the fine.

Two hundred fifty dollars.

I almost laugh at the absurdity. Who gives $250 parking tickets?

Then I see who.

Troy Sullivan.

I fling it onto the passenger seat with a disgusted snort and pull out.

Of course it's fucking Troy.

I'm sure he recognized it from being in his driveway the other day and saw the chance for a power play. Given what I know about him, I should probably feel lucky that my truck wasn't sent through the compactor, but I don't.

All I feel is rage.

Melly is waiting by Penny when I get back, leaning against her bike and scrolling her phone.

When I slam the truck door, she straightens, and I know fury is bright across my face. I shove the ticket at her. "Can you believe this shit?"

She lets out a low whistle. "Fuck your life."

"No shit." I let myself into Penny and she follows, leaving the ticket on the counter. "You think he knew you were at his house and did it deliberately?"

"I think he did it deliberately because I was at his house the other day and was asking for Jodie. Or because he could. Because he's a dick. Who knows?"

From the bedroom I hear a thud as Zoe jumps off the bed, and she trots out, winding herself around my legs. I breathe deeply as I pet her from ears to tail, knowing I need to relax and let this go.

But it's hard.

"So," Melly says, after I've had a moment. "What next?"

She doesn't mean my impending financial crisis.

I pull in one more long breath, and when I let it out, I'm back. I'm focused. "Now we figure out where the cabin is."

* * *

Having the ability to monitor Jodie eases enough of the stress that I can start to think clearly. Simply knowing she's alive has lifted the worst of the guilt from around my neck, and while she may not be safe yet, she will be.

I'll make sure of it.

But it's going to take work and it's not going to be instant, and I'm no good to anyone passed out from exhaustion.

At least, that's what I keep telling myself as I sit snuggled into Noel's side on the couch. During dinner we worked on menu descriptions for next weekend's pizza fest, and it was like any other night. When he asked how my day had been, I left it at busy. I was too tired for a lecture on the dangers of breaking and entering, and I didn't think he needed to worry about my car. If he knew, he would offer to pay, and I don't want that. The orchard may be solidly in the black these days thanks to the cider side of things, but I'm not about to pilfer from his profits. It doesn't sit right with me.

Noel leans down and kisses the top of my head. "So I've been thinking."

"Oh god," I joke.

He squeezes me closer. "I'm serious."

It's a warm and comforting kind of snug, and I burrow in a little more. "About what?"

"Winter. It's coming."

"Thank you, Ned Stark."

"Still being serious," he says, laughing. "Winter is coming, and, I don't know, I was thinking maybe we should make this a regular thing? You being here?"

I turn so I can see his face, and it's a tangle of excitement and worry and hope. "For winter?"

"Or, for, like, always?" He grins that sweet, lopsided grin of his, and I hate that I'm not the kind of person who can give him an easy yes. He must see something pass across my face, because he quickly adds, "I'm not saying get rid of Penny. Never that. But you could park her in one of the empty barns. And park yourself here, with me?"

There's so much warmth in those brown eyes that I can't help smiling. I do love this man. I have my reasons for being hesitant about this step, but none of them have to do with what I feel for him. I pull his head down for a kiss. "I'll think about it."

I feel his grin widen against my lips. "I'll take that."

Chapter
Twenty-Eight

I wouldn't have thought I had room in my head for anything extra, but I do find myself thinking about Noel's hopeful invitation in the gaps between far darker thoughts. It niggles like a broken tooth, refusing to be ignored no matter how much I try to push it to the side.

And push it aside I do. Repeatedly.

Because if there is one thing I'm good at, it's prioritizing. And as much as the sweet and settled part of me wants to make Noel my main focus, the rest of me knows it isn't an option.

The rest of me has a woman to save and a cop to convict. It may not be a murder he's going down for, but he's still going down.

Way down.

I check on Jodie compulsively. It's like she becomes a high-stakes Sims game that I have to monitor all the time. I don't enjoy it, intruding on her privacy like this, but I can't help it. I have to know she's safe. Just because she's alive now doesn't mean she'll stay that way. She's in a cabin, in the fall, with no obvious heat source. One bad turn of weather could kill her as easily as Troy.

I watch him too. The difference is, I don't feel intrusive when I do. He lost his right to privacy, to anything resembling human decency, when he kidnapped the girlfriend he couldn't stop hurting.

So fuck him.

He's intensely boring, Troy. He goes to work, comes home, and gives me absolutely no clue where that cabin might be. It's not like I expect him to leave a map on the kitchen island with a big red X marking where I need to go, but still. Some hint would be nice, just to narrow my options.

But really I'm watching them both to make sure they're alone. As big a threat as the weather could be for Jodie, Troy is worse. The longer he stays away from her, the safer she is.

I haven't been able to get a glimpse inside the cabin fridge or cabinets, but there must be a decent amount of food stashed, because the bowl and plate regularly switch between the sink and the draining board. I feel better knowing she's eating, but who knows if it's enough. Troy might want to keep her alive, but does he have any clue about the nutritional needs of pregnant people?

Doubtful.

Unfortunately, thanks to the not-so-small amount of money I owe for my truck, I no longer have the luxury of devoting entire days to the case, so I resort to multitasking.

My laptop lives on Penny's serving counter so I can easily switch between it and customers while I'm parked at the college. It's not ideal, but little about this situation is.

After a mini-rush of students in need of post-lab cutie pies, I check the cabin feed again. Jodie is where I last saw her, curled in the corner of the sofa, cocooned in the plaid blanket with her head resting on her drawn-up knees. Whether it's out of a need for warmth or an inability to take up more than the smallest of spaces, the sight of her so drawn in on herself is painful to watch.

It's like she's completely given up.

And I can't even blame her. She has no reason to believe anyone is coming for her. Troy wouldn't have even had to work hard to convince her of that. She was already so isolated. I was her lifeline and I was too late.

I wish there was a way to beam a message to her, to let her know that she's not alone, that we're going to find her.

And we are, even if I'm not quite sure how yet. It is impossibly hard to track down a cabin when the only thing you can see is the interior.

A thought jolts me upright, the sudden movement making Zoe raise her head quizzically.

"It's a fishing cabin," I say. Zoe, my only audience, tilts her head in further confusion, but my pulse picks up. I could hit myself for being so stupid.

The interior is spartan, sure, but not completely barren.

There are mounted fish on the walls.

Sure, it's not an address or even a state, but it's a start.

I switch tabs over to the radius map and zoom in. I need more than outlines of states. I need terrain. It takes a good amount of dragging the map around to find them all, but there are lakes. Plenty of them. Too many to keep track of, maybe. Once again I envy those TV detectives, superheroes so unlike their real-life counterparts, with their big crime boards full of maps and red trails of yarn linking pushpin locations. That would be handy right now.

And then I remember where I'm parked.

I can probably make that happen, to a degree.

I open multiple map tabs, each zoomed in on a different portion of the radius blob. When I have them all ready to go, I slide my serving window closed, flip my sign to BE BACK SOON, and assemble a small box of pies.

It would be better if they weren't my standard campus blend of academic enthusiasm, but they'll have to do.

After all, pie bribes are pie bribes and simple sugar can be as enticing as magic.

I trot up the steps to the library, a box balanced on my laptop, and follow a pair of students inside.

It's quiet inside, which I expect, but with only rhythmically tapping keyboards to disturb the hush, I feel like a spectacle as I approach the service desk.

I smile brightly and place the box of pies on the counter. The librarian eyes it like it might be a bomb, but I smile brightly. "Hi, I have the pie truck outside. I thought you all might like a treat."

The librarian's face shifts with recognition, the smile taking years off her face. "Oh, how lovely. Thank you, dear."

"You're welcome." I hoist my laptop and give her my best puppy eyes. "I don't suppose it would be possible to print something out while I'm here?"

There's a beat of silence when I think she's going to refuse me, but then she nods toward the bank of copiers along the wall. "Use the far one. Instructions are on the front."

"Thanks so much." I give her a grateful look and make my way over, snagging a highlighter from a communal pen cup. Within minutes I'm linked to the printer and soon have a warm stack of copies ready to be assembled. I thank the librarian again on my way out, and she raises a pie in a silent salute.

Never underestimate the power of a pie bribe.

Outside I find a line has formed four deep at Penny, and I apologize as I let myself back in. As much as I want to get right to work, I leave the printouts on the counter and get everyone their pies first.

When they're gone, I fish around my junk drawer for the roll of tape I know lives there somewhere, and then it's just like doing a puzzle.

The end result isn't quite TV detective quality, but it's good enough. All the copies are taped together to form a blown-up version of the radius map, big enough to cover the entire counter. It had to be zoomed in tight to get the smaller lakes to show up, but this way I can see them all at once.

And I can write on it.

Using the pilfered highlighter, I highlight the name of each lake in pink. The ones too small for names get pink outlines, and I underline the name of the town they're in.

When it's done, there's a lot of pink on the map, but I'm not deterred. There's significantly less pink than there is other stuff, and that matters.

That makes it manageable.

I'm no longer looking for a needle that could be anywhere in a haystack that fills seven states. I'm only looking at these pockets.

It's not perfect. I still have no way of knowing if the cabin is actually on a lake or if it's only close enough to be a reasonable base point, but it's a start. I'm still hoping to figure out a way to narrow it down further, but if I have to personally visit each and every one of these spots and their surrounding areas, I will.

Hell, there are enough map apps that I should be able to virtually put eyes on even the most isolated options and narrow things down from there.

The cabin is rustic, so it's probably not going to be on one of the bigger lakes in a more developed town, where waterfront property is inhabited year-round and comes with a hefty price tag and plenty of neighbors. It shouldn't be too hard to figure out which areas are too high-end or busy for Troy's falling-down cabin.

And I should be able to automatically exclude some of the tinier ponds that are plunked dead in the middle of woods. The cabin might be rustic, but it's still accessible. Which means a road. Maybe not a nice, paved road and maybe not a direct-to-the-door route, but still, something that can get you close.

The map may be large, but it's starting to feel manageable.

Jodie may have given up hope, but I haven't.

Not by a long shot.

Chapter
Twenty-Nine

The first few Saturdays without farmers' markets always feel strange, like I'm forgetting something important, but this week I'm grateful for their absence.

My bank account is somewhat less grateful, but it doesn't get an opinion today. Today I have a date with some diner pies and a long afternoon of map work.

The diner is hopping, which isn't a surprise. Weekends quadruple the rest of the week's business, and things aren't exactly slow then either. It's exactly the energy I need to jump-start the day.

"Man, I feel like I haven't seen you all week," Juan says above the bustle of breakfast rush.

"Miss me?" I tease. In reply he slides a bowl of steaming potatoes down the bench to me. Their crispy fried edges are red with fragrant seasoning and they're smothered in sliced jalapeños, melty cheese, and sour cream. "Ooh, I need to make myself scarce more often."

"Don't even," he says, and I clock the dark circles under his eyes before he turns back to the flat-top, spatula moving in a blur as he plates up order after order.

"Is my little pie pal wearing you out?"

He groans. "You have no idea."

"Where is the monster? Out front?"

"Home. Thank God." There's a ragged note in his voice that makes me look up from my potatoes, but he's already shaking his head. "I don't mean it like that."

I slip around Alex—present, for once—and park myself at the end of the flat-top. It kicks up enough heat to make this side of the kitchen feel like a different climate, but I don't care. I don't even care that my corgi dress is going to soak up all the breakfast scents. I care about Juan.

He gives me a look like he knows it but says, "If you're standing there, you're working."

I pop a potato in my mouth and set the bowl aside with a shrug. "I excel at multitasking." He passes me plates, which I arrange by table for the servers, and when we're in enough of a rhythm, I wade in. "Bad week?"

He sighs, cracking a trio of eggs for sunny-sides. "It's just a lot, you know? Like, Eric is in line for this promotion, and he's so excited and deserves it so much. I get that he needs to be gone a lot right now, but it's hard. Doing it all." Using the edge of a spatula, he folds an omelet in two quick flips and slings it onto a plate. "I mean, my mom was a single parent and she never complained and she's helping so much, but I feel like I'm floundering. All the time."

"You're doing the best you can, same as your mom did. You think she didn't have bad days? Of course she did. You just didn't notice because you were cared for. It's the same with Ana. She's not going to remember you floundering. She's going to remember how much time you spent with her and getting to come into the kitchen and be part of things. And then when Eric's schedule is more settled, she's going to remember all the museum and library trips they'll have. You guys got this." It hurts my heart that he even doubts it, because I can't imagine a better pair of parents than the two of them. "And you're allowed to need a break. You have people who can help you."

I'm about to offer a pie van sleepover night, knowing it's the last thing I have time for right now but wanting to ease Juan's burden anyway, when I catch sight of River, the dishwasher, waving a long-handled slotted spoon at me.

"Yo, D," they call. "I think your dog is losing her shit."

Now that they've drawn my attention to it, I hear it too. Barking, deep and angry.

Concern for her and Juan crash against each other.

"Go," Juan says, tipping his chin at the back door.

I'm almost running, shoving past Alex, who can't seem to get out of my way, and fling the back door hard enough that it crashes into the wall.

And freeze.

It's not the first time someone has tried to break into Penny, but it's the first time a cop has.

His back is to me, but it doesn't matter. The shaved white head and the way the uniform stretches across overdeveloped shoulders tells me everything I need to know.

He's cranking on the door handle, seemingly undisturbed by my not-so-subtle appearance, and in the seconds before he turns, I see the many ways this can play out.

None of them are good.

Inside, Zoe is indeed losing her shit, every rattle of the metal door setting off a fresh volley of barks.

I see the gun on Troy's hip, and I don't need the statistics to know what happens to aggressive pit bulls.

Cops love to shoot first, ask questions never.

So as much as I want to throw myself at him, tear him bodily away from my home, I don't. I can't risk that. I clear my throat, loud enough to be deliberate. "Can I help you?"

He turns, a sneer twisting his already ugly face into something worse. He stands with his feet apart, hands on his hips. It's like he wants to draw my eye to the gun. Like I could forget that it's there. "That your dog?"

"And my RV. We're parked here legally with permission from the owner." I tip my head at the diner like it's a stand-in for Frank. The world seems overly sharp. Every nerve in my body is on fire, the rush of blood deafeningly loud. But I breathe slowly. I don't make any sudden moves. "Again, is there something I can help you with?"

"I've got a report of stolen property being found at this location. I need a look inside."

My vision tightens, blocking out everything that isn't this very real threat. "Do you have a warrant?"

"Do I need one?" His grin turns nasty. "Surely if you have nothing to hide, you won't mind me having a look around."

"There are plenty of places to look around." I spread my arm slowly, indicating the expanse of blacktop. "I mean, this is a parking lot. Lots of cars come through that may have had stolen property."

"I have reason to believe you have it."

"I don't even know what it is."

"I think you do. I think this is the third time I've seen this rust bucket"—he kicks the bumper of my truck, setting Zoe off again—"and that can't be a coincidence. What do you do, use your little pie deliveries to scout houses to rob?"

My heart ticks like a bomb, loud and hard against my ribs, as I try to work out if he knows it's me or is merely fishing. If he saw the surveillance footage before I deleted it, he has grounds to arrest me and he hasn't yet. That must mean something. "I'm sorry, I don't think I can help you."

"Open the door," he says. "Otherwise I break it down."

There's a hardness to his eyes that makes me think he *wants* to break it, and I'm also tempted to calmly unlock the door, if only to take away his chance to destroy something.

But I can't.

Because he is, of course, right. I do have his stolen property. I also still have the highlighted map spread across my counter, impossible to hide.

And I have Zoe.

But I also have a suspicion.

He might be in uniform, but I don't think he's here officially. He certainly didn't file a report for his missing iPad, the one live streaming his kidnapped girlfriend's every move. And he hasn't arrested me, so he doesn't know for sure it's me. He can't prove it. And if he thinks I'm nothing more than a petty thief with a crappy truck, all the better. He might be worried about what I'll stumble across on that iPad, but he doesn't know that's why I have it.

He has no reason to suspect I'm onto him.

I let that steady me. "If you don't have a warrant, I'm afraid I can't let you."

He closes the space between us in two long strides. "So you're refusing to cooperate with an officer of the law is what I'm hearing. Is that right?"

I'm not a small woman, but he towers over me. Troy has all of Noel's height, but the raging bulk of him makes him seem like a whole different species. Birdlike Jodie would've been positively eclipsed by him.

"Huh?" he prods, backing me against the side of the RV. His right hand is on the butt of his gun. "You're interfering with a police investigation?"

My pulse roars. Every video I've seen of how quickly this can go wrong flashes behind my eyes. If I were Black, it probably already would have. As much as I want to rage, that gun reminds me that clear and calm is the safer choice. "I have not seen documentation of a police investigation."

"You've been given an order by an officer," he shouts. It's punctuated by a slam, and for a flash I think it's his fist.

But no. It's too far away from that.

"What the hell is going on out here?" Frank barks as the diner door clatters closed. Juan and River are on his heels.

Troy pushes away from Penny, and I spin out from under him. River has their phone up, no doubt recording, and I'm already planning their thank-you pie. I direct my words to them, where they'll be picked up clearly. "He's trying to enter my home without a warrant."

"Put the fucking phone away," Troy snaps. "She's resisting police orders."

Frank marches up to Troy and stabs a finger right in his chest. "Son, you listen here. I have owned this establishment for forty-eight years. This young lady is one of the best employees I have ever had in all that time, and if I hear so much as a whisper of you hassling her, I will be on the phone to Marty Cline so fast your head will spin. Do you hear me?" He doesn't yell. If anything, his words are almost hard to hear, the fury weighing them down to near whispers.

Juan and I exchange wide-eyed looks. I've seen Frank angry. It's practically his natural state. What I've never seen is Frank be scary.

It's incredible.

River is still recording and looks more than a little giddy with what they're capturing.

Troy grinds his teeth. It's clear that name means something to him, and I make a note to find out what.

"Are we clear?" Frank asks. He might be more than twice the cop's age and half his size, but Troy is the one to step back.

"I'm looking into this." He slams the side of his fist against Penny, making Zoe unleash another series of echoing barks. "All of it. If this thing isn't perfectly legal, I'm impounding it and you'll both be charged. And then I'll deal with that mutt."

It isn't an empty threat. That's obvious and enough to make my knees nearly give out. It's one thing to come after me. I could even excuse the RV, if I had to. But my dog?

Nobody messes with my dog.

I feel a touch on my arm and look down. Juan's fingers are curled there, gently holding me back.

I let him.

I have to.

For now.

Frank gives Troy a final dismissive wave. "Get yourself off my property. You're not welcome here."

Chapter Thirty

It takes a long time to settle Zoe, and in the end I wind up bringing her back to the kitchen with me.

It's wildly against health codes and something I never do when Frank is around, but she's spent plenty of nights in there with me while I've worked on diner pies and knows how to behave.

Plus, I don't have a choice.

Every part of me would rather be in the truck, getting away from here, but after what just happened, it's not an option. Not when Frank and Juan saw the whole thing. There's no way they won't have questions, and as much as my first instinct is still to flee, I owe them more than that.

That's the problem with setting down roots.

They set up in you too.

The kitchen is back to its normal bustle when we slip in the back door, and I point Zoe to her spot by the laundry. She spins around a few times, then curls up with her head on her paws, but her eyes remain alert. It's safe here, but she's wary. Up until today, Penny had always felt safe too.

The fact that Troy has violated her sense of security is enough to make me want to skip the pies and kill him with my bare hands.

Once we have Jodie back, maybe I will.

Before I can sink too far into that fantasy, reality pulls me back with a sharp crack. The swinging dining room slams into the wall as Frank stalks through the kitchen.

At first I think it's Zoe he's coming for, but no. It's me.

"You want to tell me what in the goddamn hell that was about?" he barks. "You remember when we started this arrangement and you had all that shit a few years back, what I said?"

A new fear, sharper than anything that happened outside, slices through me. Because I do remember. Clear as day. I repeat the words from so long ago. "The first bit of trouble, I'd be gone."

"And that"—he jabs a shaking, liver-spotted finger at the back door—"looked like twelve goddamn tons of trouble."

"I can go." The words are barely more than a whisper, because the lump in my throat has stolen my air. I knew this whole arrangement couldn't last forever, but I wasn't ready for it to end, not like this. Not because of Troy. Even as I remind myself that I have a place to go, that Noel will be so, so happy when I tell him, tears burn my eyes. Around us, the kitchen has gone still, but in my head it's a fast-forward blur of baking and banter, late nights and early mornings with Juan and the crew, all the hours I didn't know were spent forming a family. "I'm so sorry."

Juan is on the edge of my periphery, but I can't look at him. I know it will break me.

"Frank, man," he says softly, but Frank ignores him.

"I don't want you to be sorry," he snaps. His face is twisted in anger, and he throws his hand in frustration. "I want you to be safe. Christ, are you fucking stupid? You've never been stupid before."

"Frank." Juan grabs the old man's shoulder. "That's enough."

Frank shrugs him off, breathing hard. "No, you're not stupid." He shakes his head, but it doesn't dislodge the anger. "So tell me what the fuck that was out there. I can't help you fix it if I don't know what you did."

I can't tell him.

Of course I can't.

But the fact that he wants to know, that he's willing to chase off cops and keep me around and even try to fix things, absolutely undoes something in me.

It's dysfunctional and it's gruff and it's not like the movies, but this? Right now? It's kind of like having a proper dad, and it's such a strange feeling that I can't even stop the tears. "I don't have to leave?"

"For fuck's sake," Frank grumbles. "Don't do that. You think I'm going back to Sysco pies after all this? Have a goddamn riot on my hands."

I laugh, and the relief is so overwhelming I have to lean against the worktop.

Frank glares around the rest of the kitchen. "I'm not paying you lot to stand around gawping like idiots. Get back to work!" There's a flurry of activity as everyone jumps back to life. Juan gives my arm a squeeze and freezes when Franks jabs a finger at him. "Not you." He whacks the table, where Alex is still doing more gawp than work. "Earn your damn pay for once. Cover the line."

"Yes sir," he says, scurrying over to the flat-top.

Franks waves a finger at me and Juan. "You two. I need a smoke. Now."

We follow him out back, Zoe rising from her spot to join us. Frank lights a cigarette, and Juan and I settle uneasily onto milk crates as the scent of clove fills the air. Frank doesn't join us, and even though I know it's because his knees have long since given up the fight of getting back up, the way he stands above us still feels ominous.

"Figured he might as well be here, since he'll make it his business anyway," Frank says, gesturing vaguely in Juan's direction. "So fill us in. You steal something like that man said? If you're not making enough, I can pay you. You don't need to do this shit."

I shake my head. "It's not like that."

"What's it like, then? Because it's not every day the cops show up to hassle young white girls over nothing. 'Specially in this town."

I don't want to lie to them. Even though I know I've been lying all along by concealing who I really am, that feels different. Omission is different than outright lies, even if only a little.

At least that's what I tell myself.

Juan leans forward, propping his elbows on his knees. "If you're in trouble, we've got you. We'll sort it out."

"I'm not." The last thing I want is for them to worry, for Juan especially to feel like he has yet another thing on his overflowing plate, so I decide to go with a version of the truth. "I tried to deliver a pie to his house, for his girlfriend. But I guess they broke up or I had the wrong address, because he was really weird about it. I don't know. I think he thought I was messing with him or something, because he had my car towed as, like, I don't know, revenge? I'm not his favorite person."

Frank looks incredulous. "He towed your car because you brought him a pie?"

I shrug helplessly. "I guess?"

"And the stolen property?"

"I have no idea." The lie feels like a brick in my stomach, but I can't tell them the truth, not when Frank is letting me stay. He might be willing to protect me from a petty theft charge, but I can't expect him to feel the same about murder.

And Juan? If he knew about Pies Before Guys and what I'm capable of, the easiness between us would go right out the window. Even if he could somehow understand, he certainly couldn't trust Ana around me anymore, and the thought of that hurts more than the lie.

"You didn't report any of this?" Frank asks.

I shake my head. "It's not worth it. What would I say? He's cranky because I made a pie delivery?"

Frank drops his cigarette and crushes the burning stub beneath his toe. "Seems fishy is all. Lot of overreaction for knocking on a door."

Juan is watching me like he knows I'm holding something back, but he doesn't ask. Whether it's out of respect for my privacy or simply because he can't come up with the right question, I don't know. All I know is that I'm having trouble looking him in the eye and I don't like it.

I spent so long alone for this exact reason. It's one thing to do what I do, to kill the people who need to be killed to protect the innocent. It's another thing to do that while trying to maintain any kind of normal social life.

There's a reason most serial killers are loners.

There are exceptions, sure—the family men who torture and kill their victims at secondary locations and then go home to their happy little families with no one the wiser. But it's rare. Because it's hard.

Having two lives and investing fully in both is a Herculean task, especially when there's zero room for overlap. When I let Noel and Melly in, it felt like my world turned upside down, but somehow it worked. I got lucky, not once, but twice, and I know better than to think that fountain will keep on giving. Noel likes me despite what I do, and while I suspect Melly likes me because of it, neither of those are normal reactions.

Normal would be fear. Revulsion. All the ugly things I don't want to risk, not with my diner family.

So I let them believe it's fishy.

Just one of those weird, unexplainable things.

"You can stay with us if you want," Juan offers. "Zoe too. We have the room, and you're always welcome."

My heart swells. Even though he knows there's more to this mess, he's still willing to help, same as Frank.

"I think Frank scared him off," I say. "I should be fine. And you know I appreciate the offer, but Noel might take it some sort of way if I moved in with someone who's not him right now."

"He better not be getting controlling," Frank says.

"He's not," I assure him, a hot flush creeping up my cheeks. So much for not sharing things. "But he has been talking about living together lately."

"And you got a problem with that?"

I shrug, looking at Penny, the pink-and-white paint shining in the sun, the soundtrack of a busy kitchen behind me. "I don't know. I'm happy how things are, you know?"

Frank grunts. "Well, if he's worth it, he'll wait."

"He'll wait," Juan says, a knowing grin flashing and fading from his face. "But you probably still should tell him about what happened today."

"I know."

But the thought of doing so is the scariest part of all of this.

Chapter
Thirty-One

Telling Noel does nothing to improve my day.

I went into the conversation knowing it wouldn't be a barrel of fun, but not expecting things to get actively worse either.

I should have known better.

It's been a half hour since he left me parked on his sofa, and each minute that ticks by ratchets my stress ever tighter.

He said he was going to feed Sunny, his flaxen-maned mare, but even I know that task can only be stretched so long.

He's hiding. Or fuming. Or plotting my death. I have no way of knowing, because instead of having a proper conversation about things, he bailed.

Frustration fills my lungs with each breath, making me restless.

Too many parts of my brain are clamoring for control, and I hate the part that's winning.

I don't want to upset Noel, and knowing that I have—and will continue to—twists my stomach into uneasy knots. I don't want to acknowledge the whisper of fear that says by ignoring his wishes I have pushed him too far, that I might lose him.

I don't like how much that thought hurts.

But I also can't forget that there's a woman trapped in a cabin, who is there because of me.

The louder, rasher part of my brain blares this fact like a siren, and as much as the soft squishy part of me is concerned about my relationship, the rest of me knows that pales in comparison to a woman's life.

And that part of me is annoyed.

I should be tracking her down, working through the map, searching the footage again for a scrap of a clue to narrow things down.

I shouldn't be sitting here uselessly wondering how to apologize to the man I love for something I have no intention of stopping.

It feels cold to think about it so starkly, but after facing Troy in person today, I know it's true. If I were going to be put off this case, it would've been then, when the danger was right in my face, but all it did was make me more determined.

I'm not letting him get away with it.

I can't.

The creak of the door opening filters in from the front hall, and I hear the familiar clomp of boots being removed. Zoe thumps her tail, but the knots in my stomach turn icy.

Maybe the focused, murder-pie part of my brain isn't winning by such a large margin after all.

Noel brings a chill in with him that I can't blame entirely on the air outside. The worry etched on his face makes my heart hurt with responsibility, and when he doesn't sit, the first waves of panic start to lap at my feet.

I go very still.

Zoe, oblivious to the tension, shadows him as he builds a small fire in the hearth. He barely seems to notice her.

Finally, when the crackle of flames is steady enough to drown out the horrible silence, he sits.

Perched on the edge of the coffee table, he's close enough to kiss, but his gaze is fixed on his clasped hands like he can't look at me.

It makes those inches feel like canyons.

"I don't do anger well," he says. "Not in general and especially not with people I love."

"I didn't mean to upset you."

He shakes his head. "I am, though. And it's not because you're still doing this. It's because you don't even realize what this is."

I'm about to protest, but he looks up then, eyes shining, and I fall silent.

"You could've been killed." His voice cracks and he clenches his jaw, the muscles bunching in hard knots that I want to reach out and soothe away. But I don't, because I'm afraid he'll pull back.

After a moment he continues. "At first, yes, it was that I worried about you getting in trouble—getting arrested—but this is different. You're not poking the bear. You're pole-vaulting off his back and clog dancing on his head." The edge of a smile pulls at my lips. It's good imagery and not wholly inaccurate, but he's not looking for laughs. "I know I have a different overall view of cops than you. They were decent to me with the whole mushroom thing, but even I know how dangerous the bad ones can be. I've seen the videos too, read the stories. I know what can happen."

He doesn't, though, not really. When he was in college, he was caught with a strain of psychedelic mushrooms he had bred specifically to limit unwanted side effects in depression patients. His research was sound, and it was only his sheer enthusiasm for the project combined with his spotless record and white-boy-next-door image that let him escape with an expulsion instead of a criminal record. And while it worked out in the long run, all the experience taught him was that those in power can be reasoned with.

But they can't, not always.

"That's why I have to stop him." I say it softly, like Noel is a horse I don't want to spook, but he still rears back, dragging both hands down his face.

"No, you still don't get it," he says, face flushed with more than the warmth of the fire. "I don't care about you stopping him. I don't. I'm sorry. Not for some girl we don't know. Not if the cost is your life. That's not an even trade. Not to me."

"Noel—"

"It's one thing when it's safe. When you're just dropping pies and going. This is different. This is dangerous. Really, properly dangerous."

"I know—"

"Don't say but." There's a desperate edge to his voice that stops me from saying exactly that. "Don't say it. Just think for a minute. Because I don't think you have, not yet. Really imagine if things went wrong today. If he pulled his gun or put you in a choke hold. Think about it. Because it's all I've been doing since you told me."

"Oh, Noel, no," I breathe. This time I don't hesitate; I reach forward and take his cheek in my hand, the end-of-day stubble rough on my palm when he presses into me. "I'm okay. It wasn't that bad."

He covers my hand with his. "But it could've been. And I couldn't bear that." He brings my fingers to his lips. "I don't want to lose you."

"You won't."

He shakes his head. "You can't promise that."

I take his hands and pull him forward. He comes easily, allowing himself to be settled into the couch beside me. It feels better this way, side by side, and I burrow into him. "You're right, I can't promise that. But I can promise I'll be careful. That I won't put myself in harm's way when I don't have to."

He exhales and sinks back against the cushions, taking me with him.

"I can't change who I am." It comes out like an apology, because despite everything, it is. "And I can't force you to be on board with everything I do. But I can stay true to myself and be what you need. I know I can."

His rests his head on top of mine, and I can feel his chin moving like there are still things he wants to say. But all I hear is the steady thump of his heart, and it sounds like enough.

*   *   *

I don't sleep.

There wasn't even a discussion about my staying over; I simply did. There was no other choice.

We went to bed early, twined together and equally exhausted from the emotions of the day. Noel dropped off quickly, warm and peaceful at my side, while Zoe curled against my legs.

Everyone quiet except my brain.

In the wee hours I slip from between them, careful to wake neither, and creep downstairs.

The wood floors are cold against my bare feet as I make my way to the kitchen, but I don't mind.

One of the things I love about Noel is that despite having far too much house for a single guy, he doesn't live like a bachelor. The pantry is well stocked and, with his home being on an orchard, there is more fruit than even I have need for, and soon my hands are deep in a bowl of flour, pressing cold butter into fat flakes.

The preheating oven provides the kitchen with a gentle warmth, and in the soft glow of the under-cabinet lighting, the world and its stresses finally fall away.

I remember the very first pie I made special for Noel, an honesty-laden apple affair that I ended up taking back before the first bite. The next one was magic-free, on principle. After that, the only magic he's consumed has been incidental, the blends tailored to location rather than individual.

This one is different.

In the early-morning stillness, I pour everything I didn't have words for into this pie until it's overflowing with intention.

In addition to sharp white cheddar and rosemary, the crust is infused with every ounce of love I can conjure in every form that exists. It's the first spark I felt when we raced across the sun-drenched orchard on his horse, the wind and the feel of him in front of me that left me breathless with joy. It's the pride of watching him busy doing what he does best, making people happy with the land that made him happy as a boy. It's the coziness of couch snuggles and fires and the comfort of long hugs. It's everything we are and yet to be.

The filling is simple—apples, a touch of cinnamon, and a drizzle of honey. I cook them down with a splash of cider, stirring in as much safety and security as it will hold, along with an amped-up version of the homeyness the diner pies get.

When it goes into the oven, it's heavy with magic, more even than murder pies get.

It's nothing as manipulative as a love spell or bid for blind trust.

It's not that kind of magic.

It's the edible embodiment of everything I feel, and I can only hope it's enough to help.

Chapter
Thirty-Two

I spend all of Sunday at the orchard, but I don't spend it all on apple things.

While Noel is busy with customers, which is most of the day, I'm busy with my own work. It's a cold, drizzly day that reminds us winter is right around the corner, and pie sales are slow, with everyone favoring the warmer, drier tasting rooms. I should be joining them, setting up closer to the entrance to avoid losing more sales, but I'm content to stay tucked away in Penny, curled over the kitchen counter like a demented shrimp while Zoe dozes on the bed.

I spend the bulk of the day crossing lakes off the map, excluding any that are heavily populated or in town centers. It's tedious, mind-numbing work, but by the time dusk rolls in, I have as many black Xs as I do pink lakes, effectively halving the possibilities. It's something. It's not the kind of work crime shows are made of, but it might be the kind that actually helps find a missing woman.

I'll take that.

I spend another night at Noel's, and we don't speak of the things between us. Whether it's avoidance or a genuine moving on, I'm not sure, but either way, it's peaceful. The fact that my midnight apple pie is more than half gone probably has something to do with it.

Of course, that's the only proper pie I've baked all weekend, so in the morning I leave Noel, sleepy and snug in bed, for a date with the diner.

I take Penny too, even though it would be easier to leave her parked at the orchard, and as I pull around the back of Frank's to park, I'm surprised that neither his nor Juan's car is in its usual spot.

I'm glad Juan managed to keep his day off this week, but I'm surprised Frank isn't here yet. It's not like him to surrender control of the restaurant to anyone who isn't Juan, and when I get inside, I'm reminded of exactly why.

The kitchen is chaos.

Half-finished prep is scattered across the center worktops, and the acrid smell of burnt bacon lingers like a ghost in the air.

Happy days.

I grab an apron, determined to ignore the nonsense and get my pies out, but that quickly proves impossible.

"It's supposed to be an omelet, not a scramble," Amanda insists, trying to hand a plate back to Alex.

"That is an omelet," he says, refusing to take it.

"If it was made by Edward Scissorhands, maybe."

The plate hovers between them like an accusation, and I sigh, wondering how bad it would be to call Juan.

It would be bad. I can't ruin his day off over an ugly omelet. Besides, Frank must be on his way.

I abandon my flour and go over to mediate. The omelet does indeed look like it's been through a shredder, with bits of pepper and onion sticking up at odd angles.

"Who's it for?" I ask Amanda. Monday mornings are always slow, mostly regulars, so chances are it's one of them.

"Chicken hat guy," she says, and I know exactly who she means. A retired train conductor turned hobby farmer, chicken hat guy is never seen without his signature *Cocky* baseball cap. On a different kind of man it would be douchey, but I think he genuinely bought it because he liked the rooster.

"Just give it to him," I tell her, already guiding her away from Alex. "Make a joke, tell him coffee's on the house, and we'll send him home with a free slice of pie."

"Okay, Frank," she jokes, bumping me with her hip as she goes out to deliver the eggy disaster.

I turn to Alex next. "Dude. Gentle folds, yeah? I get that you're not Juan, but maybe try to do him proud when he's not here? He wants you to succeed. Don't let him down."

He looks chagrined and mumbles, "Sorry," before reaching for the next ticket.

I spend a few minutes straightening the worktops before boxing up a big slice of leftover cherry pie, because even though I'm the furthest thing from in charge, someone has to be the adult here. The last thing I need is Frank to walk in and drop dead from the state of things.

Plus, I need room to work.

And for a while I do. Things hum along, if not smoothly, at least better than when I walked in. I'm lining a quartet of pie crusts with parchment and sugar for blind baking—I always use sugar instead of beans, because who wants roasted beans when you could have roasted sugar?—when the dining room door flies open and I look up, expecting Frank, finally.

But instead it's Amanda, red-faced and worried.

So much for running smoothly.

"What's wrong?" I ask. Even Alex looks over with concern.

"They're back," she says.

And I know instantly who she's talking about, and I wish more than ever that it had been Frank throwing open that door.

"All of them?" I ask.

"No, two." There's a pleading look on her face that I doubt she's even aware of, but I understand.

I pour a mound of sugar into my last crust and shake the tin to level it out. "I'll take care of it."

"Same table," she says, relief brightening her face. "Thank you."

I pull off my apron and take her order pad. "Don't worry about it. Do you know when Frank is due?"

She shakes her head. "No idea. He unlocked this morning, then took off."

"Huh, that's weird."

"Yup." I can see part of her is relieved, though, because had he been here, she probably couldn't have handed her table off to me so easily, not with so few already seated.

I head to the dining room, nodding hello to chicken hat guy, who's happily lingering over his coffee and newspaper at the counter, and fix my Pie Girl smile in place. It turns rigid the moment I clock the table's occupants.

Sitting in the window are two uniformed officers, one with a mustache and one with linebacker shoulders and a shaved white head.

You have got to be kidding me.

There is nothing like the audacity of entitled white men, except, I'm seeing, the audacity of cops.

If Frank were here, he wouldn't stand for it. Cop or not, he told Troy he wasn't welcome.

Yet here he is.

I can't help thinking it's deliberate, a stupid power play, but joke's on him, because Frank isn't even here to see it.

He gets me instead.

I stride across the dining room like it's a runway, like I have no idea who he is and can't bother caring. He will not get the satisfaction of thinking he can be intimidating.

194

Across from the two men is a woman with a stubby, slicked-back black ponytail, crispy with too much hair spray. She's in faded jeans and a burgundy sweatshirt. Off-duty cop?

Doesn't matter.

She has the men hanging on her every word, though, and as I approach, I give zero fucks about interrupting their conversation.

Until I hear it.

"I mean, what's a better local legacy than a Turnbridge family connected by the thin blue line?" the woman asks, gesturing widely to encompass the men. "Did you both always know you wanted to go join the force?"

And then the sweatshirt clicks. It's not just burgundy. It's Turnbridge University burgundy.

As if this could be worse. Melly is going to lose her mind when I tell her one of her classmates is profiling not only the police for her project, but an actual predator.

I am not getting paid enough for this day.

"Good morning, folks. What can I get you?" I keep my pen poised over my pad, smile in place as I wait.

Troy pulls his eyes away from the woman, lips curling in a smug smile I want to punch right off.

"Well, hello there," he drawls, eyes roving down my dress. He's playing the game too, acting like we don't have a very recent, very ugly history, and I wonder if it's for my benefit, his cop buddy's, or his rapt biographer's. "I think you could get me some of that meat pie and another coffee." Something about the way he leans into *meat pie* makes me want to take it off the menu forever, but I keep smiling, write it down, and look to his sidekick. "And for you?"

"Big stack with sausage, bacon, and real syrup," he says. "None of that fake shit."

"You got it," I chirp. If I covered him in syrup, I wonder how long it would take ants to eat his body. The prospect injects some genuine joy into my smile.

"And how about you?" I turn to ask the woman, and drop my pen in shock.

The outfit is wrong.

The hair is very, very wrong, and some part of me registers the hard shellac of hair spray as being more than mere fixative.

But it's the eyes that give it away.

The freckles.

I bend to get my pen, feigning a giggle at my clumsiness as the world tilts around me. "Sorry about that."

Then I take Melly's order.

Chapter Thirty-Three

I don't want to believe it.

I can't.

But gut-churning flashes of finding Melly at my pie van that night so long ago, when things were bad between us, fire behind my eyes with each blink, the remembered betrayal as visceral and immediate as it was then.

I peek through the dining room door while Alex puts their order together, wondering if there was some way my eyes deceived me, but now that I know it's her, I can't unsee the shape of her neck, the easy roll of her shoulders as she moves her arms, gesturing away as always.

She's completely relaxed.

"Did they harass you?" Amanda asks when she catches me, and I jump at her closeness.

"No, they were fine," I say, although it couldn't be further from the truth. Nothing about this is fine. "Just being nosy."

I turn to Alex, wishing he would hurry up. How long can some eggs and pancakes really take? I want them fed and I want them gone. The sooner the better.

I grab a serving tray and hover, not caring that it's putting Alex on edge.

"Plate me," I tell him. I have no qualms about serving these dicks medium-rare pancakes.

"Hold your horses," he mutters, carefully sliding Melly's over-easy egg onto a slice of buttered toast. I'll be surprised if she even eats it, given her stance on breakfast as abomination.

When the tray is laden with steaming plates, I stuff all the roiling emotions into their appropriate brain box and slam the lid. They can be let out for air later. Or not. But for now, they're not on display for anyone.

I approach the table with a smile that falters only for a moment when I see Frank's car drive past the window beyond them. He's not going to be pleased if he sees Troy here, but I can't let that be my problem right now.

The animated conversation pauses as I lay the plates down with a breeziness I don't feel. Melly doesn't acknowledge me more than she would any server. It's like we're in an alternate universe where we never met, where she has the kind of journalistic objectivity that allows her to interview people she categorically despises.

The Melly I know doesn't have an objective bone in her body.

It's what makes her so intensely—and occasionally infuriatingly—who she is.

Or so I thought.

"Anything else I can get you folks?" I ask. Perhaps a raging case of mites? Bit of spontaneous human combustion? I think they're going to say no and I'll be dismissed, but a smirk twists Troy's thin lips, and any hope of an easy escape vanishes.

"This one of yours?" he asks, waving his fork over the steaming slice of meat pie.

"Nope. That's a Frank special, one hundred percent."

"Thought you were some kind of pie queen." There's a challenge to his stare that's at odds with his tone, but I refuse to take the bait.

"You could say that, but the meat pie is a Harrow family recipe. Hasn't changed since this place opened." It's true and it's one of the only things Frank still makes, although I've noticed he tends to pilfer dough when I have a stockpile, so I always make sure there's extra for him. "Please enjoy."

I turn, letting the smile fall from my face like a dropped weight.

As I go, I hear Melly pick up what she was saying when I interrupted. "That ride-along would be great. It'd let my readers get a firsthand look at what you guys really do to keep Turnbridge safe, maybe get them to see the better side of policing."

I almost gag.

Mustache man snorts. "Hippies in this town have no clue. These libs wouldn't last a day in uniform."

I don't know how Melly isn't punching him.

My fingers twitch and I wonder if murder pancakes could be a thing, if I should've elbowed Alex off the line and made breakfast myself.

Maybe next time.

In the kitchen, that thought instantly evaporates. Frank is haranguing Alex for the state of his station, and I realize I don't want that job. Not even a little bit.

Let me make my pies in peace.

"What the hell are you doing out there?" he snaps at me.

"Not getting paid," I remind him in the cheerful tone always used for such statements.

"Well, she is." He jerks a thumb at Amanda.

"I offered," I say, not wanting Amanda to get in trouble. "I had a friend come in."

It's not quite a lie, but it feels like one.

"Well," Frank huffs, looking around the kitchen like he's never seen such a disaster. "Can't be gone for a damn hour without you lot turning this place to hell."

Alex looks suitably chastened, and I don't feel as bad for him as for Amanda. He was hired as Juan's second-in-command and needs to step up his game.

"Everything's fine," I assure Frank. "Happy customers all around. Where were you, anyway?"

"What are you, my damn mother?"

I hold my hands up in apology. "Just curious. Always thought it'd take an act of God to break your morning routine, that's all."

"Act of goddamn insurance companies is what it is," he grumbles.

"What do you mean?"

"Nothing." He slams a coffee mug down and fills it from the carafe, drinking half in one go. "I'm starving." He bangs the work-top, making Alex jump. "What do I have to do to get some breakfast in my own goddamn restaurant?"

"Ask?" Alex suggests hesitantly.

"I'm not asking you anything, I'm telling," he snaps. "Scrambled eggs and French toast, now."

"On it."

I send a silent prayer to the breakfast gods that he gets it right.

"Fasting bunch of bullshit," Frank mutters to himself as he folds an apron in half and ties it around his waist.

That gets my attention. "Is everything okay? Seriously?"

He waves me off. "Doc starved me for blood work, that's all. Like I have time for this shit first thing in the morning."

"Blood work for what?"

"Vampire tasting samples," he says, and I roll my eyes.

Would it kill a single person I know to be straight with me today?

"You're the worst," I tell him.

"Damn right." It seems to please him, so I don't push. He's old and it's probably simple, routine health stuff that he's being a typical curmudgeon about.

Besides, I have a bigger problem right now.

Instead of waiting patiently for Alex to finish his food, Frank heads to the dining room.

"Frank, wait," I call, but it's too late. I hurry after him, stopping only long enough to grab Alex's arm and point at the French toast sizzling on the flat-top. "Do not fuck that up."

There's no way this is going to end well, and I don't want Alex adding himself to Frank's shit list.

The reaction comes before I hit the door, loud enough to make us freeze.

"Boy, what part of *not welcome here* didn't penetrate that thick skull of yours?" Frank asks. I join Amanda behind the counter, careful not to let the swinging door bang.

The last thing I want to do is draw attention to myself.

"Are we gonna have a problem, old man?" Mustache asks, getting to his feet. He stands with his feet wide, hands planted on his hips. I wonder how often they practice that pose, if they're coached on how it draws extra attention to their guns or if it comes naturally.

"We're going to have a problem if you don't vacate my establishment." Frank directs this to Troy, like the other man doesn't exist. If he's recognized Melly, he doesn't show it, and that makes me think he hasn't. If there's one thing she and Frank have in common, it's a complete absence of tact.

"It's a public business," Troy says, crossing his arms and leaning back so his chair is on two legs.

It would be so easy to topple.

"It's my business," Frank says. "And you're not welcome here."

"Business owners can't discriminate against customers," Troy says, almost making it a taunt. "If bakeries can't refuse to serve the gays, you can't refuse service to police officers."

"A job title isn't a protected identity, you simpleton." Frank stalks forward and grabs the back of Troy's chair, slamming it forward. Melly scrambles up and away from the table, and I think this is it, this is the moment she'll come back to herself, but she only watches as Troy turns to stare up at Frank, murder in his eyes.

"My *job title*," he sneers, "makes me one of the most discriminated-against people in this country. And if you—"

Frank grabs the chair and, with more force than his frame would suggest, yanks it away from the table. "Nope. We're not having that shit here. You can take your bigoted bullshit and harassment elsewhere. I have told you once already that you're not welcome here. This is the last time I'll repeat myself."

Troy doesn't fall, not exactly, but he has to do an inelegant scramble to regain his balance after losing his chair that pleases me.

Melly catches my eye then, lingering for a fraction of a second before looking away, but I catch a flash of something close to glee.

It fades quickly, though, because Mustache has his hackles up, and even though the dining room is mostly empty, a small audience is still an audience, and that's never good when small men feel like they're being challenged.

"You want to start your day arrested for assaulting a police officer?" he asks, dropping his hand to the butt of his gun.

Frank barely graces him with a glance. "Son, you're getting yourself involved in something that's not your business, so I suggest you take your lady friend and wait outside." He shakes his head and snorts. "Assaulting a police officer. Is that really the stock response these days?"

Troy pulls himself to his full height like he's some kind of bear. "You're the one involved in things that aren't your business."

Frank waves him off. "You came to my actual business, harassed my employees, and couldn't have the good grace to stay away when you're not welcome. She doesn't have your stolen shit, and I don't have any more patience for this. See yourselves out. Permanently."

Mustache's brows furrow in a quizzical look that Troy ignores.

Interesting.

He didn't tell his partner about our little dustup here.

For a moment the situation sits on a knife's edge and I think if anyone is going to escalate, it's going to be Mustache, because now he's riled up and confused, which is never a good combination.

Melly, perhaps sensing this same thing, is the one to break the stalemate. "We should get going, guys. Busy day ahead."

She doesn't look at me as she goes, oblivious to the knot that tightens my stomach with each step she takes toward the door.

After a tense moment, the cops follow, and even though it's like the whole room exhales in their absence, I know this isn't the end of it.

Not even close.

Chapter
Thirty-Four

The knock comes late.

Zoe raises her head, then bounds across Noel and onto the floor. Her nails click on the stairs as she makes her way down, and Noel and I exchange a look.

"Expecting someone?" I ask.

"No. And I really don't want to put pants on."

My phone vibrates with a text, and I realize I've missed the previous two.

Shit.

"I'll go," I say, climbing out of bed and pulling on the flannel shirt he's left slung over the chest at the end of the bed.

"If it's Jehovah's Witnesses, tell them we already have gods and to come back when they have cookies."

"I can make you cookies."

"Yeah, but if people ring the bell, they should pay a cookie tax."

"Fair enough." I keep my tone light, like I can convince myself the knot in my stomach isn't actively tying itself into a noose.

Downstairs, Zoe is nosing at the door, and I close my eyes, steeling myself before I pull it open.

"We need to talk," Melly says. Her blue curls shine in the porch light's glow, all traces of black dye washed away. She sheepishly holds out a paper bag. "I brought bribes. Please. Just hear me out."

From upstairs, Noel asks, "Who is it?"

I ignore him and sigh. "Why here? Why now? It's almost midnight."

She seems only then to take in my disheveled hair and lack of proper clothes. "Were you sleeping?"

"Trying to. It's been a day."

She cringes. "Please. I'll explain."

"Babe?" Noel calls, and I can hear stirring above me.

"It's fine," I shout back. "I'll be up in a minute."

But it's too late. Noel is at the top of the stairs, plaid pajama pants slung low on his narrow hips, bemusement on his sleepy face.

Melly raises a hand in greeting, but there's a set to her jaw that makes it clear she wasn't looking for a group meeting. "Just borrowing your girl for a minute."

"It's fine," I say again, although at this point I don't know who I'm telling. "Zoe, go back upstairs." She doesn't want to, not when the nighttime air is so tempting, but she does. "I need a minute."

I leave Melly on the porch and follow Zoe upstairs. Noel is still on the landing, forehead creased with worry.

"Is everything okay?"

"Yeah, but I need to talk to her."

"Now?"

"It would seem. We'll go outside; you can get back to bed." I didn't tell him what happened this morning, and the last thing I want is him overhearing it from Melly. I stretch up to kiss him, knowing this is absurd but also knowing I can't tell her to leave. Not with so much unanswered.

I dress quickly, looking for warmth, not style, and go back downstairs. Outside, Melly is leaning on the porch railing, leather jacket hugged around her. When she glances up, there's a seriousness to her face that I'm not used to.

She tips her head at the bag she put on the hanging bench swing. "I brought falafel."

"Belly's kind of full of stress," I say, pulling Noel's barn coat tighter around me.

She nods, full lips pursed. "I didn't expect to end up at Frank's."

I scoff. "That's your opening?"

"That's the truth." She sighs. "Look, I know it doesn't make sense. I should've told you beforehand, but I thought it would be better if I could just, I don't know, do it and tell you later, when I had something. Which I do, by the way."

I move the falafel to the floor and settle into the corner of the swing, legs curled up against the cold. "What are you talking about?"

"It was all bullshit—you know that, right?" She searches my face. "You don't think I was really profiling those guys as heroes?"

I didn't want to think it. I spent the whole day trying to think of literally any other thing, but all I say is, "It looked like you were."

At this her dimples pop, both cheeks betraying the smile she can't hide. "Yeah, because I'm that fucking good."

Giddiness overtakes her, and she hops off the railing to throw herself into the other corner of the swing, making it careen wildly as she arranges herself, back against the arm so she can face me. "So fucking good, right? Like, I can get anyone to talk to me."

I don't tell her it's because she's a spectacular bullshit artist. She knows, and confirmation will only convince her it's a good thing. But it's unsettling, the ease with which she can drop herself into these personas. "Is that ethical?"

"Do I care? Listen." She cocks one leg up to her chest and leans forward, eyes sparkling. "Did you know those two are related? Troy grew up in Colorado because his mom moved there for college, but the rest of her family is right here in Turnbridge. They're the Greene Farm people. The other cop is Tommy Greene. They're cousins."

Greene Farm is huge. They have a year-round farm stand but always did the Saturday morning farmers' market with us. Their tent is three times the size of mine and Noel's put together. But I don't see why any of this connection is relevant, and I say as much.

"Because now we're starting to know about Troy as a person. I get your thing with the map, and that's cool, but it's still too much. Even if you have half crossed off, we can't possibly search all of those lakes one by one."

My heart starts to speed up, and for the first time today it's not from stress but excitement. "You know where it is?"

"Not exactly. But listen. You know what Tommy Greene has? Social media. Coming out of his ass. And you know what's on it? About eight thousand pictures of fishing trips. Know who's in most of them?"

"Troy."

"Bingo. So I'll bet you anything Tommy Greene knows where this cabin is, and there's half a chance if we dig through those pictures, he was dumb enough to tag the location."

"That would be too easy," I say, but hope is already filling my chest. We're due a break.

Maybe this could be it.

Melly's knee jiggles against the back of the swing, and I know she's not done.

"What else?" I ask.

"We're not the only ones who want Troy's nuts in a vise."

I sit up straighter, something tugging at my brain. It's not only through the Greene Farm that I recognize the cousin's name. Troy mentioned Tommy when he was on the phone in the garage. And someone else.

"Is it Kenny?"

She cocks her head at me. "Okay, Sherlock. That was actually kind of spooky. It's not Kenny, but he was the one delivering the message. How'd you already know?"

"Something I overheard. What was the message?"

"*That bitch is coming for you. Both of you.* Dude was pure panicked, practically screaming it. I only know it was Kenny because Troy said his name like twelve times trying to shut him up. That was all I heard before he got out of the car. Tommy was shook, though. He obviously knew what it was about, but he wouldn't say. I tried to joke with him about girl troubles, but he clammed right up. And no offense, I don't think you were the bitch in question this time."

I wrap my coat tighter around my knees, mulling it over. "I don't think so either." I recap the conversation I heard in Troy's garage, and it's obvious this is a direct continuation. "They're into something. Something bad. And I think it's separate from Jodie."

"Well, yeah," Melly says, stretching one leg out to poke me with her booted toe. "She's not exactly coming for anyone right now."

I give her a look. "Not funny."

"Not trying to be." She leaves her leg extended, and for a moment we sit in silence, letting the motion of the swing stir our thoughts around.

"So it's two things," I say, plotting a way forward. "We have Jodie, who needs saving. We also have Troy and his merry band of ballbags who are unsurprisingly into something shady. Jodie is priority, of course, but I think we need to know what else is going on. We're going to want all the dirt we have on Troy when the time comes."

Melly's eyes light up. "An undercover exposé on the Turnbridge cops? Yes, please."

Chapter
Thirty-Five

I stay up far too late going through Tommy's social media posts, making a list of all the locations he's tagged in fishing pictures that also include Troy. It's a long list. Long enough to make me wonder how these fools have time for anything else when every spare minute is spent with a pole in their hand. Even the winter photos are fishy, with groups of guys standing around holes drilled through frozen lakes.

Absolutely nothing about it looks appealing.

Neither does the prospect of getting out of bed. Through the window the early-morning sky is a solid sheet of slate, the kind of clouds promising a wet day. But as much as my body wants to stay cocooned in the snug of covers, my brain is already back on Troy and Jodie.

This line of work is nothing if not motivating.

I park Penny at the campus library, knowing if the rain comes it will drive all my customers inside, but the prospect bothers me less than my bank balance.

Even Zoe is content to stay inside, only trotting out to visit the first wave of the pie-for-breakfast crowd. Already a consistent bunch, their numbers more than doubled when I added pop-pies to the menu this year. The frosted rectangles are a blatant Pop-Tart rip-off, but let's be real. Mine are extra flaky, are full of actual fruit, and have a peppy dose of good-morning magic to get the day off to a sweet start.

Kellogg's has nothing on me.

The rain holds off until the second morning wave goes through, but when it arrives, it's with a vengeance. Drops ping like popcorn off Penny's metal roof and sluice in wide rivers down the windows. No one is venturing out in this.

Perfect.

Uninterrupted research time is exactly what I need right now. Before I start, I open the iPad to check the feed and almost drop it when I see Jodie staring straight at me. She's perfectly still, lank hair framing her face as she stares up at the camera like something out of a horror movie. It's the first time I've seen her acknowledge one of the cameras, and I wonder if it's because she's only now noticed it or if there's something else.

I wish there were some way I could use the camera to communicate with her, but even if I could get it to turn on and off, what would I do? Morse code her? I don't even know if it has a recording light I could control.

I sigh, barely able to hear my own exhalation over the pounding rain, and then bolt up.

The rain.

There's no audio on the feed, but I switch views to the bedroom. There's a small gap at the top of the window that usually shows up as a strip of bright sunlight in the morning, but today it's dark, same as here. It's not enough space for me to tell if it's raining, but it's definitely overcast where she is.

I open my weather app to radar and zoom out so all of New England and New York fills the screen. A thick band of dark green slices through New York, over the top left corner of Connecticut, and then through half of Massachusetts and all of Vermont and New Hampshire before covering most of Maine too.

That's a lot of gray skies.

But it's something.

I grab a Sharpie and my paper map, drawing a heavy line over the borders of Rhode Island, much of Connecticut, and all of New Jersey.

There are a few lakes still on my radar in northwest Connecticut, but removing this much territory feels like a win.

Invigorated, I switch over to the laptop and plug Tommy Greene into my databases, just to see what pops. He's been a Turnbridge resident his whole life, never married, and owns his own property not far from his family's farm. I street-view the address to make sure there isn't a cabin tucked away there, but it's a well-populated street and Tommy's house is no different than the others that line it.

What is different with Tommy, at least compared to Troy, is his online presence. Melly wasn't exaggerating when she said he lived online. He has active accounts with all the major social media platforms and dating profiles on more sites and apps than I knew existed.

Using a burner email, I sign up for several of the more niche ones to get a feel of what he's doing and instantly wish I could undo it.

I'm all for consenting adults doing whatever floats their individual boats, but right or wrong, I can't help being bothered by what I find. The common theme across Tommy's accounts is control, and not in a wholesome-BDSM kind of way. In fact, one of the bondage sites I find him on lets users rate their encounters, and Tommy has a slew of one-whip reviews, all of them citing a lack of respect for safe words.

A cop engaging in rape fantasies?

Houston, we might've found our problem.

I search some of these shadier sites for Troy, but I don't find him. Maybe this is only Tommy's deal, or maybe Troy is hiding behind a fake name and email, same as me.

Either way, I've had enough of the darker side of dating for right now and switch back to Facebook. Tommy's friends list is public, and I type *Ken* into the search at the top, watching as it autofills with two options: Ken Conway and Kenneth Hansen.

Before I can click either one, there's a knock outside, and I scramble up, shushing Zoe's startled bark. "Sorry, coming," I call. I knew I should've been working near the serving window, but it was so much easier to spread out at the counter. Plus, I thought for sure the rain would deter even the most loyal of pie fans today.

And I was right, because I barely make it two steps when the door opens and a waterlogged Melly barrels inside. "It's just me," she says, shaking her head and sending droplets of rain scattering across my tiny entryway. "I didn't want to give you a heart attack by bursting in."

"I appreciate that," I say dryly, watching as she shrugs out of her dripping jacket and hangs it on Zoe's leash hook. Despite the cold, she's wearing only a loose black tank top underneath. "What's up?"

She squeezes her hair, wringing out more of the water before coming up to the kitchen. "Saw you here," she says, straddling a stool. "Wanted to say hi. Or check in. Or, you know, apologize."

"What for?"

She jerks a shoulder up, a sharp motion she doesn't seem to control. "I don't know. Showing up? Last night? There?"

For someone who is usually so confident in her speech, the way Melly is making everything end in a question unsettles me. "What? No, it's fine."

Her bare shoulder twitches again, and this time she does notice because she props her elbows on the counter and rubs at the muscle like she can force it still. "He just didn't seem thrilled. You know, to see me there?"

"And you care?" I'm genuinely curious, because she never seemed to before.

"I don't know. I don't want to get you in trouble or, like, make things difficult." She shakes her head and rushes to backpedal. "No, I don't mean in trouble. Obviously he's not that kind of guy. But I get being less than jazzed about some chick pulling your girlfriend out of bed in the middle of the night." She flashes a wicked grin that erases the awkwardness. "Especially one that looks like me."

"Good god." I laugh. "You're insufferable."

"Yeah, but also seriously—tell him sorry if I upset him?"

"You could do it yourself," I suggest carefully. "If you're that concerned. He's easy to find."

She wrinkles her nose. "Yeah, because we know he'd believe me."

I give her a look, but she's right. While he respects the fact that I've forgiven her for how things went when we first met, I know he hasn't.

"Anyway," she says brightly, and surveys the chaos spread across the counter. "What's all this?"

I go around the counter, sliding the map closer as I go and explaining the updates I've made.

She fingers the paper clipped to the top of the map. "And this?"

"The list of the places Tommy tagged in pictures with Troy." I stretch across to grab it, and as I brush against Melly's arm, I realize how much cold is clinging to her and feel a wash of shame for not registering it before. When I sit back, I notice the neck of her tank top is wet where her hair dripped, and I get up, leaving the list in front of her to read. "I need to mark them on the map, but I think that should help narrow it down more."

"I can do that," she says, grabbing my Sharpie. "Stars good?"

From the bedroom I ask, "Don't you have class?"

"Don't you trust me to prioritize?" she shoots back.

I shake my head, grinning even though she can't see it. "Fine. Yes. Stars are good."

I give Zoe a quick kiss on the head and return to the kitchen, towel and cardigan in hand. I flip the kettle switch on my way by.

Melly doesn't look up from where she's kneeling on her stool, bent over the map, already at work. One finger marks her spot on the list, and she silently mouths the name of her current target as she scans the lakes. I drape the towel over her wet head, and she turns in surprise.

"Don't drip on the map." I wrap the roomy cardigan around her like a cape, not caring if it gets wet. "And yes, it's pink. You'll survive."

The look she gives me does something stupid to my stomach that I shouldn't acknowledge. Not now. Feeling suddenly flustered, I set about making the tea while she goes back to the map, but even though she has her head down, I'm very, very aware of her dimples.

I fill her in on what I've learned about Tommy while the tea steeps, just to give my brain something to do. It has an appropriately sobering effect.

"Dude, that's gross. I'm about as kink-friendly as they come, but even I have a problem when it's a cop dabbling in that. It's like a chef considering cannibalism. Too close for comfort."

"Right?" I set a mug of blood orange tea on either side of the map and sit down, tapping the keyboard to wake up my laptop. "I was looking into who Kenny might be when you showed up."

"Another cop," she says confidently. "Townie friend of Tommy's since they were kids."

I tip my head in a silent request to elaborate.

"It came up in the interview. The local legacy thing. Apparently they think they're the Three Musketeers."

I look at the two profile pictures displayed below my search of Tommy's Facebook friends and click the younger.

Kenneth Hansen is, without question, the Kenny in question. His profile picture shows a thirty-something white guy with a ginger buzz cut, and even though he's in plain clothes, his sunglasses choice screams cop. A quick scroll confirms it—plenty of pictures in uniform, plenty of the same extremist right-wing shit Troy posts.

"Okay, fucko," I mutter. "Time to figure out what you three are up to."

Chapter
Thirty-Six

We fall into a comfortable silence, Melly working on the map while I troll the internet for any detail of Kenny's life that might lead somewhere.

It's easy to see why these three get along. Everything they volunteer about themselves paints similar pictures: solidly middle-class men who have somehow come to identify as proud rednecks. Kenny in particular has an affinity for Confederate flag pictures and posts long missives about the importance of heritage that belly right up to white supremacy without outright claiming it.

Like Tommy, he posts a lot of personal photos on social media, including a disturbing amount featuring him decked out in camo, proudly holding up the heads of various dead animals, a rifle slung across his back.

There's even one with a giraffe.

Everything about it is horrible, but somehow the worst isn't the way the body is arranged, the long neck curled around crumpled legs, like it's trying to protect itself. No, it's the unabashed glee on Kenny's face as he poses atop the creature's spotted flank, gun thrust toward the sky in manly victory.

I understand that there are people who hunt to feed their families, but that isn't what this is.

Not even close.

He did this for fun.

I don't notice I'm grinding my teeth until Melly asks, "What's wrong?"

I spin the screen so she can see.

Her lips curl in disgust, and I see my own anger in her eyes. "That fucker."

"I don't even care what he's involved in or what we can prove," I say. "I want to take him down for this."

"I support it."

And there's something about that, the utter frankness of it that is almost unbearably refreshing. Because it isn't an empty platitude. She knows exactly what I mean, and she doesn't merely accept it.

She encourages it.

"Okay," she says, oblivious to my little moment as she caps the Sharpie. "Done."

I close the laptop and look. The constellation of stars clusters tightly over Massachusetts and fans north into New Hampshire and Vermont. There are a few sprinkled across Connecticut below the new border, in the area I had discounted based on weather. I factor them back in, just to be safe.

Four states.

We started with all of New England and some beyond, but now we're down to four states.

That's manageable.

I trace a finger over the map, playing connect-the-dot with the stars as I think. "This is good."

"So what now? Road trip?"

I shake my head, refusing to let the disappointment crowd out this fresh optimism. "Not yet. I mean, we can check the closer ones for sure, but that's still too many. Between driving and searching, it would take days, realistically a couple weeks, to get them all. We need to keep narrowing it down." I explain how I've been using street-view and topography maps to investigate from afar.

She raises a pierced brow. "Smart. Not exactly thrilling, but smart."

I laugh. "Welcome to the tedium of real life."

"I feel betrayed by TV."

"Tell me about it. But that's how I'll be spending my night tonight. Who knows, maybe I'll get lucky." I grab the iPad and turn it back on. We may have narrowed down the field of play for Jodie, but I also want to narrow down what else Troy is up to. When I blow up his life, it's going to be scorched earth. I click through his app folders for the dozenth time, even though I know I won't find what I'm looking for. "I wish he synced his texts to this thing. If we could see what he was talking to Kenny about, it would be so much easier."

"That's probably exactly why they're not synced. If they're doing shady shit, he isn't going to want to leave proof on multiple devices. Hell, they probably don't even text about it, just talk."

"I don't know. He's so cocky. He thinks he's so untouchable he can kidnap the woman and carry on with his life like everything's dandy. I bet he doesn't think twice about what he texts, especially to his cop buddies. Shit. That's it."

"What's it?" Melly asks.

"He doesn't think," I repeat as I open up his web browser. His messages might not be synced, but if he's signed into the same accounts on both devices, his search history should be.

"Again with the smart," Melly says, nudging me as she leans over to get a better look.

I ignore her, clicking through to settings.

"Got it." At first, it's nothing helpful. A lot of porn, which I scroll past, and innocuous searches for takeout menus, streaming torrents, and sports news.

When I get back to Monday's history, the day Melly heard Kenny's panic call, the pattern changes.

But not in a way that makes sense.

"Why the sudden interest in Sue Vestry?" I ask after the fourth article about her.

"Vestry? Doesn't she work for the mayor?"

"Apparently." I keep clicking. "It's a bunch of articles where she's mentioned. Town stuff, nothing exciting."

I open my laptop and type her name in. My search delivers the same articles Troy was looking at, but also a picture of a middle-aged white woman I would have a very hard time picturing as the bitch Kenny referred to.

I add Troy's name to hers, then try various combinations of her name and the other cops', but nothing jumps out. In terms of local news, they've never crossed paths. I try linking her name to Jodie's, but again, nothing.

"Is it a coincidence?"

Melly, having taken over scrolling the iPad's history, shakes her head. "It's the only thing that's out of the ordinary. Everything else he looks at is entertainment and online shopping."

I run Sue through my records database, wondering if maybe she has some kind of legal encounter with Troy too small to make the news, but the woman has never had so much as a single speeding ticket in her whole life.

"It has to mean something that Troy searched her the same day he got that call," I say, trying to justify the fact that I'm completely invading this woman's privacy. Like most older women, her social media is limited, but what exists is an open book, and soon I know all about her nibling's school achievements (she's very happy her niece is at Turnbridge U), her aging mom's latest health scare, and her affinity for potted plants. There isn't a single mention of a single police officer anywhere on the page. "I don't get it."

But Melly isn't listening.

She grabs my arm, wide eyes never leaving the iPad, and something about the touch instantly shifts all my bewilderment to cold, sharp fear.

When she speaks, her voice is raw with rage. "He's there. Right now."

She moves the iPad so it's between us, and my entire world shrinks down to that glowing rectangle.

On-screen, Jodie shrinks into the corner of the couch as Troy towers above her, shaking a cereal box in her face.

I cover Melly's hand with mine and squeeze, unable to look away as Troy hauls her off the couch by her arm and drags her to the kitchen. Melly's nails dig into my skin as he throws her into a chair. It rocks precariously and I think she's going to fall, but he grabs her shoulder and shoves her down before slamming the cereal box onto the table in front of her.

"She's not eating," Melly whispers.

I think of the dishes, always the same ones, always in the same spot on the counter. Did I miss the start of a hunger strike when I assumed she was particular about her routine?

"Son of a bitch."

On some level, I get it, though. She can't fight back, she can't escape, but she can decide whether or not to eat. And she's decided it isn't worth it anymore.

There's no audio, but there doesn't have to be. It's clear he's screaming. I file away the fact that the cabin has to be remote enough to allow for that even as the rest of my brain is gripped with fear.

I'm viscerally aware that at any moment this could turn into a snuff film.

I reach blindly for my phone, double pressing the power key to launch the camera. If he kills her, he'll purge the footage. It might be stored remotely, but I can't risk him interfering with that too.

I hit record and pray I'm not about to capture Jodie's death.

Troy bangs a bowl on the table, and she flinches, then goes very still as he upends the cereal box, pouring until the bowl overflows. He jams a spoon into it and seizes the back of her neck, pinning her to the spot.

She doesn't move.

Melly's fingers tighten on my arm.

Troy wrenches at her neck, shaking her small body like a doll's. His neck cords with rage as he screams words we cannot hear. He grabs the spoon and forces it into her mouth, making her gag.

He doesn't release her or relent until the bowl is empty.

As horrible as it is to witness, a tiny part of me starts to relax. He's not going to waste all this effort making her eat only to kill her, not today.

When it's finished, he drops into the chair next to her, sagging like he's just finished a long day of physical labor.

And then he talks.

He talks with a perfectly placid expression on his face, like she isn't pressing her whole body into the slats of that wooden chair to keep as much space between them as possible. He talks like they're any normal couple, sharing a nice, normal, dinner.

I stop recording when he takes her to the bedroom.

When Melly exhales, it's long and shaky, like she's been holding her breath the entire time. She releases my arm, and neither of us comments on the half-moon indents left behind.

"Okay," I say, desperate for a task, something to make this more than voyeurism. "We need to clock when he leaves. We can't assume he's necessarily going straight home, but he might be. If we compare the time he leaves to when he gets home, it might give us a more accurate idea of where on the map he might be."

Melly nods. "Right. Okay. We don't even need to monitor the home feed—we can check it later, rewind it back. But we do need to watch until he leaves, just in case."

"Of course."

And we do.

Shoulder to shoulder, we wait, bearing witness until the monster departs.

Chapter
Thirty-Seven

In the dark hours before Thursday dawns, the Pies Before Guys account pings with a new order.

It's like this sometimes, the concentrated flurry of requests after weeks of silence.

The sound should wake me, but I'm already up, having spent the better part of the night staring at the ceiling, where a ghostly image of the map seemed to float regardless of whether my eyes were open.

It took Troy three hours to get home. Regardless of whether that was direct or included stops doesn't matter; either way, it effectively halves our radius, even if that area still includes the highest concentration of spots we know for sure Troy has been before based on Tommy's photos.

At this point, even if we can't narrow it down further, visiting each lake on the map isn't out of the question. It will take time, a lot of it, and even though Troy has kept Jodie alive this long, we'll still be racing against one bad decision from him. Because that's all it will take.

A man like that, already prone to fits of explosive violence, can snap at any minute. It doesn't have to be deliberate. A single moment of resistance from Jodie on the wrong day could make it her last.

I'm frozen by that knowledge. I can pick any direction on the map to start, but there's no guarantee it's the right one. I could be a hundred miles away on the day he loses it and all of this will have been for nothing. I will still have failed her.

So with that swirling in my head, I let myself welcome the distraction of this unusual order.

Tammy02816 is not my normal client, if I even have such a thing. The people who contact me are trapped in circumstances they can't control. They're looking for a way to protect themselves, and I am their last resort.

Tammy is ready to be her own last resort.

Hello.

I'm writing to you because I don't know where else to turn. No, that's not true. I do know. I bought the gun. But I also know going that route will damn me. I will free my daughter only to lose her forever.

I am convinced the only way to save Jenna is to kill the man she 'married' and I am prepared to do that, if I have to. I know there will be consequences beyond Jenna hating me, but I can accept them. I'm working on making arrangements for my 17yo should the worst happen. He doesn't deserve a mother in prison, but my daughter doesn't deserve to live in one either.

And she does.

When I confessed to my friend what I was planning, she said she would take my son in, but that there was a better way. A safe way.

She gave me your name.

Caleb Werner is a cultist. He doesn't look like it, but that's what he is. It's why he's so good.

At least eight other women are living with them, including my daughter. Two are pregnant.

Jenna's birthday is next week and I have convinced her and Caleb to come for dinner.

If you can do what Rose says, I would like to request a pie for dessert.

It's essentially a proxy request, and even though I understand where this mother is coming from, I don't immediately reply to her. What she's asking for is one step removed from me choosing my own targets. I act on behalf of the person in danger. They have to want it. I've had plenty of people start the pie process only to back out, either out of fear or because it motivated them to find another way out, but it's always their decision.

But at the same time, I've made exceptions in the past. While I never pick targets for personal gain, I have chosen them for public good, even when no one requested it. There was a violent rapist not too long ago who walked on all charges because he was a clean-cut, all-American college basketball star and the judge didn't think one drunk night should ruin his whole life, even if it ruined Anna Hargrave's. Whether he meant to or not, the judge gave him a free pass to do it again, to someone else, by proving that the rules don't apply to guys like him.

I made sure they did.

So I mull it over.

If Jenna had written to me directly with a tale of getting sucked into a cult and having no way out, I would already be assembling ingredients. Even if Caleb isn't laying a hand on her, psychological abuse is every bit as deserving of Pies Before Guys' attention as physical.

Cults aren't something I'm well versed in, but I feel like the fact that it's still small and that the leader is willing to allow visits with outside family, even supervised, is hopeful.

I write back to Tammy, asking for as much information as she can give me. I include a contract.

Then I get out of bed.

There's no way I'm going to sleep now, not with thoughts of Jodie and corrupt cops and now cults colliding in my brain.

Zoe raises her head but doesn't follow me to the kitchen. She's seen enough midnight baking to know it's not going to result in treats for her.

No, these cutie pies are meant for one mouth and one mouth only.

* * *

The mayor's office is in a historic brick building that began life as an elementary school and was later converted to serve as the town hall. While it might seem strange that the police and fire departments have brand-new, state-of-the-art facilities while the literal mayor does business out of a repurposed school, I can see why she prefers it.

There's a certain charm to this old building, and with offices the size of classrooms, there's enough space to never get on your coworkers' nerves.

That alone probably makes it worth keeping.

Black metal signs hang from iron rods beside each door, identifying the departments and people within. On the walls where bulletin boards would've once showcased children's artwork, displays about Turnbridge history and prominent local figures encourage visitors to stop and peruse on their way to more boring business.

I don't stop.

Every so often I pause to consult the signposts at the junctures of different hallways. Made in the same style as the office signs, the black arrows are labeled with white block letters and point in all directions like some sort of maze key. They're both cute and effective, and I find myself at the mayor's suite with no wrong turns.

The nearest door is marked GISELLE WASHINGTON, EXECUTIVE ASSISTANT. As tempted as I am to find Sue Vestry and deliver directly, Giselle seems like the more logical choice.

Besides, her door is wide open, so there's no way I'm getting by unseen.

I knock on the jamb and step inside as a pretty mixed-race woman in a purple wheelchair looks up from her computer. "Can I help you?"

I offer her a sunny smile. "Good morning. I'm the Pie Girl." I hold out the two boxes laden with cutie pies, both stamped with my logo and tied with pink twine. Sometimes the best way to hide is in plain sight. "I wanted to drop off some treats, a little something to brighten up the day."

"Ooh, a visit from an actual pie fairy. I love it," she says, rolling out from behind her desk. "Tell you what, why don't you leave one here and I'll put the other in the conference room." She winks at me. "That way I don't need to share this whole box with everyone walking by."

"Fair enough." I laugh, placing one box on her desk and passing her the other. I want to follow to personally make sure Sue is invited to have some, but I'm aware of how weird that would be, so I tell Giselle to enjoy them and see myself out.

"Come back anytime," she calls in a singsong that makes me smile.

The simple power of pie to inspire joy can't be underestimated, magic or not.

With nothing left to do now but wait, I head back to Frank's. I figure by the time I top up the diner stock, the cutie pies should've made their way through the mayoral staff. For most of them, the magic will simply make their days feel more meaningful as they work to serve the people of Turnbridge. They'll want to go above and beyond to make their constituents happy.

Each of them will find themselves being more helpful than ever before.

It's a harmless blend, really, almost a workplace equivalent of the campus pies, but it should be enough if I play my cards right.

I'm so absorbed in practicing what I'll say to Sue that I don't notice the sirens right away.

They start as background noise, an added layer to the normal soundtrack of busy morning traffic, but the closer I get to the diner, the louder they get, until they're all I hear.

Panic grips me when I realize they're not near the diner but at it. My mind immediately jumps to the worst-case scenario: fire.

I think of Penny, Zoe trapped inside, and step on the gas, flashing my high beams until the car in front me pulls over to let me around.

I tear into the back lot to find everything bathed in red, but not from flames. Swirling emergency lights paint crimson streaks across the diner and Penny, but both are intact and standing.

My relief short-circuits when I register that it isn't a fire truck screaming.

It's an ambulance.

And I'm in its way.

I pull forward, throw the truck in park, and jump out in time to see Juan sag through the diner's back door, a glazed expression on his face as he watches the ambulance peel away.

I bolt to him, thoughts of Ana and all the danger she could find in the kitchen filling my head. But no. If it were Ana, he wouldn't be here. He'd be in the ambulance with her.

I don't have a chance to be relieved by this, because when I reach him, I know whatever it is, it's every bit as bad. "What happened?"

The Last to Pie

His eyes take a minute to find mine and focus, but when they do, my heart drops. Each beat becomes a sledgehammer blow, loud and echoing, like my body is trying to drown out what he's about to tell me.

"It's Frank."

Chapter
Thirty-Eight

A heart attack.
    Frank.

He's not even supposed to have a heart, never mind an attacking one.

"We have to go. Now," I say, pulling Juan by the arm.

He shakes his head, still numb with shock. "I can't leave the diner. He'd kill me."

"He doesn't have family," I remind him. "He has us. We have to be there." I don't add the *just in case* to that sentence. I can't.

"My mom's due to drop Ana off in an hour. She has an appointment she can't miss, and I can't leave Ana with Alex."

I understand what Juan is feeling, the foggy unreality that comes when you realize death is truly near. I felt it with my mom and in the aftermath of that first pie.

But we don't have time for it.

I march into the kitchen and find Alex and the servers clustered together and talking over each other. When they hear the back door bang shut, they spring apart and fall silent. The diner is in the lull between breakfast and lunch, and if we're closing things down, now is the best time.

"Frank's on his way to the hospital," I say, even though they know that better than me. They saw everything. "Me and Juan are going there now. You guys need to finish out service, and you"—I pin Alex with a look that dares him to let Frank down—"need to close up. The right way."

"I got his back," River says.

"Thank you."

Amanda sniffs and wipes at puffy eyes. "You'll keep us updated?"

"Of course."

"What about tomorrow?" Alex asks.

"That'll be part of the update."

I can't look too closely at this knot of people who, for better or worse, are part of the diner family. I can't think about what we all stand to lose right now.

I leave without saying goodbye, because I have no intention of saying that to anyone today.

Outside, Juan is on the phone, and I grab his free arm as I go by. "Come on."

"Ten minutes," he says into the phone. "Love you too." Then, to me, "We need to get Ana first."

"I know." I open Penny's door and call for Zoe. She bounds down, tail wagging and blissfully oblivious to the world crashing down around us. "Can she stay at yours?"

He nods, and the three of us climb into the truck. I don't know how long we'll be at the hospital and I don't like the idea of leaving Zoe unattended for that long, not when Troy has already threatened her.

At Juan's, we swap the dog for the girl and speed for the hospital.

"Is Uncle Frank going to die?" Ana asks, kicking her feet on the bench seat between us. "Lita said he might."

"We don't know yet, baby," Juan says, and even though it breaks my heart, I like that he doesn't lie to her.

She's silent for a moment, picking at the handles of the over-stuffed tote bag of snacks and activities Magdalena packed in the ten minutes it took us to get there. "Did his heart really explode?"

"No, it didn't explode." Juan's voice is hoarse, and he coughs to clear it. "It just stopped working for a minute. Sometimes that happens when you're old."

"But the doctor will fix it, right?"

I follow the blue signs for Turnbridge Memorial Hospital, tears stinging my eyes.

"They're going to try."

*　*　*

The hospital staff doesn't know what to do with us at first.

"Immediate family only," the lady at the desk says apologetically.

"I'm his granddaughter," I lie. "Please, we need to see him."

She eyes Juan skeptically. "I thought you said you worked for him."

"He does," I say, praying no one contradicts what I'm about to say next. "But he's also my boyfriend. Please, just tell us where they took him."

"I want to see Uncle Frank," Ana says, tugging at Juan's hand, and it's her little voice that seals the deal. The woman, clearly of grandmother age herself, finally relents.

After a moment of tapping, she says, "It looks like he's still in surgery and will likely be for the next few hours, so I'm afraid there isn't much I can tell you. But there's a waiting room on the east fourth floor that you can use. I'll notify them that you're here."

"Thank you so much," I say, barely hearing the directions she gives to get us there.

The three of us are silent in the elevator, the white-coated doctor with us a grim reminder that Frank's life is in the hands of humans.

Highly educated and very skilled humans, to be sure, but still. There will be no miracles today, no gods or magic to make things okay. Only people, trying their best to do their jobs.

It seems wildly inadequate.

When the doctor steps off on the third floor, Ana looks up at me curiously. "You told a lie."

"I did."

She considers this for a minute, then nods. "I think that was good. Why didn't that lady want to let us in?"

"Hospitals have rules."

"And we broke them?"

"We did. Because we had a good reason." I exchange a look with Juan, knowing he's going to have to reckon with all of this later, but he gives me a small *What can you do about it?* kind of smile.

Luckily, the elevator dings before she can continue examining the ethics of honesty, and we step back into the harsh reality of why we're here.

The wide halls are quiet, a reverent hush for the lifesaving procedures going on around us. We find the waiting room, empty save for a man wearing headphones and pecking away at a laptop. We set up in the far corner, where there's a table for Ana to put her things.

"I need to call Eric," Juan says. "Can you watch her?"

"Of course. Go."

While he's gone, I take out my phone to text Noel.

He replies immediately. *Do you want me to come?*

No, Juan's here. I think it's going to be a lot of waiting right now. Just wanted to let you know.

Do you need me to get Zoe?

Left her at Juan's. All good.

Ok. Let me know if you need anything or want me to come. I love you.

Love you too.

"I'm going to make Uncle Frank a card," Ana declares, pulling a drawing pad from her bag along with a box of colored pencils.

"Excellent idea."

"Do you know what his favorite dinosaur is?"

"I bet it's a T. rex."

She grins. "Because he acts like one?"

"Because he acts like one." The words burn my throat. Because they're also a lie. A joking one, perhaps, but a lie. Frank is a lot of things, and while in some ways dinosaur might be one of them, that's not the whole picture. He might stomp around and roar, but he's also the glue that holds the diner family together. Even if he doesn't know how to say it out loud, he loves it.

He loves us.

Okay, maybe not all of us. Alex's days are probably numbered, but Juan? Amanda?

Me?

Love.

When Juan returns, his eyes are red, and I know it's every bit as mutual for him as it is for me. More so, given the years it's had to solidify in Juan's case. Frank doesn't have to say Juan is the son he never had. It's too obvious to need words.

"Eric's leaving work early to get her," he says, collapsing into the chair beside me. Ana has wrangled her chair to face the table and is busy sketching away, content that the grown-ups are going to make everything okay.

Being the grown-up is overrated.

I squeeze Juan's hand, and he huffs a breath, shaking his head. "This day, man."

"I know. Surgery's a good sign, though," I say, as much to remind myself as him. "Whatever's wrong, there must be hope of fixing it if they're in there trying."

He nods, but his eyes are bright with tears. "Like, I get that he's old, but it always seemed like he'd live forever, right? He's too stubborn for anything else."

"I know." Just thinking about the diner without Frank is enough to destroy me, so I refuse to. Not until I have to. "It'll be okay. No matter what."

He laces his fingers into mine, gripping tight like the only thing keeping him above water is that hold.

We stay that way for who knows how long. Ana finishes her card, eats her snacks, and plugs into her iPad while Juan and I continue to start at every white coat that passes, thinking this one, finally, will have answers.

None do.

Eventually Eric arrives, and Juan stands just long enough to collapse into his arms.

I slip unnoticed out into the hall. I don't want to miss the doctor, but I have a call to make, and I'm running out of time.

Chapter
Thirty-Nine

After giving a very cheerful Giselle a fake name, I'm put on hold to wait for Sue Vestry.

Without knowing when—or even if—she had any of the cutie pies, it's hard to judge how active the magic will still be. I had planned to call sooner, when the scales would be tipped further in my favor, but this day had other ideas.

"This is Sue," she chirps. While the bright tone may be her default setting, I still take it as a good sign.

"Hi, Sue," I say. I've rehearsed various ways of approaching this, but now, with half my attention still watching for white coats, I just go for it. "I was wondering if I could ask you some questions about the Turnbridge PD? Particularly Troy Sullivan, Tommy Greene, and Kenny Hansen?"

She whistles, disapproval ringing across the connection, but when she speaks, her voice is calm and modulated. "I'm not prepared to comment on that situation. May I ask who's calling?"

I repeat the fake name. "So there is a situation."

There's a crackle of silence, and I wish I could see her face to gauge what kind. Is she suspicious? Angry? Scared?

It could be all three.

I play the best card I have—the truth. "They hurt my friend. Well, one of them did."

The silence stretches on her end, and I wonder if she's fighting the pie, if there's something more powerful than magic at play here.

I hear the intake of breath before she speaks and tense, readying myself to be told off. Instead, she asks, "Did she tell?"

I push off the wall I've been leaning against, suddenly alert. "Did she tell what?"

"What they did to her?" Now Sue sounds like she's fishing for information as much as I am, but a note of hope is hooked to the question. "Did it work?"

"She can't tell," I say carefully. Again, the truth.

But maybe not the same truth as Sue's.

She sighs, and even though I can't see her, the frustration is clear. But then something shifts.

"Okay," she says, some of the chirp returning to her voice. "Sweetie, I don't know how you got my name and I don't know anything about your friend, but I think I might know someone who can help."

"What do you mean?"

"Well, me," she says, and it's pure pie-induced helpfulness filling her voice. "See, it happened to my niece too. Enid. Your friend should talk to her. We're working on something to stop this from happening again. Maybe your friend wants to be part of it."

Now it's my turn to fall silent, confusion whipping my thoughts like a whisk.

Troy kidnapped someone else? And now she's what? Free? With no consequences at all for him? If Sue works for the damn mayor, how did her own niece's kidnapping stay completely under the radar?

I want to ask all of this, but I'm out of time. A somber-faced doctor strides down the hall, and I know in my bones he's here for us.

"Enid. Right," I say, heart hammering faster with each step that brings the doctor closer. "That would be great. Thank you so much for your time."

I hang up before she can say goodbye and pocket my phone.

"Daisy?" the doctor asks.

I nod numbly.

She gestures to the waiting room with a steady hand. "Why don't we take a seat?"

I go past her, fighting a wave of dizziness. Juan and Eric both clock our entrance and rush to meet us. Juan takes my hand as Eric puts an arm around him.

We don't take seats.

"I'm afraid it's not good," the doctor says.

My fingers tighten hard on Juan's and a veil drops over me, just like when I found out about my mother. Only fragments filter through.

Stress.

Infarction.

Oxygen deprivation.

Intubate.

Coma.

"What does that mean?" Eric asks.

"It means he needs another surgery, but right now he's too weak to survive it."

"But he's alive?" I ask.

"For now, yes. We're doing everything we can to stabilize him, but I don't want to give you false hope. I would think about notifying any other family members who might wish to be here. If he's religious, this would be the time for clergy." She gives us a moment to process this, like such a thing is even possible. "Do you know if he has any advanced directives in place? A health care proxy?"

I look at Juan, and he shakes his head, wide eyes reflecting everything I'm feeling. The floor tips beneath me as I turn back to the doctor. "I don't know. I don't think so. What happens if he doesn't?"

"It's not a problem," she says calmly. "We're going to do everything we can to get him through this, but in the event he is unable to advocate for himself, you'll be able to as family."

I don't register anything else she says after that.

I'm dimly aware of her laying out the plan for what comes next, but it washes over me in deafening waves.

Because I know what she means.

I stood up as family, and they believed it.

They had no reason not to, because in the truest sense of the word, I am.

So that means it's going to fall to me, when the time comes, to decide when to let Frank go.

Chapter Forty

They allow us to see him, briefly, although the nurse suggests it's best that Ana doesn't go in.

For her own good, she says.

"We should head home anyway, huh, bug?" Eric says, swinging her up onto his hip.

"I'm not a bug, and I want to see Uncle Frank," she insists.

"Tomorrow," Eric promises. "Give Papi a kiss."

She pouts but does as she's asked. "You better give him my card."

"Promise," Juan says, smoothing her hair. He kisses Eric, and for a moment they stay joined, foreheads pressed together.

Eric cups Juan's cheek. "Call me if you need anything. Anything at all."

Juan nods, and we watch them disappear down the hall before steeling ourselves.

It doesn't help.

No amount of visualization could prepare for the reality of what we find.

Frank has never been a large man, but his big personality made that easy to forget. In this hospital bed, surrounded by wires and machines, there's nothing to him at all.

It's like he's already gone.

I refuse to cry, because the last thing he would tolerate is people sniffling over him. I know that. But that doesn't make it easy.

Juan leaves the dinosaur card on the windowsill, and that tiny splash of cheer is almost the thing to break me.

There's no question of leaving tonight, not for either of us.

We might not be the family Frank signed up for, but we're the one he's got, and we're staying.

While Juan goes in search of coffee, I text Noel an update, then call Melly. "I need help." I don't mean to let my voice crack, but it does.

Melly instantly catches it. "Are you okay?"

It takes me a minute to even pretend that I am. "Frank had a heart attack. It's pretty bad. That's not why I'm calling, though."

"Okay," she says slowly. "Am I supposed to ask how you're holding up, or are we passing over it in silence?"

"Silence."

"Fair enough. What do you need?"

"I called Sue Vestry, and it was weird." I recount the conversation almost verbatim, and something in me steadies at being able to focus on what I can control. "So we need to talk to Enid, but I obviously can't leave. Not now."

"Don't worry, I'm on it."

"You can't talk about Jodie, though, not outright."

"Yeah, I'm not stupid," she says. "I'll see what her deal is and report back. You said she goes to Turnbridge? It'll be cake. Or, you know, pie."

I smile, despite everything. "Okay. Just tread carefully."

"You got it. I can make a pit stop at the hospital if you need anything. Emotional support snacks? Phone charger?"

"No, it's fine."

"Liar. What do you need?"

"It's a pain in the ass."

"As am I. Just tell me."

"You don't have a picture of the lake map, do you?" It might be something to pass the time.

"I can get one."

"No, it's in Penny, and I have the keys. That's a lot of back-and-forth—don't worry about it." I probably wouldn't be able to focus on it anyway. "Enid is the priority. If you can talk to her tonight, that'd be great."

"Dude, I got you. Don't worry."

"Thanks. I owe you. Seriously."

"Damn right," she says, and I can hear the cheeky grin in her voice as she hangs up.

It's not ideal, sending her in my place, but it's better than not getting answers. I'm in no position to be picky right now, and like she said before, Melly can get anyone to talk to her.

When Juan returns with coffee, it's nowhere near drinkable, but it doesn't matter.

We settle in to wait.

* * *

Noel arrives without warning around seven, and as much as I thought I was doing fine, the feel of his arms around me is a balm I didn't know I needed. I'm tempted to stay cocooned there for the night.

"Thank you for coming," I say into his chest. "You didn't have to."

He shrugs, letting me go. "Course I did. I thought you guys could use some proper food," he says, unpacking one of the insulated Hollow Hill bags.

"You weren't wrong," Juan says.

"It's nothing fancy," he says, but it's a total lie and he knows it. No one brings thermoses of hot and cold spiced ciders, three kinds of cheeses, and a salad made exclusively of local, organic ingredients and thinks it's not a little bit fancy, especially when even the dressing is homemade. His showstopper is a huge slab of quiche, studded with roasted butternut squash and rich green spinach, the crust adorably wonky. When he catches me noticing, he grins. "You left dough in the freezer. Figured I'd give it a go."

"It's perfect, thank you."

I wouldn't have expected to have an appetite, but the freshness of the food is an unexpected relief after so many hours in this sterile building.

Noel stays, even though there's little we can do but wait. Juan and I take turns checking on Frank, going often enough that the nurse promises to alert us immediately if there's any change.

"It wouldn't hurt to get some rest," she suggests. "We can call you if anything happens."

While I know we'll eventually have to, neither Juan nor I can bring ourselves to leave just yet.

So we wait.

Eventually Noel stands, looking apologetic. "I have to do night check," he says. "But I can come back."

"It's okay. I know Sunny will take the barn down if she doesn't get her bedtime hay." I smile fondly, thinking of all the times the horse's thundering kicks have reminded us when she's felt forgotten. "I'll let you know if anything changes."

"You're sure?"

"Positive. No need for both of us to be up all night."

I walk him to the elevator, leaving Juan slouched and dozing in one of the chairs. While we wait for it to arrive, Noel pulls me into a long, tight hug. "He's going to be fine, you'll see."

We both know that might not be true, but it's nice to hear. "I hope so."

The elevator pings its arrival, and we break apart.

"Call me for anything," he says.

"Promise."

The doors slide open, and before he can get in, Melly, wild-eyed and breathing hard, tumbles out in a flurry of bags and frenetic energy. The fact that she's already on top of me pulls her up short. "Dude. You are not even going to believe what I found out."

There's an awkward moment when the three of us stand there, the ding of the elevator echoing its empty departure.

Melly, however, does not seem to notice. "Where can we talk?"

Flustered, I gesture down the hall to the waiting room. "Give me a minute?"

"You're gonna want to hear this," she promises, but gives me the space I asked for.

"What's that about?" Noel asks. He's trying to sound casual, but there's a coolness to his voice that doesn't quite sell it.

"She was doing an errand for me. Talking to someone." I have no desire to lie to him, but I also don't want to open this all back up, not right now and certainly not in a hospital hallway.

"I could've done it." He might not mean to sound defensive, but he does. And more than a little hurt.

"No, you couldn't have." I take his hands in mine and kiss his fingers. "But what you did, coming here to sit with us, that means more."

Several heartbeats pass when I think he's going to protest, push for more details, but he doesn't. Instead he hits the button for the elevator and drops a kiss on my head. "I love you."

"I love you too," I say, wrapping my arms tight around his narrow waist.

The elevator dings, and he steps back. "You better go find out whatever it is you're not even going to believe. And like I said, call me. If you need anything else."

The Last to Pie

When he steps into the elevator, I feel like he's taking part of me with him, a soft, scared part that doesn't want to be cut off when the doors slide close.

But he's right.

I have to find out what Melly has to say, so I let that part go and set off to find her.

Chapter Forty-One

S he isn't in the waiting room, because things are never that easy with Melly.

A short, sharp whistle draws my attention, and I see her down the hall, leaning against the wall. She tips her head toward the room behind her.

The door is marked FAMILY ROOM, and it's significantly smaller than the waiting room, with a sofa along one wall and a scatter of armchairs filling the remaining space. At the center is a low coffee table with a box of tissues pushed to one end and Melly's pile of bags on the other.

"First, I brought you things, and I don't want to hear anything about it." She tosses me the biggest bag, a battered black backpack covered in faded patches. Hers, no question.

I sit on the edge of the sofa and unzip it, wondering what this could possibly have to do with Enid.

Not a damn thing, it turns out.

Inside I find a neatly folded dress, the fluffy pink cardigan, and a set of pajamas—fresh undies included. Further sifting reveals a big ziplock holding deodorant, dry shampoo, a toothbrush and paste, and a pouch of makeup wipes. A smaller bag contains all the makeup that usually lives in my tiny bathroom medicine cabinet.

I stare into the gaping mouth of the backpack, at all these things from home, then back up at her. The lump in my throat is too big to speak around, but she has her phone out and doesn't notice.

My own phone buzzes with a text, and when I make no move to check it, Melly indicates with hers. "That was me. The map picture you wanted." When I don't say anything, she winks. "I told you I got you."

"But how?" The words come out as a croak.

She shrugs. "Not my first rodeo. Plus you never changed your lock, so it practically picked itself."

My throat closes like a fist and I screw my eyes shut. Hot tears find a way down my cheeks anyway.

"Whoa, wait, I'm sorry," Melly says quickly. The cushions shift as she sits beside me. "Shit. I thought you could use a change of clothes and I knew you wanted the map. I was just trying to help."

Maybe I should be angry—this is, after all, the second time she's forced her way into my home. But as my shoulders shake, I realize it's as much with laughter as sobs.

I've never been a big crier, and I'm not prepared for how it steals all my air and leaves me gasping.

Melly passes me the tissues without making a fuss. "Look, they planned ahead."

"How considerate," I choke, wiping my face and forcing my lungs to cooperate with the basics of breathing.

Melly side-eyes me. "We still passing over this part in silence?"

I nod. "What else you got?"

She hesitantly points to the brown leather weekend bag, like I might break again. "For Juan. Figured he was here too and Eric hooked him up." My eyes well, and she holds her hands up in mock surrender. "Zero B and E on that one, I swear."

I laugh. "At least there's that."

She reaches for the last bag, white paper, and opens it to reveal familiar foil-wrapped cylinders. "And falafel. Natch."

It's been hours since Noel's picnic spread, but I realize that was the only thing I've eaten all day. And even if it wasn't, I don't need permission to have falafel for dessert, not when everything else is going to hell around me.

"But first," Melly says, "I have so much news."

"About time."

She gives me a look. "Hey, I'm not the one having a total breakdown here. You had to get that out of your system before you could pay proper attention."

I don't argue, because she's not wrong.

"Okay," she says, drawing a leg up as she spins to face me. "So Enid was easy to find. Super easy. Told her I was in J-School, blah, blah, and I was investigating allegations about the police department. You could tell, right then, she had something to say. It took some coaxing, but I stuck to your story and said I had a friend it happened to too, and that did it. She was pissed. She kept blaming herself at first, but I shut that shit down, told her what happened to her wasn't her fault, it was theirs. I used names. So she told me her story."

Her eyes harden and she rolls her neck, visibly trying to keep calm.

"She was stopped walking back to campus one night. She was drunk, but not like falling-down or anything. She thought they were doing a safety check, you know, making sure she could get home all right, but they—Troy and Tommy—put her in the back seat and told her they could lock her up for public intoxication. Made a whole fuss. Then they gave her a way out."

Melly's hands furl and unfurl into fists as she talks, and I feel each squeeze around my stomach.

"They threatened her, of course, when it was over. Said they'd arrest her for solicitation, that her accusation would be her confession."

She stops, lets me take this in, and flexes her hands. She cracks each finger in turn, the pops the only sound to punctuate the horror of this new information.

"Where does Sue Vestry fit?"

"Enid's close to her. She told her what happened and why she can't report it. Sue understood. Apparently the current mayor has a blind spot where the cops are concerned, and Sue's trying to fix that. Two ways." Melly holds up one finger. "She's been spearheading the organization of a citizen-led oversight committee, and"—she raises a second finger—"her and Enid are quietly organizing a class suit to take directly to the district attorney. She's not the only one this happened to."

I think back to what I overheard in the garage that day, how Troy said "it" wasn't a form of bonding for the new guy. This has to be the "it" they were talking about. Troy, Tommy, and Kenny have a history together, but trusting someone new with their secret would be dangerous for all of them.

"How many more?" I ask.

"Four others confirmed, but they're only willing to go public as part of a group. Who knows how many beyond that."

"Holy fuck." I exhale hard and sink back into the sofa. My temples throb with a headache brewed equally from stress, exhaustion, and the remnants of tears.

"No shit. But it's answers, right? And even bad answers are good to have."

I snort. "Thanks for that, Yoda."

"Hey, learned it from you."

With the weight of the day heavy on my eyes, I give in and close them, just for a minute.

The cushions shift again as Melly stands. "Stretch out," she says. "Get comfy. That's what this room is for."

She says it like she's spent time in one too, but I don't ask. Cowardly or not, I can't take one more bad story on top of what I just heard, not after spending an entire day in a hospital.

I do as she suggests, because I'm too exhausted not to.

There is so much still to do, information to process and people to save, but I can't do any of it in this state.

"I'll let Juan know you're down here," Melly says softly. "Get some sleep."

Her combat boots clomp as she crosses the room, her steps falling silent as she flips off a bank of overhead lights.

Even with my eyes closed, the dimness is a relief, a softening of this harsh day.

"Melly?" I whisper.

"Yeah?"

"Thank you. For all of this."

Exhaustion pulls me under before she can reply, and for a while I drift, blissfully unaware of the entire world.

Chapter
Forty-Two

Sometime in the night, Juan and I switch, and while he sleeps, I stand watch. I know it's unnecessary, that the nurses can wake both of us, but it feels wrong not to have one of us clearheaded at all times.

The last thing I want is to have to make a life-or-death decision before I'm fully awake.

It's harder to work the map on my phone, toggling back and forth between the image and my various location apps, but it does help to pass the time, and I'm grateful for the distraction as much as anything.

The satellite maps take the longest to load, but the wait is nothing compared to the time it would take to do these searches in person.

Taking a gamble, I assume that Troy's latest three-hour trek home was more or less a straight shot. Even factoring in a few stops for snacks or gas, my gut says the outer reaches of the radius are where I'm going to find the cabin. Sure, it's possible he took a half-hour jaunt west to Lake Ellis, which is plunked at the edge of a small town and rimmed with the kind of ramshackle buildings Jodie might be in, but I doubt it. The two trips we have travel times on don't suggest she's close.

After enough pinching and zooming to make my eyes cross, I discover something about rural Vermont and New Hampshire towns that surprises me—a complete willingness to build shit regardless of access roads. If it were one or two instances, fine, I could forgive that, but as I search the wooded areas around the more remote lakes, I find several small clearings with structures on them, some barely the size of Penny, and easily half of them don't have driveways. There are roads vaguely adjacent to them, sure, but it's not like UPS is delivering anything to these doors.

Those are the ones that feel right.

I screenshot all the most likely options, knowing the GPS coordinates are the only way I'll find them again.

When the nurse comes in, announcing herself with a soft knock, I have four of particular interest, but any excitement I have at the development evaporates with her arrival.

"Juan, wake up." I shake his shoulder and he bolts up, disorientation written all over his face. When he registers the nurse's presence, he's instantly awake, though.

"I didn't mean to disturb you," she says, "But I wanted to let you know that we're moving Mr. Harrow to surgery now."

She must catch the fear that flashes across my face, because she quickly reassures me. "This is good. He's stabilized nicely over the past few hours, and the team want to take advantage of this window. If you want to go home and get freshened up, this would be a good time. We can of course call you if anything changes, but you have a good few hours before you're likely to hear anything. I know it can be hard, but you have to remember to take care of yourselves too."

When she's gone, Juan and I stare at each other, barely daring to breathe, never mind hope.

But like the early-morning light, it starts to seep in, slowly at first, then in a blaze.

Frank made it through the night.

He's strong enough for surgery.

He still has a chance.

We fall into each other, joy, relief, and exhaustion all wrapped up in a long, hard hug.

"I knew he was too stubborn to die," Juan says. "Not without a fight."

"Now he's got to keep fighting."

"He will," Juan says, because there's no way we're entertaining any other alternative, not right now. He taps his phone to life, and when he sees the time, he jumps. "Shit, I never called Alex about the schedule."

"You should go home," I tell him. "See your family and sort out the diner stuff. I can hold down the fort while you're gone."

Juan looks torn, but he fumbles under the edge of the sofa for his shoes. "You should come too. You heard her—there's nothing to do right now but wait. I'm sure Zoe is wondering where you are."

Even though I know Juan's dogs and Ana's unrelenting affection have probably kept Zoe from even noticing I've been gone for so long, I'm hit with a sharp pang of guilt. The only other time I've left her overnight was to film the baking show, and that was the single hardest part of that whole ordeal, murder included.

"Come on," Juan says. "You know dog snugs and a hot shower will change your life right now."

"You're not wrong."

"Seldom, if ever." He grins. "Plus you're my ride."

"Oh god, you're right, sorry." I gather up my things, not wanting to leave anything behind in case someone needs the room while we're out. "We can swing by the diner first for your car."

I text Noel an update on the way to the truck to let him know I'll be stopping by. Despite the obnoxiously early hour, he replies in seconds. *I'll make breakfast :)*

I have never been happier for his adherence to the absurd farmer schedule he keeps.

Our arrival at Juan's sends the house into a frenzy of chaos, with Ana and the dogs equally excited by the early-morning appearance. Zoe is reluctant to leave, but I'm even more reluctant to linger. Juan has enough going on here without two extra guests, and the prospect of a hot shower and breakfast is calling me from across town.

"I'll head right back," I tell him on my way out. "Don't feel rushed."

"I don't know, I think it might've been more peaceful at the hospital," Juan jokes as Ana clatters around the kitchen with Eric, but the affection is obvious.

I realize with a start that what he has here is exactly what I put in the diner pies, but he doesn't even need magic to achieve it. It's simply love and a house that contains everything that goes with it—the chaos, yes, but also the comfort, the closeness that comes from tying your life to others.

It's something that could be worth changing everything for, someday.

That sentiment follows me all the way to Noel's, burrowing into the bit of brain not occupied with Frank and Jodie and the stopping and committing of murders.

It blooms when I step into the kitchen and melt into Noel's warm embrace. What I do with Pies Before Guys is real, it's important and life altering, but this is too. Having someone care enough to make you breakfast and worry when you're gone—that matters. Lives can be saved with pies, but they can be endlessly enriched by things as small as warm toast and tea, easy conversation, and quiet nights in.

The things that make a life worth saving are the same that make it worth living.

As much as the soft part of me wants to wallow with these fuzzy feelings in Noel's house all day, I don't have that luxury. Not yet.

"You're sure you don't mind keeping Zoe?" I ask after I'm showered and dressed in the clothes Melly packed. "I know Fridays get busy, and I'm not sure when I'll be back."

"Course not. She's the best barback around." He grins and ruffles her ears. "Okay, maybe she's not great at cleaning, but she excels at customer satisfaction. People like having her around." He plants a kiss on my forehead. "I know there are plenty of other worries in there, but you don't have to worry about us."

I wrap my arms around his waist. "You know I hate leaving her."

"And I also know she'll be fine." He kisses my head again. "Go take care of what you need to take care of. And keep me posted on how Frank does. I'm sure this next update will be a good one."

"I hope so."

I give Zoe a long cuddle before I grab my keys and kiss Noel goodbye.

I'm still tired—I'll be paying for last night's broken sleep all day—but I feel a little more human for having left the hospital for a bit.

I'm halfway down Noel's long drive when I catch him waving in my rearview mirror. I grin and wave back before realizing that he's chasing me. I brake and roll my window down.

I'm expecting another kiss, a second sweet goodbye, but instead he stops at the door and holds out my phone.

"You forgot this."

"Oh god, thank you. I would've lost my mind. I think I already am." I laugh, but he doesn't.

The screen is bright when I take the phone, a cascade of notifications that must've arrived while I was in the shower crowding the display.

Among them is a PBG banner with no preview, two missed calls, and a text from Melly with enough of it showing to explain the stony look on Noel's face.

Hey Sleeping Beauty. Call me ASAP. We need to talk.

Chapter
Forty-Three

I check the Pies Before Guys account while I drive. It's a reply from Tammy with a completed contract for her cult pie.

She needs it for Monday.

I send a confirmation, knowing that the last thing I have time for right now is a trip to Rhode Island, but I can't turn her away. Especially not if this pie can stop a cult from spreading.

Luckily, her only flavor request was *something with chocolate*, so I'll at least be able to whip something up in whatever window of downtime I find and freeze it. I'm already thinking of a rich, dark-chocolate ganache spiked with orange, a halo of candied peel for garnish. The peel won't freeze well and will have to be added last minute, but it can be prepped in advance.

Totally doable.

I check the dashboard clock, almost tempted to bang out part of it now, before heading back to the hospital. But no, I have the whole weekend. There will be more time later, once Frank is out of surgery and on the mend, and if there's one thing that shouldn't be rushed, it's murder pies.

With that at least planned, I dial Melly, switching the call to speaker and dropping the phone into my lap.

She picks up before the first ring finishes, like she's been waiting. "Where are you?" She sounds agitated, and I swear she learned phone etiquette from the movies, where no one ever says basic things like hello or goodbye.

"Heading back to the hospital. What's up?"

"Three things, and you're not going to like any of them."

I groan.

"Actually, one you should see. Are you near the diner?"

Dread fills my chest. "I can be. What is it?"

"Just get here. I'll wait." She hangs up without explaining more, and I curse her. This is not the kind of drama I need, not right now.

I pull around the back of the diner, surprised to find the lot full of staff cars. Even Juan's green BMW is already back in its spot.

I assume this is why I'm here, to help get things moving before going back to the hospital, but I don't get why Melly would be the one to summon me.

I spot her leaning against her bike, facing Penny, and I pull up along the back of the RV.

She flicks her head around at the sound, but any welcome I expected to see on her face is covered by a mask of rage.

Once again, I find my body knowing the truth before my brain, somehow comprehending the worst of things I don't want to acknowledge.

Melly watches me come toward her, and her chin tips in the direction of Penny's door.

The door I hadn't noticed was hanging ajar on loose hinges when I dropped Juan off in the early light of dawn.

"You broke my door?" For some reason, the sight of it makes me want to cry. Melly seemed like an angel last night, bearing the comforts of home, but now I just have one more thing I need to take care of. I swallow the frustration and exhaustion, reminding myself that she meant well and that matters. "It's fine. I can get it fixed."

She shakes her head, face stony. "Not me."

And there it is, the tremble in my legs that told me this was bad as soon as I got out of the truck.

Melly inclines her head in a silent invitation to enter my own home.

It's suddenly the very last thing I want to do.

The door is even worse up close. The lock I assumed Melly had picked has been warped by brute force, wide silver gouges scarring the pink paint around it.

It hasn't been picked, it's been popped.

Violently.

I pull the door carefully, unsure if the bent hinges will hold, but they do.

The echoing cacophony of the diner's kitchen and the morning birdsong are drowned out by the rush of blood in my ears as I climb inside.

My things are strewn everywhere, as if a giant picked Penny up and gave her a good shake before tossing her aside.

Aprons and dishcloths are thrown across the floor, pans piled in haphazard cairns before the gaping mouths of cabinets. Even my food has been rifled through. A broken bottle of saffron sits in a heap, the vibrant little threads irreparably mingled with sparkling shards of glass beside my laptop.

Something lodges in my throat, a scream or a sob, something so big it can't get out.

My limbs shake with each step, but I have to see the rest.

The bedroom is every bit as bad. Discarded dresses pool like deflated ghosts at the foot of the bed, half buried by a tangle of sheets. Every cubby that can be opened has been, their contents spilled, and amid the wreckage I find a crumpled envelope. The achingly familiar handwriting is enough to take my knees out, and I sink down, carefully smoothing it out before realizing it's been opened and the letter isn't there.

Panic seizes me, hands shooting out to sift through the detritus. It has to be here. There's no reason for anyone to take it. It has to be, it has to be, it has to be.

I don't know how long Melly has been watching me or that I'm even saying those words out loud until she asks, "What is it? I'll help you look."

"The letter," I gasp. "From my mom, when she gave me Penny. It has to be here."

"Okay, we'll find it." She crouches down slowly, like I'm a wild animal she's worried about spooking, and starts going through the mess, making piles as she goes.

When she finds it, she doesn't make a fuss and doesn't try to read it.

She simply hands it over and, in doing so, gives me back my ability to breathe.

The paper is wrinkled but intact. It's all that matters. I slide it back into the envelope, then tuck it into the nightstand. The rest can be dealt with later.

"Okay," Melly says. "I know this kind of thing would usually call for tea, but I don't even know where it is in this mess."

"It's fine." But that's obviously not true. Nothing is fine. The search for the letter temporarily hijacked my brain, but now that I can focus, I realize what else I haven't seen.

The map.

The iPad.

"This was Troy." The realization punches me in the chest. "He must've been after the iPad."

"Yeah, about that," Melly says. There's not quite a spark in her eye, but there's a definite gleam that gets my attention.

"What about that?"

"That's the rest of what I need to tell you."

But she doesn't tell me. Not right away.

She surveys the wreckage of the RV, then seems to decide something. "You need to get back to the hospital, right? We can talk and drive."

She's right, I do need to get back. At least someone does, and when I stick my head into the diner, it looks like I'll have an easier time getting away than Juan.

"As soon as Alex gets here, I'll be over," he promises, flipping two fat slices of French toast sizzling on the flat-top.

"You don't have to do this," I tell him. "No one would blame you for closing."

"Frank would. I don't want him to wake up to things falling apart."

The way he says it, I'm not sure if he means the diner or himself, but after my little meltdown in the RV, I know better than to ask.

Instead, I pull him into a quick hug. "He's lucky to have you. I'll call if there's updates."

"You better."

In the truck, I find myself equal parts impatient and worried to hear what Melly has to say. "The fact that you're being so cagey isn't exactly inspiring faith."

"Not cagey," she says, propping one foot on the dash. "Thinking of how to best lay this out. Your plate is kind of heaped as it is."

"Understatement."

"Right. So, good news first." She flips open her messenger back and pulls the iPad out like it's a magician's rabbit. "Took it when I was getting you clothes last night."

"And the map?"

Disappointment darkens her eyes. "That I didn't take. Only a picture of it."

Anxiety curdles in my stomach. "So he saw it. And presumably has it."

"And knows we're onto him," she confirms. "For the timeline—Troy's break-in occurred after I came to see you, so late. I found your door open this morning when I came to return the iPad."

"I wonder why last night. Because I was gone?"

Melly purses her lips. "Maybe, but I think it's more than that. I'm not sure if he has a way of knowing we've been watching or if he just sees the iPad as a potential loose end because the security app is installed on it, but I don't think the timing was a coincidence."

"What do you mean?"

"I figured I'd take the iPad, check in on Jodie, right?" Her foot bounces on the dash. "And something's wrong. I watched the footage back, and she's been on the bathroom floor for hours. I checked while I was waiting for you, and she's still there."

"Morning sickness?"

"I don't think so." The beat of her agitated foot increases. "She's not moving."

The truck jerks when I turn to look at her, the steering wheel accidentally following my gaze, and I correct hard. "She's not moving? For how long?"

"Too long. Hours. I played it back, and yeah, the morning sickness has still been a thing, but the last time she went in there, she fell. Not tripped, more like dropped."

"Did she hit her head?"

"On the floor, yeah, but I can't see blood."

Possibilities tumble through my mind. A complication with the pregnancy, weakness from the hunger strike, something completely unrelated. We have no way of knowing, not from here.

"That's not the worst part," Melly says.

My lungs freeze, trapping my breath. What can be worse than all of this already?

"I went back through some of the footage at Troy's house too. Just to be nosy. And he's been . . . shopping."

"Shopping?"

"He has stuff on the table. Tarps. Some cleaning stuff. Duct tape. A whole murder cleanup starter kit."

"Son of a bitch." I follow the signs for the hospital, barely aware of the drive at all. "That doesn't make sense, though. She said he wanted the baby, the heir to his name. He wouldn't kill her while she's pregnant."

"He might if she loses the baby."

God, she's right. She's absolutely right.

On the dashboard, her foot stills. "Or if she's already dead—if she doesn't get back up off that floor—he still needs to hide her body. She's kidnapped and malnourished, and he's been beating her for years. There would be evidence of that in an autopsy. He can't let that be discovered."

"We have to find her. Now."

Chapter
Forty-Four

At the hospital, I pull right up to the main entrance and leave the engine running. Melly raises an eyebrow when I hop out.

"I need my laptop."

Melly slides across the bench seat. "On it. Anything else?"

"Just that for now. I'm going to search property records for the more likely options, see if we can zero in on the best place to start."

Had Troy known what I could access with that computer, there's no way he would've left it behind, but I'm grateful he did.

It's going to be the thing that sinks him.

"Be back in a flash," Melly promises.

I head inside, wondering exactly how much more the universe can possibly throw at me before instantly squashing the speculation. The last thing I need to do is jinx myself.

Upstairs, I check in with the nurses' station to let them know I'm back.

The nurse on duty tells me Frank's still in surgery but that they should be wrapping up soon.

"And everything is okay?" I ask.

She gives me a sympathetic smile. "I'm afraid I don't know more than what I've told you. The doctor will be out as soon as they move him to recovery, though, so feel free to have a seat."

I do as I'm told, although I feel perilously adrift in the empty waiting room, like I'm stuck in limbo.

Or purgatory.

Luckily, Melly is good to her word and arrives with the laptop in record time.

"And tea," she says, handing me a takeout cup with a monocled dinosaur printed on the cardboard collar that Ana would adore. "Maybe not as fancy as you're used to, but it's from Tea Rex, so it's not trash."

I take a sip, closing my eyes as the malty richness of Yunnan coats my tongue. "It's perfect, thank you."

"It's also a bribe," she admits. "Can I keep your truck for while? I need to take care of something, and I don't want to waste time waiting for a bus."

"Yeah, no problem. I'm here for a while anyway."

"Cool." She turns to go, then stops. "Good luck. With the search and, you know, with Frank."

"Luck would be nice," I agree.

When she's gone, I settle into a corner chair and get to work.

The databases I pay for may be the same ones private investigators use, but thinking that makes me a skip tracer is like thinking possession of a cookbook could make Melly a chef. I'm good at using the tools I have for the specific job I do, but this is new territory.

Luckily, you can do anything with the internet and perseverance these days, and I'm not starting from scratch.

I know Troy took Jodie somewhere he's comfortable. He had the time to install cameras and cover the windows. That means it's a property he has full access to, which means there will be a record of it.

Somewhere.

I'm so immersed in the search that I don't notice Juan come in until he sits down.

"Any news?" he asks.

"When I got here, they said he was in surgery still, but finishing up." I check the time on my laptop and realize that was almost two hours ago. "It should be soon."

He nods and cranes his head to look at my screen. "Whatcha working on?"

"Research project." It's not a lie, but it's nowhere near the truth either.

"Genealogy?"

"Something like that."

"Eric was into that for a while. I think he was hoping to find a celebrity in there somewhere." He smiles wryly and settles back in his chair. "Closest he got was a distant cousin who survived the *Titanic*."

"Better than finding out you're related to Mussolini or something." Relieved that he's not overly interested in my search, I continue scrolling as I speak.

"True. I bet Frank was, though."

That's enough to snag my attention. "What? Why?"

Juan shrugs. "Maybe not Mussolini, but something scandalous. There has to be a reason he never talks about his family."

"I thought he didn't have one."

"Everyone has family, at some point."

I think of all the pies I've delivered for fathers and husbands over the years, how that family label can warp beneath the weight of violence and hate. "Maybe he has a reason for forgetting them."

"Maybe. Can't imagine it, though. With Ana?" He shakes his head. "We don't pretend she's not adopted, and she understands that we chose her specifically because we wanted her in our lives, but how long will that be good enough? Someday she's going to wonder why her birth parents didn't keep her, and I have no idea what I'm going to say, because no part of me can even imagine doing what they did, not ever."

My heart contracts, but I understand. He's right to be concerned. Adoption, even in circumstances as great as theirs, doesn't erase the trauma of being abandoned in the first place. "Families are complicated."

"But worth it."

"I'm going to remind you of that next time Ana's sugared up and doing pterodactyl impressions in the kitchen."

He laughs. "You better." As soon as he says it, the smile drops from his face and he abruptly stands. Startled, I close my laptop and follow his gaze.

I'm on my feet before I fully register the doctor coming toward us. I have the impression of a white coat and measured stride, but I don't want to look at her face. I don't want to risk seeing there what I fear most.

My hand finds Juan's already reaching.

"Daisy, Juan, good morning," she says. She sounds as tired as I feel.

"How is he?" Juan asks.

"Well, he's in recovery and coming around," she says, and there's a hint of lightness to her voice that finally lets me see her face.

She's tired, yes, but there's satisfaction there too.

Hope flutters in my chest.

"He won't be heading home anytime soon," she says, "I think we're out of the woods. He'll need to take it very easy for a while, and we're going to keep him here to make sure he does precisely that, but his overall prognosis looks good. He's very lucky."

Relief threatens to take my legs out, and I feel Juan's arm press into mine.

"He's going to be the worst patient." I laugh. "I'm so sorry."

The doctor smiles. "Trust me, our staff has seen it all. We'll just be glad to get him back on his feet."

"As soon as he is, he'll be trying to leave," Juan says.

"Well, we'll be keeping him in ICU for another day or so, but as long as he remains stable, we'll move him to a regular room, where he can have all the company he needs to stay entertained." Her expression sobers. "I do want to be clear. Even though the surgery was a success, he does have a long road ahead. He's not going to wake up and walk back into his old life, not at his age. It's going to take time, and it's important to manage expectations."

We both nod, but what she's saying doesn't matter. Not right now.

Frank is alive and on the mend.

"Is he awake? Can we see him?" I ask.

"He will be, and yes, briefly, eventually," she says. "He's going to be very groggy and won't be up for much, but once he's back in his room, the nurses will let you know."

"Thank you so much." My throat tightens with gratitude, and the urge to hug this woman is nearly overwhelming. But I refrain, barely.

However, what I will be doing, if the dust ever settles on the chaos that is currently my life, is making sure this unit has a never-ending supply of thank-you pies.

It's the least I can do.

* * *

The wait to see Frank is almost the hardest one yet, because we know it's so close.

We call the diner together to spread the news, and the resulting cheers echo through the waiting room. It takes a lot of backpedaling to convince everyone to stay put, that visitation is limited for now.

I text Noel and Melly to let them know things are looking up, and when Juan steps away for a longer call with Eric and Ana, I get back to work.

The only property records I can find in Troy's name are for the house he's living in, which means he either has the cabin under a fake name—possibly a company—or it isn't his.

I remember his mother grew up in New England and enter her into the search, but every piece of property she's legally attached to is in Colorado, which I guess makes sense if she left for college. What eighteen-year-old would have a New England fishing cabin in their name?

It takes a bit more digging, but I find Troy's grandparents and something electric buzzes through me, a whisper that this is the right path.

When he was alive, Walter Greene, Troy's grandfather, purchased multiple properties across Massachusetts, all of it farmland that has since been passed down to Patrick—Tommy's father and Troy's uncle.

It's enough to make me want to sketch out a quick family tree to keep track of who's who. Turns out this research isn't so far from genealogy after all.

I switch to the grandmother next, and my heart punches when I see what comes up. Like her son, Alice Greene has inherited property.

In Vermont.

I plug it into the map, and holy shit, yes, there's a lake nearby.

I pull up the details, hope deflating. It's an undeveloped parcel, a narrow triangle of mostly woodland, the narrow point barely reaching the waterfront.

My disappointment doesn't have a chance to take hold, though, because Juan returns, a smiling nurse at his heels.

"He's awake."

Chapter Forty-Five

T he nurse explains the rules as she leads us to Frank's room, warning us that he's going to tire very easily and that we shouldn't
expect miracles quite yet, but the words float by like dandelion fluff.

He's awake.

That's all that matters.

But when we reach his room, I see I was wrong. I should've lis-
tened. She was trying to prepare us, and I let my joy drown her out.

Stupid, stupid joy.

I thought Frank looked bad when he was in the coma.

This is worse.

"Is he okay?" I ask, frozen at the door.

Frank is propped up in the bed, head slumped to the side. Wires
snake out from the covers like spider legs, and that's still not the
worst part.

The worst part is the open neck of his hospital gown, the gaping
fabric revealing an edge of white bandage secured to a sunken chest.

It's like seeing him naked somehow.

"He's doing very well," the nurse assures us.

From the bed is a stirring, and although his eyes don't open right
away, Frank's head straightens. "It's my heart ain't working, not my
hearing. Stop talking like I ain't here."

The gruff grumble is so familiar, so comforting, that tears fill my eyes, and it doesn't matter how frail he looks or how much he's going to hate being so vulnerable.

He's alive.

Something between a sob and a laugh bubbles up, and I tumble into the room. Frank's eyes open, and it takes a moment for him to focus, but when he does, something very near a smile lights his face.

Just for a second.

I take his hand, the skin stretched paper thin over knobby bones. "I'm so glad you're okay."

He waves me off with his free hand. "Bunch of nonsense."

"It's not nonsense. You almost died."

"Could've used the break." Then, clocking Juan, he huffs. "What is this, my goddamn funeral? Everyone coming to pay their respects for once?"

Juan's grin isn't dimmed at all by this badgering. "Good to see you, boss."

"Don't you have a job to be doing?"

"Everything's covered and running like clockwork," he promises. "Nothing to worry about except getting better."

Franks scoffs, but it quickly turns into a coughing fit. I pour him a cup of water from the plastic jug on the table and help him sip. "Goddamn throat," he mutters. "Worse than having my chest pried open, I swear. Don't ever get surgery. It's like they intubate with razor blades."

I laugh. "I'll try to avoid open heart surgery for the time being. And don't worry about the diner. Juan's right. We have everything under control."

"Well, even you lot should be able to handle things for the weekend. Get back to normal on Monday."

Juan and I exchange a look.

"I'm not sure they're letting you go quite so soon," I say carefully, wishing the nurse were still here to back me up with more specific info.

"They'll let me go when I'm good and goddamn ready to go," Franks says, but there's already a fading to his bluster.

"We can figure that out later," Juan says. "Why don't you try to get some more rest?"

"Don't need more rest," he says, but it's only to be contrary. His eyelids are already drooping.

I pat his hand. "We'll be back soon. If there's anything you need, let us know. The nurses can get us."

He nods vaguely and lifts a hand, the normally dismissive gesture barely a flutter.

But he's trying.

We check in with the nurses on the way out, and they assure us he'll be sleeping for most of the day. He might be cranky, but his body can't deny the wringer it's been through.

We hover at the waiting room, neither of us sitting.

"You think it's okay to leave?" Juan asks. "I don't want to, but I feel like I'd be more useful back at the diner than keeping vigil now that things are looking up."

"You know it's what he'd want anyway," I assure him. "They'll call us if anything changes, but you saw him. He's weak, but he's still Frank. He's going to have the fastest recovery in the history of this hospital thanks to spite alone."

"You're right." Juan exhales like it's the first full breath he's taken since this began. "Okay. I'll hit the diner, come back later. Maybe let Ana say hi."

"They'd both like that." We head to the elevator together. "I'm going to try to catch up on some Pie Girl stuff, then I'll swing by and sort out diner pies."

"I can double-check, but I think we still have a few in the freezer. I can toss them in the oven if you have other things to do."

"Actually, that'd be great," I admit. Right now, anything I can delegate feels like a lifeline.

As the elevator delivers us to the ground floor and we step out into the bright sun, I groan.

"What?" Juan asks.

"I need one more favor. Melly has my truck."

He laughs. "No problem. It's not like we aren't heading in the same direction anyway."

* * *

My truck is already at the diner when we get there, parked in front of Penny.

It's locked, and more importantly, so is the RV.

I run a hand down the door, the scratches catching at my fingers, but the handle is no longer bent at such an awful angle, and the door sits flush on the hinges.

Maybe it wasn't quite as bad as it seemed earlier.

I find the keys in the kitchen, but I don't linger. I know I should go get Zoe, but first I need to make the RV habitable again.

I unlock the door carefully, worried that one wrong move will return it to its battered state, but it swings open without a creak.

I climb the stairs, already dreading the task ahead on top of all the other things I need to do. Then it hits me.

A smell.

Lemon, but not the fresh kind.

Disinfectant.

It takes a minute to register what I'm seeing, or rather, not seeing.

The mess is gone.

Completely.

The counter is clear of broken glass, the expensive saffron wiped away. Pots and pans have returned to their spots behind closed doors, and my drawers no longer spill their contents across the floor.

The bedroom is equally straightened, the piles Melly created tucked away, the dresses out of sight. Even the bed is made.

I sink onto it in stunned silence, gratitude closing around my throat like the warmest scarf.

I pull out my phone, not even knowing how to begin thanking Melly for this. In the end, I text, because I don't trust my voice to speak.

This is amazing. Thank you.

Her reply dots bounce into action. *Figured you had enough to do. Any updates?*

And just like that, we pass over it without fanfare. Which is fine, because she's right. I have work to do.

Getting there, I reply.

Not having to clean the RV means I can pick up right where I left off at the hospital. The relevant tabs are still open on my laptop, and I start a new search.

The genealogy angle feels right, but I've already gone through Troy's parents and grandparents. He doesn't have siblings.

But he does have a cousin.

I run Tommy through and find records of his house and some of the Greene Farm land. All of it's in Turnbridge, though, and there's nothing that could be a cabin.

Okay. Not Tommy, then.

I try his father, Troy's uncle. I knew about the Greene Farm properties but underestimated exactly how many there are. They take a while to sift through, but buried among all that farmland is a single outlier.

An undeveloped parcel of land.

In Vermont.

Adjacent to the one in Alice Greene's name.

My heart cannons against my ribs.

This can't be a coincidence.

I pull the address up on the satellite map and am rewarded with a bird's-eye view of verdant treetops. I zoom in, but the dense forest gives nothing away. I pull back, widening the view to include the large, kidney-shaped lake. Most of it is surrounded by woodland, but if I go the long way across, there's a sandy shore at the end, a boat launch, and a handful of houses.

It's populated, but not heavily. And not at all on the side where the Greene property is.

But there's no cabin.

At least not that I can see.

One thing I've learned in all the years I've been making murder pies is that people are really good at hiding the truth. But they're not perfect.

Nothing is, not even technology.

I should've realized it right away, but I'm not looking at a live map. The trees are in full bloom, vibrant green canopying the ground below. If the image were live, those trees would be a blaze of autumn color. In another month, they would be bare. They wouldn't hide the things beneath them.

I pull up the number for Suffolk, Vermont's town hall. This would be easier with a pie, but that doesn't mean it's impossible.

While the phone rings, I think of Giselle at the mayor's office, her bright and friendly manner, and focus on channeling her energy.

It takes a few passes, but I'm connected to the records office.

"Hello," I say. "I was wondering if you could give me some information about a property."

Chapter
Forty-Six

" I have a lead. A good one."

"Seriously?" Melly asks, a guarded note floating through the phone that I can't fault her for.

I barely believe the words myself, but my body buzzes with the possibility that this may finally be over.

"It's not guaranteed. It's not like I can digitally peek in windows or anything, but there's a property in Vermont. When it was bought by the Greenes, it was undeveloped. It shows up as nothing but woodland on the map, but there were building permits pulled on it two years ago. This could be it." There's silence on the other end, and I give her a minute to let the news sink in. I certainly needed it.

Finally, she lets out an impressed whistle. "Nicely done, Sherlock, nicely done."

I grin. I can't help it. It's not a victory yet, but it's the closest thing we've had. "So what's your weekend look like?"

She scoffs. "Saving damsels in distress with you. Obviously."

"Just checking."

"Like I'm letting you do this on your own." There's a beat, and when she comes back, her voice sobers. "This is good. The timing. Because I think we have a problem."

276

My elation turns to ice with that single sentence. "What do you mean?"

"The shit on Troy's table is gone. All of it. The murder cleanup kit."

"Doesn't mean anything," I say, trying to convince myself as much as her. "He might've put it away."

"No. He bagged it and took it out to the truck."

"When?"

"This morning. I checked both feeds after I straightened up the RV. But we still have a head start. He came back in and got dressed for work. The truck is still in the garage."

"And you're only telling me this now?"

"It wouldn't have changed anything," she says. "You had the world on your plate already. What good would a countdown clock be on top of that?"

She's right, but knowing that doesn't make me feel any better. Had she told me the moment she discovered it, it might even have derailed my search.

But still.

"There is good news," Melly says. "He's on shift until eight tonight."

"How you know?"

I can hear the smirk across the line. "I might've called Tommy, told him how great I thought their story was, that I'd love to continue the conversation. Maybe over drinks, maybe with the two of them? There was shit implied. It was gross, but it was effective. He said they both got off at eight and suggested a place."

I let out an appreciative huff. "That was smart, calling him rather than Troy. If Troy's planning to go up there with that kit, he's bound to be amped up. He might've gotten suspicious."

"Not an amateur," Melly says, the pride evident in her singsong.

"No, you're not," I agree. "Okay. And what about Jodie?"

She sobers. "Same. She's still in the bathroom, but there's been movement. Very slight, but she's still alive."

I breathe a sigh of relief. "Okay. I have two things I need to take care of before we leave, but that'll still put us well ahead of Troy if he's going up after work. I only need an hour or so."

"Then we be heroes."

"Then we be heroes."

* * *

The first task is the easiest.

I bake.

The best thing about pie is that there's one for every occasion. They can be as simple or as complicated as you like, but at the end of the day, pie is pie.

These ones are simple.

They have to be.

I keep the ingredients basic and almost identical, so I only have to pull supplies once.

The first pie is for Tammy. I crush the gingerbread cookies by hand, each snap and break multiplying the magic until every crumb is charged. I stir in melted butter, channeling everything I can that will get Caleb Werner to see the error of his culty ways, then press it into a shallow disposable tin. A mountain of dark chocolate gets drowned in steaming cream, and while the heat works its magic, I work more of my own, adding in the zest of two oranges as the final step. The zing of citrus will pair nicely with the warmly spiced ginger crust, even if the candied peel has to wait.

The next pie follows the same process, with very different magic. Because while there's a part of me that thinks Caleb the Cultist just might be redeemable, Troy Sullivan is not.

I crack each chunk of gingerbread like they're his bones, doubling all the rage and violence he's ever directed at others. The plea to stop is in there, that most fundamental part of a murder pie, but it will feel like a scream when he swallows it. I mix the butter in with bare hands, squeezing handfuls of moist crumbs into grenades.

I want him to choke on the truth of who he is.

Each shard of chocolate I slice from the block gets cut with fury singing through the knife blade. Unbridled power pours from my heart along with the simmering cream, and I force myself to stir with slow, deliberate strokes, each one folding the magic in a little deeper.

He will stop.

There will be no other option for him.

I add the nuts last, toasted pecans that I crush in clenched fists before sprinkling them across the finished pie.

They're the only element that doesn't get any murder magic. Instead, every handful is suffused with the aching truth of exactly who we are, Troy and I. Each morsel harbors the inescapable clarity of what I can do and why.

Troy will not go gently into that good pie coma.

No. He will know exactly who it is he lost to.

I scatter the nuts across the surface of the finished pie with a flourish, watching as they settle into the thick grave of ganache.

It's a simple pie.

Nothing fancy.

But it'll do.

Chapter
Forty-Seven

With both pies tucked in the freezer, it's time to tackle the second item on my list.

Hollow Hill is quiet when I get there, the cidery lot mostly empty. Fridays are always busy, but not until the after-work crowd is set free, so at least that's in my favor.

I park, and the thud of my door is enough to summon Zoe. She bounds out of the storeroom, tongue lolling as she barrels into my legs.

"Hey, good girl." I drop down and give her a proper snuggle that doesn't release the tightness wrapping around my chest.

Noel comes out after her, hefting a box of apples for the older Black lady at his side. He grins when sees me, a genuine flash of warmth that floods me with relief. If he was upset about the text from Melly this morning, it seems to have passed as he's gotten about his day.

He takes his time walking his customer to her car, carefully storing the apples in the trunk. I can hear him tell her to make sure she gets help unloading, but she waves him off with a mischievous chuckle.

"I'm a lot stronger than I look," she says.

"Most women are," he agrees.

"Smart boy."

"On occasion." He sends her off with thanks and a request to hear how her sauce comes out, then turns to me. "This is a nice surprise."

I try not to wince, because I know it won't be for long. "I was hoping I could ask a favor. Two, actually." His smile falters a fraction, and I steel myself. The last thing I want to do is upset him, but I need his help. "First, do you mind if Zoe stays with you tonight? I'm sure Juan could take her if it's a problem, but—"

"Of course she can stay," he says. "But it doesn't sound like you're joining her, so what's going on?"

"I have a lead. On the Jodie case. I need to check it out, and I don't know when I'll get back. Late, though."

"You have a lead," he says slowly.

I nod. "A good one."

He tilts his head a fraction, enough to reveal the tightness in his jaw. "Is this safe?"

"It's safer than leaving her there."

"And you're going alone?"

"Melly's coming."

He chews his lip, nods once. "Right." An electric silence passes, and then he asks, "What's the second favor?"

I don't even want to ask now, not with the air so charged between us, but Tammy is counting on me to save her daughter as much as I'm counting on saving Jodie. "I have a pie delivery. On Monday. If something happens and I don't make it back in time, would you deliver it? Nothing else, just drop it off and go."

"If something happens? Something like what? What is it that could possibly hold you up for an entire weekend?" He's not shouting, but there's a frantic edge to the questions that makes it even worse.

"I don't know, it's just in case. I can't let this woman down. She's trying to stop a cult. And she actually might. It's early enough that the pie could work before anyone gets hurt." It seems important that he understand it's not a guaranteed murder pie this time but one with real potential to stop something before death is on the table.

The distinction doesn't seem to matter. He runs both hands through his floppy hair and down his face. He hides there for a minute, long enough for my stomach to lace into knots. When he sighs, they tighten.

"So let me get this straight. Your 'good lead' might get you, what, killed, arrested, or otherwise incapacitated to the point where I need to deliver a murder weapon."

"It's not like that."

"I think it is. If this lead is so good, why aren't you telling the cops?"

"Because I can't trust them."

"Do you understand how you sound right now?"

"Do you?" I retort, the stress in my belly turning sour. "If I call the cops with this address and they run it, they're going to realize it's been developed by, you guessed it, another cop. If you think they're not going to immediately get on the phone to him and ask what's up, you're more naïve than I thought. Cops protect their own. They cover each other for all sorts of shit."

He throws his hands up in exasperation. "Fine. But it's a different state. That makes it federal, right? Skip the cops. Call the feds."

I soften. "Noel, I can't invite the FBI into my life. You know that. They would want to know where I got my information, and if they start poking . . ." I trail off, knowing that some part of him understands this. I can see it in his face, the frustration tinged with something more grudging.

He sighs and rubs his head again. "So, what, you and Melly are just going to do a job that's apparently beyond the scope of the cops and FBI?"

"In this case, yes."

"Why is she even involved?" The vehemence of the question seems to startle him as much as me.

"Are you mad that I'm going or mad that I'm going with her?"

"Both! None of this is right. I can't believe you even trust her after what she did to you. I don't think it's good how she's continued to insinuate herself into your life. She's reckless, and now you're being reckless too."

"I'm not being reckless."

"You are, though." His eyes shine with unvoiced fear. "You could call the cops anonymously, hand this over to the professionals. You're choosing not to."

"I have to do this. She's in the cabin because of me." I hold up a hand to forestall any protest on semantics. "I got her into this mess; I have to be the one to get her out."

"How can you leave now, though? Even for a day? Frank just got out of surgery. What if something happens?"

"The doctor said he's fine. And if something happens, they can save him. I have to save Jodie."

"This is selfish."

The accusation lands like a slap. "Maybe. But it's what has to happen."

"You can't keep putting yourself in danger for everyone else. At some point, you have to think about yourself." He shakes his head, and a wave of profound sadness washes away the frustration from his face. "Is this really the kind of life you want, that has you leaving behind the people you're supposed to love?"

"That's not fair."

"Isn't it? Because you're looking at this as a right here, right now problem. But what about the next time? And the one after that? What about five years from now?" His voice catches and he swallows hard. "Is this what you want forever?"

Fear closes around my throat, choking any reply I might have.

"Because I don't think I do," he continues hoarsely. "And I don't think it's what your mother wanted when she gave you the magic. When you told me about her and all the grandmothers' grandmothers, it was clear they embedded themselves in their lives. Their real lives. All of them. They had families and meaningful connections and used their power safely. They weren't lone wolves risking everything with it."

The grass beneath my feet seems to undulate as my blood rushes to my head. For a disorienting moment, I feel like I'm floating outside my own body.

"I don't need a lecture on my family power." The words are disturbingly calm even to my own ears, but behind them, I hear the tick of a bomb. I pat my leg. "Come on, Zo, let's go see Juan."

"Daisy, wait—" Noel says, but I keep floating toward the truck with Zoe at my heels.

"We can talk when I get back."

It's the best I can offer right now.

Or maybe ever.

Chapter
Forty-Eight

E ric is home with Ana when I drop Zoe off, apologizing for
infringing again.

"She's always welcome," he assures me, studying my face. "You're
sure everything's okay?"

"It will be."

Because it has to be.

I pop into the diner to tell Juan I'm going to be gone for the
rest of the day and ask him to let me know if anything changes
with Frank. Like Eric, he only wants to make sure everything is
okay.

"I have to help a friend with something," I say, hating how the
vagueness sounds like a lie. "I should be back late tonight."

"Don't wear yourself out," he says. "All of this is going to catch
up to you at some point."

"Trust me, I know." I toss him a cheeky grin that I'm sure doesn't
reach my eyes. "But not today."

While I wait for Melly, I debate hooking Penny up, thinking
it might be more comfortable for Jodie to have the bed on the ride
back, but in the end, I decide against it. We'll make better time without the RV, and besides, we may very well be going straight to the
nearest hospital rather than on the run.

The roar of the motorcycle announces Melly's approach, and I fetch the chocolate pecan pie from the freezer. Now that the chocolate is set, it will hold its shape at room temperature, but I throw it in an insulated bag with a couple of freezer packs anyway. I secure it in the plastic tote bungee-corded in the truck bed along with a blanket and a change of clothes.

Just in case.

Melly parks the motorcycle tight against the RV and locks her helmet away. She shrugs off an overstuffed backpack and slings it into the footwell.

"Supplies," she explains. "Food, water, first aid. The basics."

"Good."

I climb into the cab, that feeling of unreality still vibrating in my head as I turn the key.

Melly, oblivious, kicks her feet up onto the dash with a grin. "Let's be heroes."

We drive north, and I spend the first hour trying to forget everything that isn't right in front of me. Melly, unfortunately, has no intention of making it easy.

"So are you going to tell me what's crawled up your butt, or is this extended silence some residual exhaustion thing? Because I can drive if it's that."

"It's nothing," I say. "I'm good."

"At a lot of other things, maybe, but not lying."

I glance over and find her studying my face. I have no idea how long she's been doing it.

"Friendly ears," she says. "Judgment-free and everything, if that's what you need." I shoot her a look that makes her grin. "Really. I can just listen, swear."

When I don't answer, she gestures to the iPad balanced on her thighs with the cabin feed open. "You nervous about this? Because we're gonna rock."

"It's not that." Not directly, not in any way I can possibly explain.

"So?" she prods, stretching the two letters to the length of ten.

It takes me a while to gather my thoughts, but she seems to see the gears turning, because she waits.

And waits.

"I had a fight with Noel," I say, and sneak a look to gauge her reaction. Where I expect something smug, there's only patience.

She catches me and points to her face. "Judgment-free, remember?"

"Okay." I nod, the threads of discontent weaving into something cohesive. "What's bothering is me that he wasn't wrong. He wasn't right, not completely, but what he said—and has been saying—is all valid. I think I'm bothered so much because he took what was already in my head and said it out loud."

I signal and change lanes to move around a dawdling minivan.

"There's shit I worry about sometimes," I admit. "About what's wrong with me."

"Nothing's wrong with you," she says, then mimes zipping her lips. "Sorry, judgment-free. Continue."

"Well, there's a lot that isn't exactly normal." I sigh. "Like even my magic. Obviously, magic isn't normal, but for my family it is. And for some reason, mine is different. And Noel was right, the other women who had it still managed to have normal lives. They had kids and husbands and regular jobs that the magic made them exceptional at. And that was enough."

"Okay, you know what, fuck it. I can't do judgment-free." Melly loosens her seat belt so she can sit facing me, back against the door. "You realize all the shit you just described is patriarchal bullshit, right?"

"Yes and no," I say. "Like, yes, it's stereotypical, but it's also normal. The vast majority of people have families and jobs to support them. They find it fulfilling. What's wrong with me that I can't be content with that?"

"Because it'd be settling," Melly says, and this time, it is without judgment. It's simply a fact. "You don't have to live your grandmother's life in order to live a good one."

"It bothers me because I know that's true, but I also feel like it's not enough, you know?" In the rearview mirror, a blue-and-gray SUV is gaining on us, fast. State cops. "Shit."

I move back to the right lane, knuckles white on the wheel, ready for the red and blue lights to flare behind us. The SUV fills my side mirror, big as life, then blows right by us.

I exhale hard and relax my grip.

"All good," Melly says. "We're doing nothing wrong. Continue your justification of adhering to patriarchal norms."

I roll my eyes, but I can tell she's joking. "Okay, so you know you're doing that legacy project?" I expect her to question this non sequitur, but she doesn't. "I worry that I'm screwing mine up. By being selfish. Because the magic is my legacy, and if I opt out of the patriarchal norm of having kids, then it ends with me. Is that my choice to make?"

"Yes, you absolutely have a choice about that. No one gets to make that decision for you, not even your fairy godmothers."

I continue like she hasn't spoken. "But the other side is, what if I did continue the legacy—whether out of obligation or desire or whatever—and the magic warps again? What if it gets worse? Because it's one thing to do what I do the way I do it, with the boundaries and the rules and the get-out-of-death-free card I bake into every murder pie, but what happens if I put this power into someone without that control? Like a proper psychopath. Is that risk worth continuing the legacy? Would that even still *be* the legacy?"

Melly is silent for a good mile, then says, "You're overcomplicating it."

"That makes me feel so much better, thanks."

"No, seriously," she says, and her voice is, shockingly, quite serious. "This is simple. Do you want kids? Yes or no?"

"It—"

"No, no hypotheticals or justifications. Factor in nothing beyond the existence of offspring. Is that something you want?"

I don't even have to think about the answer. "No, I don't. I like kids—Ana's awesome—but I don't want one. And maybe it is selfish, I don't know." I gesture at the highway stretched out before us. "But I couldn't do this with a kid. I don't think I could do Pies Before Guys at all, not if I had to worry about a kid being motherless if I ever got caught or had a target come after me. And I don't think I can give this up. Not for anything."

"There you go," Melly says. "You don't have to have kids to pass on your legacy. You do that every time you make a pie that saves a life. Those women are your legacy. They get to live and fill the world with their influence, and then their kids get to and their kids, and then it's kids and legacies all the way down."

I laugh. "That was almost profound."

"Almost," she agrees with a grin, then sobers. "So what's this all mean for you and farm boy?"

I shoot a look at her, wondering if the question is as sincere as it sounds.

She shakes her head. "Not angling, I swear." She stretches her feet back up onto the dash. "I want you to be happy. If it's with him, great. I'm happy having this." She shrugs and settles the iPad back on her legs, tapping it back to life. "But if he keeps being the reason you're all stressed out, then I might have to kick his ass."

I snort. "It's not his fault, really. This is all stuff that's been bothering me—it just sort of came to a head."

"The fuck?" she mutters, but it isn't directed at me. She jabs harder at the screen in her lap. "Oh, come one. No, no, no."

My breath catches. "What's wrong?"

Melly's eyes are wide. "It's gone. The cabin feed is gone. The cameras aren't linked to the account at all anymore. We have no access."

I take a steadying breath. "That's okay. We know where we're going. We don't need the feed."

She shakes her head, her mouth a grim line. "That's not it. Troy already left his house. In regular clothes. In the truck."

"What? Why? I thought he was working until eight?"

"Apparently not anymore."

Chapter
Forty-Nine

I check the rearview, knowing it's impossible that he'd be on our tail already but feeling him there all the same.

I curse each minute I spent baking and arguing with Noel when I should've been driving.

I curse my little plan to wait, to be the one Troy found inside that cabin instead of Jodie. All I had to do today was get her out. Fuck the pie. Vengeance keeps and would've been every bit as satisfying served later.

I curse every decision that led to this, from my initial reaction to her request to the amount of time I spent finding her.

"What's our head start?" I ask.

She scrolls back through Troy's feed to the moment his truck backed out of the garage. "Forty minutes."

"Shit."

I'm already doing seventy-five to stay with the flow of traffic, but I push it to eighty, getting close to the Honda in front of us.

It moves over.

"Easy," Melly says. "We can't get pulled over."

"We can't lose our lead either."

"We have enough," she says. "And we technically don't know that he's even following us."

"He cut the feed and packed his kill kit. Where do you think he's going?"

"On the plus side, he's not going to see us on the cameras. We have that going for us."

It's a small win, but not enough to silence the bomb ticking in my brain. "He doesn't want a record of what's going to happen. You said she moved, that she's definitely alive, right?"

"Yeah, but it was subtle. Like a shift of weight, that's it."

Brake lights flare ahead of us, and I slow, adding traffic to my list of curses. "Could he have missed it? I mean, if he thinks she's already dead, why would he bother leaving work early?"

"No idea," Melly says. "Maybe he saw it and wants to try to save her—or the baby—or maybe he didn't, thinks she's dead, and is panicking. It's one thing to kidnap your girlfriend, it's another thing to kill her. It could be either. Schroedinger's crime scene."

The speedometer drops to forty, then twenty-five, as traffic snarls around us, and I crane my head, trying to see what's holding us up.

"GPS says we're looking at a ten-minute slowdown at the next exit," Melly says, showing me the app. "Not worth it to reroute."

I stick to the left lane, but it takes everything I have not to use the shoulder.

"Huh." Melly taps the iPad, and I glance over as she moves the slider across Troy's feed, rewinding his life in a blur. She lets a portion of the garage interior play and pauses. "We might have a problem."

"Another one?"

"Watch the road," she says, but lifts the iPad into my line of sight. Troy is in the truck, arm outstretched toward the windshield, something long in his hand.

"What am I looking at?"

"I think that's a light bar."

And just like that, the safety of our lead goes out the window.

We may be ahead of him, but if he can use that to get around traffic and, more important, traffic laws, we have no way of predicting how quickly he's gaining on us.

If we hit the wrong traffic or take the wrong route, he could even beat us.

And without the camera feed, we won't even know until we get there.

*　*　*

Traffic picks up, the road opening out before us as the sun begins its descent, the specter of Troy chasing us all the while. Every black pickup is a potential threat, every siren a sign we're too slow.

It's worse when we get off the highway and have to surrender higher speeds to the winding back roads. I curse my truck for not being something smaller, something agile that could dart around these curves in a way my rambling truck simply can't.

Given the growing list of curses today, it's a good thing for everyone that my magic works only under very specific parameters.

"How much longer?"

Melly checks the GPS. "Fifteen minutes."

Something stirs, the thing I haven't wanted to acknowledge for the past two and a half hours. "What if I'm wrong? What if this isn't the right place?"

"It has to be," she answers without a second's hesitation. "It doesn't make sense that he'd use some random shack when he already has one in the family. If nothing else, it's safer. Imagine someone stumbling onto the kidnapped woman you stashed on their property? Can't risk that. This will be the place."

We pass the next ten minutes in silence punctuated only by cheery directions from the GPS.

Suffolk is the kind of town the world forgets, a no-stoplight little place with more train tracks than businesses. We pass a post office and a rickety gas station that's straight out of a horror movie, its single pump lit by an overhead fluorescent, the storefront barely more than a pile of peeling boards held together by decades of repainting and luck.

An empty rocking chair sways gently by the door, and I'm glad we filled up back in Bethel.

We continue by, the tiny center of town giving way to rural wilds, and the GPS chirps its final command. *"In four hundred feet, turn left onto Access Lane B. Your destination will be on the right."*

I slow and turn onto a rutted dirt road. The GPS dings, telling us we've arrived.

My heart hammers at my throat, the wings of panic beginning to brush my back. I bring the truck to a crawl. "This isn't right. There's nothing here."

"Including Troy, so that's a plus. Just stop for a sec."

I park, letting the headlights slice through the trees while Melly toggles between the GPS app and the plot diagram the woman from the town hall emailed after our conversation.

"No, this is right. Look." She points to the blue GPS dot showing our location and the corresponding spot on the diagram, then looks at the woods around us. "There has to be a path or something. Come on."

"Wait." I put the truck in reverse, executing a crude three-point turn that leaves us facing the way we came. I take the keys but leave the doors unlocked. I want as few things as possible slowing us down on our way out of here.

"Smart," Melly notes, swinging her backpack over her shoulders. I leave the pie behind. If there's time to lay the trap, I'll fetch it later, but Troy could be here any minute, and we need to focus on getting Jodie out.

Or rather, first, on finding her.

I had never hiked a day in my life until Troy came into my orbit, and now here I am, facing my second one.

In the dark.

If I hadn't already made his pie, I would have added this to the list of reasons he deserves it.

The sun isn't fully down, but this far from any light pollution and under the cover of trees, it might as well be.

We walk the edge of the road, shining our phone flashlights in the direction GPS tells us the lake should be.

And Melly is right.

The path isn't marked or manicured like a proper walking trail would be, but when we finally spot it, it's impossible to unsee, nature's version of an optical illusion. What looks like solid forest is anything but. An unnaturally straight vein runs through the woods, and although the ground is littered with fallen leaves, the well-trodden earth below is packed flat.

This has to be it.

"We get in and we get her out," I say. "Everything else can be sorted on the road."

She nods. "Let's do this."

The path is barely wide enough for us to walk side by side, but we manage. Things rustle in the woods beyond, animals either bedding down for the night or beginning their nocturnal rituals, and I try not to think about the dangerous beasts that could be hiding. Bears and moose are bad enough, but Troy is out there too. Somewhere.

Humans may like to think they're predators, but there's always something that can make us prey.

Chapter Fifty

The cabin appears in a sudden widening of the path, squatting low in the forest like part of the terrain. In the void beyond, an expanse of lake mirrors the darkened sky above.

"In and out," I remind Melly.

"Trust me, I'm not trying to stick around here longer than necessary."

We creep closer, ignoring each NO TRESPASSING sign we pass.

The cabin is built with its back to the woods, its roughhewn exterior only a single generation removed from the trees around it.

"This way," I whisper, veering toward the left, where the edge of a porch juts out.

"Why are you whispering?"

"I don't know." Nervous laughter snags in my throat and dissipates when we reach the side of the cabin. A thin sliver of light glows through the edge of the boarded-over window. "Come on."

The porch is as rustic as the cabin, but it's clear care was put into it. The railings are made from knobby branches, bits of bark still curling around them, and the view beyond them must be amazing in daylight. A steep set of stairs leads down from the center to the water below, and I can see why this parcel was undeveloped for so long. Between the lack of road and that embankment, there's not a single thing easily accessible about this place.

The floor creaks as Melly drops her backpack, the thud impossibly loud in the twilight stillness.

I search the front of the house, looking for any sign of life or danger. The boards covering the windows are intact, and the door, a simple wooden thing, is secured with a padlock clipped through a heavy metal latch.

Another NO TRESPASSING sign is stapled at eye level.

In a sea of things that are already wrong, nothing looks recently out of place.

"He hasn't been here. We still have time."

"Good." Melly draws a hammer from her backpack like it's Excalibur and offers it up. I take it, the weight reassuring in my hand while I wait for her to find the crowbar.

"What do you think?" she asks, using the crowbar as a pointer. "Door hinges or window board?"

"Wait." I knock on the door, a series of sharp raps that echo across the lake.

"Dude. She can't answer the door." Melly taps the padlock with her crowbar.

"I know that." I knock again and press my ear to the door.

Silence.

"Jodie?" I call. "If you can hear us, don't be afraid. We're going to get you out of here."

I listen for a response, anything to indicate we've made it in time, but nothing comes.

"Hinges," I decide, if no other reason than to be petty. He did destroy my door, after all. "The window's probably faster, but if we need to carry her out, this will be easier."

That's all the encouragement Melly needs. She tucks the edge of the bar into the gap near the top hinge and holds a hand out. "Hammer."

I pass it to her like a surgical nurse delivering a scalpel. She strikes the crowbar, the sharp reports ringing through the night air.

The animals fall silent in the face of our racket.

Melly drops the hammer and leans her full weight onto the crowbar. The door groans, a splinter starting somewhere deep. But it's not enough.

She moves the bar lower, repeats the process. "Get the hammer in here," she says, pushing the bar to open up a gap. I tuck the claw end in and hold while she positions the crowbar where she started the first gap. "On three."

She counts in a rush, and on three we both haul on our tools. When the hinge gives, it's with a completeness that sends us staggering.

"Okay, same thing on the bottom," Melly says.

This one goes faster because we know exactly what to do, and soon the door is dangling askew on the padlocked latch.

Hiking and B and E. Two things I can now add to my résumé thanks to Troy.

"Jodie?" I call again. "We're coming in. It's okay."

Stepping into the same cabin I've spent so much time watching on the iPad is surreal. The space is both familiar and somehow not, like visiting a movie set.

The light is on in the main room, and even though we're on a rescue mission, I feel like an intruder. "Jodie?"

"She's probably still out," Melly says.

The bathroom's bifold door is closed, and I knock, stupidly, as I slide it open. It moves freely, and in the light that spills in from the main room, I see the floor is bare.

My heart cannonballs against my chest.

Too late.

We were too late, and he got her and locked everything back up tight. Panting fills my ears, short, ragged gasps that I don't feel.

I don't feel them because they're not mine.

298

A look confirms that they're not Melly's either.

She nods once at the drawn white shower curtain.

I reach forward carefully, not wanting to scare someone already so panicked. "Jodie, we're not here to hurt you. We're here to get you out."

Before I can slide the curtain aside, it flies toward me, a shrieking ghost made of plastic.

"Fuck," Melly snaps, bundling the thrashing curtain in her arms. "Calm your tits. I don't want to hurt you."

"Let me go," Jodie sobs. "Just let me go."

"We're here to help," I say, moving the curtain away from her face. She struggles in Melly's arms, wild eyes skating right past me.

Melly widens her stance to better brace herself and shakes her head. This is obviously not the hero's welcome she expected. "She's in shock. Trauma response. Something. I don't know."

Jodie's chest heaves with ragged breaths, but the fight drains out of her quickly. When her eyes manage to land on my face for longer than an instant, I nod at Melly.

"I'm going to let you go," she says. "Don't freak out again?"

Jodie nods, and Melly's grip relaxes. The shower curtain puddles to the floor, and Jodie looks about to follow it. Melly and I both catch an arm, gently this time, keeping her upright.

"You know, you're pretty spry for someone who's spent most of the day passed out," Melly says.

Jodie pulls away from her, panic filling her face. "Who are you? Did he send you?"

"No, no, nothing like that." I guide her out of the bathroom, equally afraid of her bolting as I am of her collapsing again.

"Who are you, then? How did you know I was here?"

The rules I have for Pies Before Guys exist for a reason. They're to keep me safe, so I can keep doing what I do. But right now, that doesn't matter. Jodie looks like she's three seconds from coming completely undone, so I break one. I have no choice. "You emailed me. About a pie."

"And you found me?" There's a childlike wonder in her voice, like maybe she thinks she's dreaming.

The bomb ticks louder in my head. "Yeah, we found you. And we're getting you out of here. We have to walk a ways, but my truck is here. Can you manage that? Are you hurt?"

She shakes her head.

"Uh, do we need to go back to the passed-out on-the-floor thing?" Melly asks. "Because I think we should know if you're going to drop again."

"I'm okay," she says, then again, stronger. "I'm okay."

"What happened before?" I ask.

"She's right. I passed out. I don't know why. Hunger, low blood sugar, who knows." She shakes her head, the dazed look fading from her eyes. "And when I woke up, I just, I don't know. Gave up. I thought maybe if I stayed there, he'd think I was dead and would let me go if he came to check. Or that maybe I would actually die and it would at least be over."

"It is over," I promise. "You're getting your life back, right now. But we have to go."

I don't want to risk spooking her, not when she's so fragile, but time is very, very much of the essence here.

"Faster would definitely be better," Melly agrees, heading for the door. "Let's move."

I keep an arm looped through Jodie's and lead her out, away from her prison. Melly stoops to grab her bag, and we set off the way we came.

Night has fallen fully around us, and it's slower with Jodie, who's rallying in the fresh air but is still weak. Our phone flashlights are barely up to the job of lighting the path, and I would curse them if I weren't so relieved to have Jodie alive and at my side.

We're halfway back to the truck when she stumbles, hard, and I have to scramble to keep her upright. My phone goes flying, the beam of the light bouncing off into a thicket of brush.

"You good?" Melly asks, turning to point her light at us.

"I'm so sorry," Jodie says, the frantic apology of someone used to making many.

"You're fine," I assure her. "You only tripped." I have to bushwhack my way to my phone, but I don't complain because it doesn't matter. Even the spider web of cracks across the screen is nothing, not compared to getting this girl her sense of safety back.

"Onward ho," I joke when I get back to the path, but neither Melly nor Jodie responds.

Both of their gazes are fixed rigidly ahead, tracking a firefly flitting through the trees.

No. Not a firefly.

A flashlight.

Chapter
Fifty-One

Jodie sinks to her knees, a mewling keen slipping from her throat as Melly and I race to extinguish our phones.

"Shh," I whisper, pulling Jodie to her feet. I press my lips close to her ear. "We have to hide. Now. Quietly."

Melly huddles in on Jodie's other side, and we shepherd her off the path. The trees are the blackest shadows against the night, and I keep an arm outstretched, searching for one big enough to conceal us all.

"Here," I breathe, pulling them around a giant maple.

"We let him go by, then we book it," Melly whispers as we crouch near the trunk.

"It's going to be fine," I add, and even almost believe it. The roots of the tree sprawl in knobby tentacles that form a crevice perfect for tucking into. "We just have to wait."

It's hard, though.

Really hard.

Jodie's breathing is a ragged metronome that doesn't ease no matter how much I try to model deeper, softer breathing.

The leaf-strewn path cushions the sound of Troy's approach, but the bobbing beam of light tells us everything.

It dapples the trees around us, swaying with each footfall. The leaves beneath his feet crunch louder with each closer step he takes.

Every so often he whistles a tune that, in daylight, in different circumstances, might be jaunty, but here in the dark of the woods, it's unnervingly sinister.

It sounds deliberate.

Jodie whimpers, once, softly. It's enough to plunge the forest into silence.

The flashlight beam stills on the path, Troy's footfalls halting. He swings the light in a slow, wide arc.

I press a hand against Jodie's arm, a silent reminder to be still. To be quiet. She practically vibrates beneath my touch.

"Saw your truck," Troy calls. The lilt in his voice tells me that whistle was indeed deliberate. A taunt. "Don't know why you're so up in my business, but you're not getting away with just a ticket this time."

I close my eyes, cursing myself. More than any other thing tonight, I curse my own stupidity. We knew he was coming. We knew he was barreling down behind us, and we parked exactly where the GPS told us to. Exactly where he was bound to do the same.

Of course he saw us.

I made it easy.

"I know these woods better than you do," Troy calls, his voice sweeping after the beam of light. "You're not going to get away."

Jodie's teeth chatter, and even though none of us is dressed for a night in the woods, I know it's not the cold that's getting to her.

It's fear.

"You're okay," I breathe, the words barely more than puffs of air.

Troy's steps pick up, the soft crunch of leaves giving way to the sharper snap of branches as he moves off the path. "Come on, girl," he calls, his voice a singsong. "Come out and play."

Something about that line breaks Jodie.

She's on her feet before either of us can stop her, bolting into the dark. She crashes through the brush, her need for distance eclipsing the need for silence.

Troy chuckles, low and deadly. "That's more like it."

Melly and I are on our feet, catching sight of her the moment he does. In the naked beam of light, we watch her find the path and take off, sprinting for all she's worth.

In the wrong direction.

Instead of heading for the truck, to safety, she's tearing down the path back to the cabin.

"The fuck?" For a moment Troy is frozen in confusion, and Jodie lengthens her lead. She's heading to the only safety she knows, a place with doors she can close.

"Fuck," Melly spits.

Troy whirls, bringing the beam back to our tree. Melly shoves me hard, back toward the cabin. "Go. I'll deal with him."

I want to argue, tell her that he's my problem, but there's no time. She's already darting toward him, using his light to guide her way. I go after Jodie, letting the even ground of the path guide my racing feet.

There's a scuffle behind me, and I risk a glance back. The flashlight is on the ground, angling across the path. Shadows tumble through the trees.

Troy's growl cuts through the dark. "Fucking bitch."

A series of dull thuds echo down the path, then a hard crash. Melly grunts in pain.

I skid to a stop, double back, freeze. For a moment I'm rooted there, torn between who needs me more.

In the space between heartbeats, when a decision should be made, the flashlight seems to float off the ground and takes the choice away.

Troy barrels down the path, straight at me.

"Go," Melly shouts from the woods. "Keep her safe."

I go.

I go faster than I have ever gone in my life, my feet flying over packed dirt. I grab a hanging branch that passes in a blur and let it snap back like a whip. It connects with a meaty thwack, not enough to do real damage but enough to make Troy swear a blue streak.

Good.

I hope it took an eye out.

If it did, it isn't enough to deter him.

My lungs burn with effort, and I reach the clearing only steps ahead of him. If I can get inside with Jodie, we might have a chance. We can barricade a door. It's two against one.

But then his hand is in my sweater, twisting, throwing me aside like trash. I hit the ground hard enough it takes my breath away, and I curl up, instinct guarding against the pain that's sure to follow.

But the blows don't come.

He's panting, breathing as hard as I am, but it isn't me he's after.

Not anymore.

She's at the edge of the cabin near the porch, watching. Not hiding. Not fleeing.

She's frozen.

He stalks toward the cabin.

I stagger to my feet and scream, "Jodie, run!" as I launch myself after him.

I have no plan. I don't have the muscle to stop him with brute force, and he left the land of reason a good long time ago. But I can't just stand by while he goes after her.

Not again.

I reach him as he turns the corner of the porch, and now I'm the one clawing at him, reaching for a handful of shirt, belt, anything that can slow him down.

It's a mistake.

He whirls and slams me against the rough wall of the house, a thick forearm pinned across my throat.

"I planned to take some time with you, but if you want to go first so bad, we can do it this way instead," he growls.

Pinpricks of light dance across my vision, and I jerk my knee up, thrusting it into his groin with all my might. It's a cheap shot, but it's enough to buy me another breath as he folds over, roaring in pain.

It should be satisfying, but it only makes me want to keep going.

But we're not alone.

Jodie stands in the pool of light spilling from the cabin door, Melly's crowbar held high. She glowers at Troy. "Get away from her."

He straightens, taking in the woman before him.

"Woman, you better not be raising your hand to me."

I move along the wall, aligning myself with her. Two against one. And if Melly left the crowbar, maybe she forgot the hammer too.

"Get out of here," she orders, and for a split second, he looks so stunned that I think he actually might.

But then he laughs, a cold, cruel cackle.

He closes the distance between them faster than a man his size should be able to, and years of conditioning take over. Jodie yelps, the crowbar clattering to the floor as she scurries across the porch.

"Don't you make me chase you," he growls, lunging at her.

And something happens then.

Something amazing.

She sidesteps, dancing just out of his reach. But she doesn't run. She spins in close, gets her hands on his back, and then she's using his own furious momentum to send him forward, through the gap in the railing, and all the way down the steep stairs down to the lake.

Chapter
Fifty-Two

For a long time, neither of us speaks. We don't move, and we barely dare to breathe.

We need to listen.

The sounds of the forest return, the soft scuttling of animals through brush, an owl calling across the night. The lake is calm in the still air.

Everything below is silent.

"Did we win?"

Jodie and I both start at the sudden intrusion of sound, but it's only Melly, limping across the porch. She cradles her left arm against her chest, and there's a scratch on her cheek crusted with drying blood, but she's okay.

"We won," I confirm. "Thanks to Jodie."

Melly raises an eyebrow, then winces. "Do tell."

I look to Jodie, giving her the floor, but she's gone back to staring down the stairs.

"He's not coming back," I tell her gently. "Not after that."

"Wait," Melly says. "She pushed him down the stairs? For real?"

"For real."

"Damn, girl, well played." Melly shakes her head. "And here I thought we were going to be the heroes."

The corner of Jodie's mouth lifts in a fraction of a smile that vanishes instantly. "We should check," she whispers. "Just to make sure."

"Dude, those stairs are practically down a cliff," Melly says. "You slayed the dragon. It's over now."

I shake my head. "She's right. I'll go. Just to be sure."

"If you fall and die, I'm going to be cranky," Melly grumbles.

I shoot her a look. "Maybe not with the jokes yet?"

"Just be careful, then," she says. "And quick. Someone's going to have to pop my shoulder back in, and something tells me neither of you have the stomach for that."

"Fast and safe," I promise.

It's easier said than done. The stairs are clearly DIY'd, because no builder worth their license would ever construct something with this kind of pitch.

But I take it slow, and the farther down I get, the more a sense of Jodie's dread starts to creep in. If this were a movie, Troy would spring up for a final battle right as I reached the bottom.

I should've brought the crowbar. Just in case.

The fear is unfounded, though, as the logical part of my brain knew it would be.

Troy's body is concertinaed across the bottom steps, his top half on rocky ground, legs akimbo above him. One arm is pinned beneath his big torso, but the other is thrown back like he never even tried to break the fall.

Maybe he didn't.

Maybe he somersaulted like a boulder down a cliff, end over end, and never even felt the final impact.

That would be kinder than he deserved.

I run the flashlight over his body once more, then turn to make the steep climb back up.

I don't check for a pulse.

With the angle of his neck, I know it's not going to be there.

* * *

I'm out of breath when I reach the top, and I can already tell my legs are going to make me pay for everything about this night, but it's a small price for what we've done.

"All good," I say. "He's dead."

"What do we do with him?" Melly asks. "Toss him in the lake?"

I shake my head, and not just because I have no desire to ever climb those steps again. "We leave him."

"What? Like in the open?"

"Yes. Right where he is. Trust me."

"You know I do."

I nod. "Jodie, is there anything in the cabin that belongs to you?"

Her eyes are wide, like she can't believe we aren't hiding the body either. "Only some clothes. He made me pack a bag when we left."

"Okay, let's get that, and then we need to go."

Having a task seems to focus her, and it takes no time at all for her to gather her things. I take the bag from her and give the cabin a final look. There are clean dishes beside the sink, but that's fine. At some point the generator will give out and whatever is in the fridge will rot, but that's fine too.

The door is less fine, but there's nothing we can do about it.

I slide the crowbar into Jodie's bag. "Did you take the hammer?"

"In my backpack," Melly confirms. "In the woods." She wiggles the fingers that cradle her elbow. "Kind of ran out of hands."

"We'll get it." I turn to Jodie. "Ready?"

"God yes."

"Let's go."

* * *

After everything with Frank, the last place I should want to be is another hospital waiting room, but when the doors of Green Mountain General slide open, it feels like a welcome.

The rural emergency room is blessedly deserted, so our entrance is less of a spectacle than it could be.

The grizzled woman at the registration desk makes no effort to disguise the nosy way she peers over her glasses, and honestly, I can't even blame her.

We're practically the start of a bad joke—a baker, a biker, and a broken librarian walk into a hospital.

"Looks like you all found yourself a spot of trouble," she says.

Surprisingly, it's Jodie who takes charge. "I got lost in the woods. So stupid, I know." She giggles, radiating charm. "They came to save me."

No, not surprisingly. This is someone who has had to lie to hospitals for years now. That sheepish self-deprecation would've glossed over many truths, let the staff believe she was just clumsy, that it was an accident, and of course she feels safe at home.

This is the last time she'll have to do this.

The woman arches an eyebrow and plucks at the lanyard around her neck. The ID badge reads BARB. "You know this isn't the time of year to be hiking on your own, right?"

"I do now," Jodie says. "I think my friend's arm is broken."

"Dislocated," Melly corrects, and Barb holds up a pen, silencing her.

"One at a time." She points the pen at Jodie. "You first."

She shakes her head, keeping that sweet smile fixed on her face. "No, I'm fine. They took care of me. It's Melly's arm that needs help."

"Nope." The woman shakes her head. "You just told me you've been lost in the woods. How long?"

Jodie shoots me a look like I have the answer to her made-up story.

"You passed out," I remind her. "Let them look you over."

Barb taps her pen, and Jodie relents with a soft sigh. Barb gets her registered, ignoring the waves of reluctance radiating off Jodie.

"Through there." Barb waves her pen to indicate the double doors to our right. "Natalia will get your vitals."

Jodie disappears into the bowels of the ER, and Barb points at Melly.

"The arm and what else?" she asks, the pen held like a cigarette as she types.

"Just that," Melly says. "The bruises will sort themselves out."

"I watched you limp in here like a three-legged racehorse," Barb says. "Be straight with me."

Melly snorts. "I fell down a hill. Took out my shoulder and slammed my knee on a rock. But I really do think it's a bruise."

"Well, when you're a professional with a radiography machine, I'll put some stock in what you think," Barb says, clacking away at the keyboard. "In the meantime, x-rays. Follow your friend."

Melly salutes with her good hand and hobbles away, leaving me with Barb.

"And your story?"

"Genuinely nothing," I say, glad it's the truth.

Barb shakes her head. "Who'd've thought the one thinking a dress like that was proper hiking attire would be the only one to come out unscathed. You kids, I swear."

"It's a lucky dress."

"Lucky you all didn't get eaten by bears," she mutters. "Waiting room's yours. It's quiet tonight, so they shouldn't be long."

It is, of course, a lie, because all hospital waits are long.

But the room is warm, the TV is set to cooking shows, and I must doze off, because the next thing I know, Jodie is sitting beside me.

"What's the verdict?" I ask.

"Dehydrated, severely anemic." She shrugs. "And still pregnant."

I know how complicated that is for her. "Well, you can sort that out however you want once you're settled."

"I just wish—" She hesitates, glancing up at Barb, who is most definitely within eavesdropping range. "It would be nice if this was a clean break, you know? I need a fresh start."

"And you'll get it," I promise. "Do you have any thoughts on what you want to do next?"

She laughs. "Sleep? For at least a week? Is that an option?"

"It is. We'll sort out somewhere for you to stay on our way back. I know a lot of people."

Jodie's eyes flick back to Barb, and I can see all the questions she would ask if we were alone. There will be time for them later.

"I don't even know where home is anymore," she says, her voice cracking. "There's nothing left in Colorado, and everything I have in Turnbridge was his."

I think of Heath at the library, his warm eyes and the obvious concern he had for his absent colleague. "Not everything. People are missing you, right now."

She cocks her head like she can't even fathom that possibility.

"Everyone at the library."

An embarrassed flush colors her face. "No. Really?"

"Really. Especially Heath." I can see this pleases her, even if she doesn't know how to admit it. "They want to be there for you. You might think about letting them."

She shakes her head, the color rising in her cheeks. "They're not my friends, though. They were only nice to me because I was free labor."

The words tumble right out of her mouth like they were put there for that very purpose.

By someone else.

"Did Troy tell you that?" I bite back the anger. It's not directed at her, and she doesn't need to hear it. "He lied to you, Jodie. All the time. About everything. It's what abusers do." I wait until she meets my eyes to continue, wanting her to understand that I'm not lying. "You have people who care about you. It might be a small group right now, but it will grow. It just takes time."

She has a long road ahead unlearning everything he's beaten into her, but if she can let people in, it will be easier.

"Maybe," she says. "I don't even know who I am anymore."

"Anyone you want to be."

"You make it sound so easy."

"It isn't. Building a life from scratch is one of the hardest things you'll ever do, but it will be worth it. I promise."

Epilogue

S ometimes the best hiding place really is right in plain sight.

When Troy stops showing up to work, it takes no time at all for them to check the cabin. After all, Tommy knows it's there. In the story that runs about the "tragic loss of one of Turnbridge's finest," that shack is referred to as a beloved family fishing spot and one of Troy's favorite places to unwind.

So of course there is nothing suspicious about finding him there at the end of a long week. Even the autopsy confirms that it's plain to see his injuries are consistent with an accidental fall.

Although it's exactly how I expected things to play out, seeing it in print is a relief.

Between all the police and Greene Farm's prominence in town, the funeral ends up being a massive affair.

Several local restaurants contribute dishes for the reception, but not Frank.

It's a decision no one at the diner dares contradict, not even when a uniformed officer stops in to inquire.

Frank may still be recuperating, but as far as his employees are concerned, his word is final.

It's a good thing I don't work for him.

It goes without saying that the entire police department will pass through that memorial service. I will never have a better chance to get them all at once.

The unburdening magic that goes into the small, badge-shaped cutie pies is crude.

It's meant to be.

I wanted them to be murder pies, not honesty pies, but that's not my decision to make.

Enid and her aunt Sue are already working on securing their own brand of justice.

I have no intention of depriving them of that.

But I will help it along.

* * *

The one thing Tommy didn't seem to know about the cabin is that Troy was holding a woman hostage there, because at no point do the police come for Jodie.

Or who knows?

Maybe he did know and thought loyalty could keep the world from learning the worst about his cousin.

It can't.

Not when Melly is working with Enid and the others to get their stories told. They're more than ready to talk, and the minute the lawsuit hits, Melly is taking their truth public. The world will know exactly what kind of men Troy and his corrupt buddies were.

But Jodie will not be part of it.

She's busy getting on with her new life.

Embracing the time-honored tradition of radical post-relationship makeovers, she started by cutting her long locks into a chic pixie that does brilliant things for her cheekbones. She decided

Turnbridge deserved another chance and has gone from volunteer to full-time employee at the library and is thinking about enrolling at the university next year. When I drop in with pies, she's always busy, showing teens the newest young adult books or chatting with patrons and coworkers at the circulation desk. Happy looks good on her.

On Tuesdays, when she doesn't have plans, she visits the meeting at Saint Stan's. While she loves her therapist, she also likes how the women in the group already understand what she's gone through.

She's figuring out that her people can come from many places and that family can form right before your eyes.

* * *

As for my own cobbled-together family, well, we carry on.

Melly got to shed the sling after two weeks, but her shoulder is still a long way from handling the motorcycle and, more often than not, I'm the one she calls when a bus isn't convenient.

I don't mind. I am, after all, at least partly responsible for what happened to her.

Plus, even though I'll never say it, I feel like I owe her for the drive up.

Giving her the messiest version of my tangled lifestyle and legacy thoughts has made it easier to explain things to Noel in a way that makes sense.

We sit on the picnic table as we talk, watching Zoe cavort around the orchard in the golden hour light.

"I never meant to steamroll over you," Noel says.

"I know. But I also don't want to stand in the way of the kind of future you want."

"The kind of future I want has you in it."

My heart aches, because while I know that's true, it's true with caveats. "A future with me has murder pies, which means it has the occasional harebrained adventure." I need him to hear this. "There will be a certain danger that doesn't go away until I run out of bad guys, and I don't think that will ever happen. And there won't be kids. Ever."

The rambling part of my brain wants to keep going, keep justifying and explaining the reasons why, but I resist it. He's already heard the "murder pies as legacy" speech. He needs to hear this part too, for exactly what it is.

To his credit, he takes it in without immediately jumping to comment. He hears it, for real this time.

And he considers it. Properly.

"You're the only one who can decide if that's enough for you," I say. "And if it's not, I understand."

He turns to face me, and the crisp, apple-scented breeze blows his floppy hair into his eyes. I want to reach out, brush it away, but without his answer I don't know if that's my right anymore.

The wind shifts, sending his hair back. His warm brown eyes are serious as he takes my hands in his.

"It is enough. More than enough. At least for now." He pulls in a shaky breath and squeezes my hands. "I can't predict the future, and I can't promise I'll always be happy with you throwing yourself in harm's way, but I can promise that you, Daisy Ellery, are more than enough, and I want you in whatever capacity I can have you. Murder pies, danger, and all."

"For now is good for me," I say.

Besides, what is forever if not one long string of for-nows?

It's enough.

It has to be.

Recipes

Pumpkin Chai Latte Pie

The ever-popular fall coffee drink gets a spicy upgrade in this festive pie.

Flaky Espresso Crust Ingredients

1¼ cups all-purpose flour
1 teaspoon espresso powder
1 teaspoon sugar
½ teaspoon salt
8 tablespoons butter, cold and cut into small cubes
¼–½ cup cold water
Splash apple cider vinegar
1 egg for wash

Method

1. Combine the dry ingredients in a bowl.

2. Add butter and mix with your hands or a pastry blender until incorporated. You should be able to feel and see flakes of flour-coated butter.

3. Add cider vinegar and enough cold water to form a cohesive dough.

4. Form into a disk and wrap in plastic. Let dough rest in the fridge for a half hour or up to two days.

5. When ready to bake, preheat oven to 375 F and roll dough out.

6. Place in pie pan and crimp edges as desired.

7. Line the crust with parchment and fill with your preferred pie weights. Bake 10 minutes, then carefully remove pie weights. Dock the bottom of the crust by using a fork to poke holes, then whisk egg and brush on edges. Return to oven for 8–10 minutes. (The bottom should just be beginning to brown when you remove it.)

8. Leave oven on and set crust aside while you prepare filling.

Pumpkin Filling Ingredients

1 15-ounce can pumpkin puree (not pumpkin pie filling)
2 eggs
1 cup brown sugar
1 tablespoon cornstarch
1 teaspoon cinnamon
¾ teaspoon ginger
½ teaspoon cardamom
¼ teaspoon nutmeg
¼ teaspoon cloves
⅛ teaspoon black pepper
¼ teaspoon salt
⅔ cup (160ml) heavy cream
⅓ cup (80ml) whole milk
Optional: Espresso beans or whole star anise for garnish

Method

1. Whisk the pumpkin, eggs, and brown sugar together until combined. (This can be done by hand or in a mixer.)

2. Add remaining ingredients and whisk until combined.

3. Pour filling into crust. Bake 50–60 minutes until center is almost set. There will still be some jiggle, but it will finish firming up as it cools. While baking, periodically check to make sure your crust isn't overbrowning. If it is, cover edges with strips of aluminum foil or pie guards.

4. Allow the pie to cool fully before topping with espresso whipped cream.

Espresso Whipped Cream Ingredients

1 cup heavy cream
½ cup powdered sugar
1 teaspoon espresso powder

Method

1. Combine all ingredients and beat on high until stiff peaks form.

2. Pipe around edge of pie in desired pattern.

Chocolate Orange Murder Pie

A ginger crust offers a cozy twist on the classic flavors of everyone's favorite whack-and-unwrap chocolate orange, but you'll have to supply your own murder!

Gingerbread Crust Ingredients

1¾ cups gingerbread cookie crumbs
6 tablespoons melted butter
2 tablespoons sugar
Pinch of salt

Method

1. Preheat oven to 350 F.

2. Combine all ingredients and press into pie or tart pan.

3. Bake 8 minutes. Remove and allow to cool before filling.

Filling Ingredients

10 ounces heavy cream
14 ounces chopped milk or dark chocolate (chips will work, but bar is better)
Zest of two oranges
Optional: Splash Grand Marnier

Method

1. Bring cream to a simmer.

2. Put chocolate in a bowl and pour in hot cream. Allow to sit for a minute, then slowly stir until smooth. If using Grand Marnier, add now.

3. Pour filling into crust and allow to set.

4. When firm, add whipped cream and candied peel in a decorative pattern.

Variation: The above recipe produces a very dense, fudgy filling. For a lighter option, allow the ganache to cool fully and beat in a stand mixer until fluffy before adding to the crust. Same flavors, different textures!

Vanilla Whipped Cream Ingredients

1 cup heavy cream
½ cup powder sugar
2 teaspoons vanilla

Method

1. Combine all ingredients and beat on high until stiff peaks form.

Candied Peel Ingredients

4 oranges
2 cups water
1 cup sugar
1 teaspoon vanilla
½ teaspoon salt

Method

1. Using a vegetable peeler, carefully peel the oranges in strips. It helps to press firmly, but try to avoid getting into the white pith. Don't worry about making each peel perfectly symmetrical—you'll trim them later.

2. When all the oranges are peeled, use a paring knife to slice each piece of peel into ¼-inch-wide strips.

3. Add them along with the sugar and water to a pot and simmer for 20 minutes or until soft but still bright. Remove from heat, add vanilla, and let sit for 10 minutes.

4. Remove peel from sugar syrup and drain on cooling racks for 15 minutes, then toss in granulated sugar. Return to rack until fully dry.

Daisy's Pop-Pies

These Pop-Tart–inspired cutie pies come together in a snap and are infinitely customizable!

Pop-Pie Ingredients

Double batch of All Buttered Pie Crust (recipe in Book 1) or store-bought dough
Jam of choice
1 egg

Method

1. Preheat oven to 400 F.

2. Roll out each piece of dough and use a sharp knife or pizza wheel to cut out an even number of rectangles. You can make them Pop-Tart sized or minis; your choice!

3. Lay half the rectangles on a parchment-lined sheet pan and spread with jam, leaving a ¼-inch border around all edges.

4. Top with second rectangle and use a fork to crimp the edges. Poke a few holes in the tops to allow steam to vent.

5. Whisk egg and brush on top of pies.

6. Bake for 15–25 minutes until golden brown (exact time depends on size).

7. Allow to cool and make icing.

Icing Ingredients

1 cup powdered sugar
1 teaspoon vanilla
2–4 tablespoons milk or water*
Optional: Sprinkles, freeze-dried fruit, sanding sugar, etc., for
 garnish

*I prefer water because I find it makes the icing a bit crunchier when dried, but milk adds more richness. Your choice!

Method

1. Whisk all ingredients until smooth. Icing should be thick but easy to spread. Add additional water in small increments if needed to achieve proper texture.

2. Spread icing on cooled Pop-Pies and decorate as desired.

Variations: To make a flavored icing, swap out the vanilla for different extracts or add powdered freeze-dried fruit to taste. This icing also takes color well, so feel free to get festive!

For Brown Sugar Cinnamon Pop-Pies, replace the jam with cinnamon filling, which you can make by mixing ¾ cup brown sugar, 2 teaspoons cinnamon, 1 tablespoon flour, 2 tablespoons melted butter, 1 teaspoon vanilla, and a pinch of salt. Assemble pies and let chill for an hour before baking so filling can firm up.

Add 1 teaspoon of cinnamon to the icing.

Acknowledgments

As always, the biggest thank-you pies go to the people responsible for getting this book into readers' hands—especially my agent, Rebecca Podos, and my editor, Faith Black Ross. Special thanks also to Rebecca Nelson, Madeline Rathle, Dulce Botello, and Thaisheemarie Fantauzzi Perez for their work in getting this book to print—publishing would fall without the hard work of the production, marketing, and publicity staff and interns. And shout-out to Rachel Keith for once again making sure I know how commas and calendars work!

I would also like to thank Stephanie Singleton for creating another fabulous cover and Tanya Eby for narrating the audiobook to perfection. You make my murder girl look and sound amazing!

Thank-you pies all around for everyone who blurbed, supported, or otherwise cheered on this wacky series of mine. You're all the best! And thank you again to every reader who picked up the first book and came back for more. I am so glad to have my books be part of your world!